Cleat Chasers

NO EASY CATCH

JAQUELINE SNOWE

No Easy Catch
ISBN # 978-1-83943-764-9

Interior text design by Claire Siemaszkiewicz
Totally Bound Publishing

Published in 2022 by Totally Bound Publishing, United Kingdom.

Totally Bound Publishing is an imprint of Totally Entwined Group Limited.

NO EASY CATCH

Dedication

As always, thank you to Rebecca for your guidance and help with Ambar and Jeff's story.

To my husband, thank you for your patience as I spent hours writing trying to meet a deadline before the birth of our first kiddo.

The characters of the Cleat Chasers series have felt like friends and, while I'm so happy to write the final book, it feels like saying goodbye to people I've known for years.

Chapter One

Ambar

Convincing the hostess to let me into the second semester sports fundraiser was easier than it should've been. With one little promise of featuring her on my blog and *bam,* the young girl ushered me into the ballroom where the school's biggest and best athletes mingled with coaches, alumni and the press.

Ah, the things people do for attention.

I tapped my pen against my lip while I took in the surroundings. It wasn't black tie, but it was fancier than a casual get-together and I sent a prayer of thanks to my roommate who'd convinced me to wear a sleek black dress. It was a little tight and I kept running my hand down to the side to make sure my love-handles weren't bulging out. My coordination was abysmal and I tripped over my own two feet sometimes, but at least I didn't stand out—which was the goal.

I needed a new story to boost views on my blog or I would be shit outta luck. No views meant no affiliates, which equaled less money, and with my less-than-stellar first two years at school, I had no internships or job opportunities waiting for me at the end of the semester. The real world was knocking with graduation looming and I hadn't a clue what I wanted to or could actually do.

But, I did have a clue about what the student body loved to gossip about more than any other topic—the latest on the hot jocks. Girls, guys, scholarships and walk-ons. Readers loved hearing about the latest flings or scandals and this fundraiser was hot-jock central.

"Ambar Henderson?" A familiar voice caught my attention and I glanced at my left to see Peyton Gentry smiling at me. "What are you here for? Sneak in for the free booze?"

"Ha ha." I plastered on a fake smile despite the flash of hurt. Peyton and I had become friends freshman year—right in the smack of my party days—and he always brought it up no matter how much I had changed since then. "I'm here for a story, not the booze."

"Right." He smirked and lowered his voice. "Is it a juicy one?" He slung an arm over my shoulder in a quick hug and, while I didn't dislike Peyton, I was glad when he removed his arm. "Heard there's something weird going on with the volleyball team with one of their new freshmen."

"Yeah?" I waited for him to respond, but his attention drifted elsewhere and he gave me a weak wave before heading off. "Great to see you too, Peyton," I mumbled to myself. He was an average player on the soccer team but always managed to make himself seem bigger, better, more handsome. I snorted to myself at the headlines I would love to write someday.

Athletes and their egos – size does really matter
The bigger and not better – egos exposed

I took a deep breath, gathered as much courage as I could and walked about the event searching for anything that could be of interest. There were a couple of girls I recognized from the volleyball team, but they seemed normal, laid-back even. Each table had a large tented sign with the sport listed and it amazed me to see how much attention was given to athletes at our Division I school. Were there events like this for scholars? For those who made the Dean's List year after year? *Doubtful.*

Schools spend money on sports, not smarts

Yeah, that headline wouldn't sell shit. I derailed those thoughts and tried to ignore the tinge of jealousy weaving its way through my body. All these athletes had futures after college. They had tutors, scholarships, teams that supported them and, as someone who came from the opposite end of the spectrum, it was easy to envy them.

A loud cackle exploded near the front where the baseball players sat talking to what I assumed to be the coaches. They wore polos with the school logo, were significantly older than them and had the whole coaching vibe with the hard face and knowing eyes. Zade Willows, Tanner Johnson and Aaron Hill all wore suits and smiles and a part of my stomach fluttered. They were so handsome and such decent human beings I wished I could've written a million stories on them. Their faces alone would get readers. But I'd already done a story on Aaron and his girlfriend, so that well was dry. Plus, they were my friends and I refused to cross that boundary.

Moving on to another sport, I weaved through tables, trying to listen to conversations for something to spark motivation. Fifteen minutes passed without any luck and the familiar sensation of failure washed over me. *How can*

I pass my senior classes when I can't even write a stupid blog post without getting writer's block?

God, I wish I could drink.

It wouldn't hurt anyone if I snuck one bottled water and I blended in with the crowd as I approached the refreshment table. That was the good thing about being average-looking. No one really noticed me like they did my beautiful and tall roommates. I undid the cap and took a huge gulp when I felt someone staring at me.

Water spilled down my mouth and onto my dress when I found cold, unamused gray eyes narrowing at me. *Jeff Maddow.* He defined my perfect male specimen with his honey-brown hair styled just enough to be cool, his massive broad shoulders that went well with his defined pecs—perfectly showcased in the dark-gray dress shirt plastered across his chest. *Good lord.*

Shit, did he say something?

Did I?

His light gray eyes were framed by perfectly dark eyelashes and, God damn, those cheekbones were enough to make me forget my own name. He blinked and tilted his head to the side with impatience as he approached me. "Ambar Henderson, how the hell did you get into this event? You are neither an athlete nor a sponsor."

"I have my ways." I jutted out my chin and ignored the sweat pooling down my back.

"Did you sneak in? No, wait, let me guess. You bribed someone." He smiled like it was a joke, but his tone made it clear he was not happy. "I should call security."

"Really, Jeff? Come on." I hated how my fingers shook when I ran them through my hair, trying to act nonchalant. "I didn't bribe anyone."

"I wouldn't put it past you." He brought up a glass of champagne to his mouth and held my gaze as he took a sip. It was annoying to be attracted to someone who thought so little of me, but, alas, that was life.

"What do you care if I'm here? I'm not bothering you or anyone for that matter."

"False." He finished the glass and took a step closer to me. For one stupid second, I wondered what it would be like to feel his full lips against mine, but the look on his face sobered that thought. "You are a known campus blogger who finds out information about people to get views. You're no better than a tabloid magazine for a college. Athletes have enough to worry about with how hard *we* have to work. They should feel safe here, celebrating and networking, not worrying about being featured on a girl's pathetic blog to get attention."

"You know that's not what I do, Jeff," I defended myself but my voice lost its gusto. "I'm here for ideas…more like motivation. Nothing more."

"Right." He shook his head and tensed his jaw as he scanned the room. "Motivation to find out who's sleeping with who? Who has a better batting average when they're in a relationship versus being single?"

I gritted my teeth and willed my skin to not turn red. My cheeks burned when I attempted to defend my reasoning for writing those blogs. "It was for entertainment, Jeff. Plus, the stats didn't lie."

He gave me a look like many of my professors had. *Disappointment.* "Do you ever think about writing something credible or for a good cause?"

"The story about Hilly and Greta was—"

"Fine, sure." He waved a hand in dismissal and gave me a look that made me feel even smaller than my just-over-five-feet frame. "But you could *actually* spend time writing stories that matter. Not dumbass pieces that exploit athletes and encourage cleat chasers to come after us." He pressed his lips together and let out an aggravated sigh. "Stay away from my team, Ambar."

Then he stalked away to the front of the room, his stiff shoulders telling me everything I needed to know. He wasn't a fan of what I did or who I was. It wasn't news, but his words hit one of my deepest insecurities. *What am I even doing with my blog? My life?*

God damn it. Find a story! I finished the water and tossed the bottle into a trash can when a familiar deep, masculine laugh caught my attention. *That's my Uncle Martin.* My mood lifted instantly and I headed toward him. He was dressed in a three-piece suit and had his hand on a shoulder of a middle-aged man I didn't recognize. He finished telling a joke—a specialty of my favorite family member—before he noticed me and ushered me over. "Ambar Henderson."

"Martin Rhett," I replied, mirroring his hugging stance and smiling into his chest when he wrapped me in a bear hug like he had since I was a child. "I don't even know why you're here, but I'm so glad."

"Business partners in the community. We love supporting athletes!" He kept his arm around me and introduced me to the gentlemen around us. "This is my favorite niece, fellas. She's a senior this year and is a hell of a writer."

Various hellos and greetings echoed around me and I relished my uncle's words. *A hell of a writer.* He never made me feel stupid or unremarkable. He'd encouraged me my entire life and seeing him at the event gave me the necessary boost of confidence.

"Nice to meet you all," I said, looking all five of them in the eye and shaking their hands. There was a brief moment where I faced the direction of the baseball table and met Jeff's gaze, but I forced myself to not stare or think about why he was watching me. "Anyone have a good story for me? I'm looking for a topic on my senior project and could use some ideas."

"Ah, my girl is always working." Uncle Martin laughed and led me away from the group with a smile that had taken years to practice. Once we were out of earshot, he changed his expression. "How did you get into the event, Ambar? I thought this was for athletes only."

"See, the thing is… I was on my way out." I gave him a cheesy smile. "Lunch next time you're in town?"

"Of course." He pulled me into another hug. "Stay out of trouble, okay? You have four more months of college and I don't want anything *more* to happen. You know?"

Like my little drug and drinking binge freshman year?

Or my academic probation?

"I know, I know." I frowned and felt every ounce of shame in my bones. "I'll head out. I really did come for ideas. Nothing more."

"I believe you. Now go through the side door. I'll cover for you." He indicated the large black double-doors and winked. "While I can't condone you sneaking into an event, it does bring me joy to know you do have a little Rhett in your blood."

"See you later, Uncle." I smiled and snuck one more glance around the ballroom before leaving. It didn't mean anything when Jeff continued to stare at me with an unreadable expression on his face. If anything, he should've been happy I was leaving his precious party. *Ugh.*

New headline.

Jeff Maddow should pull the stick out of his own ass to get a better batting average.

Chapter Two

Jeff

Aaron Hill and Tanner Johnson had the tempers, not me, yet the urge to slam my fist through a wall grew stronger the more I thought about Jaime Smith. The fundraiser had done nothing to appease the growing frustration, nor had working out harder than normal that morning. It was bullshit. I left the shower and called him again, hoping he'd answer to explain what the hell had changed since the previous month. The kid had talent and deserved a scholarship and a place on the team—so what had made my coach take it away?

"Yo, Maddow," Jaime answered without the normal pep in his voice.

"I'm fucking pissed, man." I clenched my fist a couple of times and asked the question I couldn't stop thinking about. "What are you going to do now?"

Now that your future's been taken away for no reason.

"Look, this guy from a community college contacted me and he seems all right. Might play for him a year or two, save up some money. My ma found a part-time job for me on the weekends, so I'll be good."

A dull headache started at the base of my skull and I needed to clarify one more thing before storming into my coach's office. "I know I've asked before, but Coach talked to you, verbally promised you a spot on the team and backed out without an explanation?"

"Yeah, dude. Said something about funds, but I can read between the lines. They gave my spot to someone else. Dude better be worth it."

"No way he will be. You *earned* this, Jaime." I squeezed my phone and let the anger roll over me in waves. "I'm talking to Coach about it. I don't care."

"Nah, don't cause trouble for yourself. My ma won't admit it, but I think she's relieved I won't be too far away to help out. She needs me for my siblings. It'll work out."

"You should be playing at a D I school, getting the attention of the scouts."

"If it's meant to be, it will be. Thanks for all the support and encouragement, Maddow. It's nice knowing guys like you are in my corner."

"Anything you need, let me know," I demanded.

"Will do. Keep that swing hot, Maddow."

He hung up but my hands shook with adrenaline and fury at my coach flip-flopping on a verbal offer. *He tells me he likes Jaime and sees a spot for him on our team, but then he pulls this shit? No.* I wanted answers.

I had my duffel bag over my shoulder and ignored the looks of younger players as I stormed down the hall toward his office. My normal calm demeanor was shot to hell and I slammed my fist against the door. "Coach, can we talk?"

His heavy footsteps carried to the door and he opened it with a surprised look on his face. "Jeff, what's wrong?"

"We need to talk." I waited for him to usher me through, but someone shouted for him down the hall.

"Coach, Martinez is bleeding!"

"I'll be right there." He pointed his finger toward his desk and spoke in his commanding tone that I used to admire. "Wait in there. I'll be back as soon as I can."

I nodded, annoyed that I had to wait, but understanding that an injury would take precedence over my grievances. I plopped down on the chair facing his clean desk and thought of how best to approach it. Did I accuse, or gain information? Did I demand an explanation or ask to see who did receive Jaime's place on the team? Or, did I ask him to explain why he would go back on his word, something I had never seen him do?

This is the type of shit Ambar should write about. Not bullshit. Seeing her dressed in a prim-and-proper outfit had messed with me—I was used to seeing the party girl in clothes that revealed a lot more skin—but this wasn't the time to think about my semi-hot, annoying neighbor.

My headache increased and I tossed my bag onto the ground, accidentally hitting his desk and causing the few papers on the top to fall to the floor. I bent down to pick them up and froze when Jaime Smith's name was handwritten on the top of the page. *What the fuck is this?*

My heart raced to the point where my pulse pounded in my ears. Jaime's name was listed with four other players I had never heard of—all in one column. Three other names were written on the other side and there was something familiar about them. *Max Miller, Cooper Killian, Dillon Cage.* The third column had the name MARTIN RHETT and a list of dates and the fourth.... a list of numbers and checkmarks.

Why was Jaime's name on the list? Who were these dudes and what were these numbers and checkmarks?

I snapped a quick picture of the paper as my mind spiraled. The name was familiar, Martin Rhett, as if I'd heard it recently, and the other names rang a bell, too. My leg bounced up and down with adrenaline—was this the proof of why Jaime didn't get recruited? The hair on the back of my neck tingled as the weight of what I'd found dawned on me. This was Coach's handwriting and not my business. I glanced over my shoulder at the crack in the door, waiting to hear if my coach was coming back, but injuries could take a while depending on if they were severe.

Injuries.

That was why I recognized the three names. Typing Max Miller's name into my social media meant I pulled up a picture of a face I knew. He'd started on the team in the fall and something had happened for him to not return. *He's injured, that's right.* That was what our hitting coach had said. *Did something stupid and tore his ACL. He's gone.*

My thoughts blurred together as I typed Cooper's and Dillon's names into social media—their faces were familiar, too—former members on the baseball team who I never saw play. They had all been injured before the season had started. *So where are they now?*

Max's Instagram account showed a recent video of him snowboarding. I clutched my phone tighter as rage coursed through me. He'd said he'd torn his ACL and couldn't play baseball, but there he was, snowboarding like he was fine.

What the fuck is going on?

Who was Martin Rhett and why was my coach writing notes about this? I wanted to research and I stormed out of there, desperate to get information and to find out who these people were, and to get an honest answer for Jaime.

Social media was a blessing and a curse. It took me less than five minutes to see where Cooper hung out with all the geotags online and my adrenaline kept me warm on my march to see him. My mind flip-flopped with wanting to punch him in the face or demand answers. *Both seem like great and valid options.*

The library had four floors and a coffee shop known for its multi-colored coffees and that was where I found Cooper Killian. The son of a bitch wore name-brand everything and had his arm around a chick that looked opposite his type in every way. His clothing all had labels displayed while she wore large glasses, a baggy gray sweater, and had stacks of textbooks on the table. Cooper wasn't a bad-looking dude—and he knew it, too—but this chick was not someone who ran in his league. *She has to be his tutor.*

My heart pounded against my ribcage as I sat down a table away from him. It wouldn't go well for me to cause a scene. I had enough coverage being a senior on the team and Coach would kill me if I got into a brawl. But I could wait until the girl left and question him.

"Cooper, focus," the girl said in a mousy voice.

"Jane, I'm paying you to do my work. This isn't *tutoring*, no matter what you think it should be. I posted the ad, you accepted, so stop trying to fucking teach me."

Paying you to do my work.

Jesus. I pressed my palms against my eyes as it dawned on me that this guy had money and wasn't afraid to use it. Who else paid others to do work? *Entitled people, that's who.* I stood, disgusted with Cooper, and left the library with the intention of researching more. But it didn't hit me until I got home.

Shit! The numbers!

Money.

I had more questions than answers, and none of them made me feel better. If anything, my anger got worse when I typed in Martin Rhett's name and found a picture of the man *Ambar Henderson* had been hugging at the event. Of fucking *course* she would be related to the man involved in something shady. How else could these guys get into school for baseball, never play a goddamn second, yet all still attend the school like it was no big deal? She had to know something to make sense of this.

How else could some party girl like her get into this university?

I threw on a jacket and stormed out of the baseball house and walked past the house that stood between ours. I slammed my fist against the door and almost barged in when she opened it wearing tiny-ass shorts, long rainbow socks and an oversize sweatshirt that hung off her shoulder. "We need to talk."

Chapter Three

Jeff

"Uh..." She looked around, chewing on her bottom lip a bit, and said, "Why?"

"Let me in, Ambar. It's freezing outside."

"Sure, yeah." She moved out of the way and closed the door behind me, her large brown eyes widening when I took off my coat.

"Well? This needs to be private."

She gulped and pointed toward a white door with chipped paint. She led the way to the basement and while I would've enjoyed the way her shorts clung to her curves, my mind was on one thing—finding out the truth.

"Look," I said, clearing my throat and rubbing my hand over the back of my neck. *Start slow.* "How the hell did you get into this school?"

She rubbed her lips together and the longer the silence went on, the redder the tips of her cheeks became. "Get into school?"

"Yes. How did you get into *this* college?" I asked again, my temper threatening to boil over. "It's prestigious and quite difficult."

"I, uh, applied to general studies and got a letter."

"You just applied? You didn't have to write an essay?"

She paced the small tiled foyer with a worried expression. "I think I did an essay, maybe an interview with some deans." She pulled on the bottom of her shirt, fiddling with it as she added, "Why are you asking me this?"

I barked out something between a laugh and a cough and made a face of disgust before saying, "Honestly? I think you're a part of a college scam of some sort with your enabling uncle, and that he paid someone *something* to get you into this school. I looked you up, Ambar, and from what I could find, you were not a quality applicant to get into this university. I mean come on, the whole drug thing freshman year? But don't worry, you're not the only one."

Ambar Henderson had to be the world's best actress. The large brown eyes watering on the sides, the bottom lip trembling just enough for it to seem genuine, and the stubborn jaw sticking out in defiance. I'd *almost* believe she had nothing to do with it if I hadn't seen her with her uncle and found almost nothing about him online—suspicious in today's society. *Martin Rhett* and my coach…it was hard to believe, but something was going on and despite my reservations about Ambar, she was the best place to start.

If only she would say something. It had been three minutes of silence, three minutes of her wounded expression and three minutes for a trickle of remorse to ebb its way into my conscious. My approach had been a little strong without any explanation and straight to a verbal accusation, but the mere thought of someone buying spots at a college over people who deserved it sent a wave of rage through me. The enabling and injustice of it all was hard to swallow. Kids who needed financial help through sports scholarships were missing opportunities for people like Ambar, who didn't deserve it. *Like Jaime Smith from back home.*

Shit, is she crying? "Ambar, look—"

She blinked and within seconds, the moisture was gone and her petite face was scrunched in anger. "No, you look. How dare you come in here, accusing my uncle of doing such things? You don't know anything about him *or* me."

I mirrored her position, putting my hands on my hips, and narrowed my gaze at her. "You're wrong. I *do* know about Martin Rhett and I want more answers. I want to know what he's doing and how he gets away with it and I'm going to start with you."

"Oh, you are? How do you envision that going, Jeff? Want me to spy on him without you showing me a single piece of proof?" she asked, shaking her head hard enough that little pieces of her black hair escaped, giving her a bit of a wild look. It fit her. Ambar Henderson had always been a bit of a wild girl.

"What do you call this, then?" I got my phone out of my pocket and shoved the image in her face.

"What am I looking at?" she asked, not hiding the disdain and irritation in her voice.

"Those are three *players* who had mysterious injuries during fall practice and do you see that name next to theirs?" My voice shook with my anger.

"Yeah, I can read, Jeff. So what? This could be written by a fifth grader. It has seven names and my uncle's name on it. What's the big deal?"

"There's a phone number, too." I snatched the phone away from her. "Those three guys were all given a spot on the baseball team their freshman year but they mysteriously went away after their injury. I did some digging and found one of them, Cooper Killian, and there was one picture with him and your *dear* uncle. Cooper is from Missouri—hours away—and he knows your uncle—who is listed as a businessman. Isn't that odd?"

Ambar tilted her head just enough for me to find a weakness. *She's hooked.* "He works with athletes sometimes. He was at the event last night. And how do you know these guys had a spot on the team? Or if that spot was taken away?"

"I can't confirm it was taken away from them, but I can tell you they all claimed to be here because of baseball and never played a second. Take Cooper. I remember him from fall ball. He tore his ACL, which is a year of therapy, at least. So why is he snowboarding right now?" I moved to the video I'd saved from his Instagram and hit play for her. "Why is there fifteen written next to his name?"

"I don't know," she mumbled.

"Because something is going on and Martin Rhett has something to fucking do with it."

She sucked in one side of her cheek and eyed me up and down in a bit of an intimidating gesture. I was a big dude, five inches over six foot, but her dismissing glance knocked me back a step. Then she brought her hand to her chest and dragged her fingers back and forth over her heart. "I'm sure there's a reason this Cooper kid knows my uncle. A perfectly rational explanation."

An idea struck, mainly to piss her off to get her to spill information, and I said, "I guarantee if I ask around other teams, they'll find similar situations. Freshmen being recruited and offered spots on the team—taking real opportunities away from people who actually deserve it."

"It's interesting, sure, but I'm not understanding what your goal was coming here and insinuating I'm a piece of shit and a part of this all."

The hurt in her voice had me pause—I wasn't a total asshole. "Never said those words, so quit the act. I want to hear in detail how you got into school because I think it could provide some key insight to all this. Nothing I've found so far dates back before our freshman year, so I'd like you to get information from your uncle, and I'd like you to write about it on your blog."

"Is that all?" she mocked. "Why would I want to do any of those things?"

I studied the way she intertwined her fingers and had an eager look on her face. Ambar was intrigued, but she was offended and was letting that stand in the way. "Prove me wrong."

"What?"

"Prove me wrong about you and your uncle. If I'm wrong, I'll leave you and your uncle alone. Hell, I'll send you invites to every sporting event the rest of the year. But if I'm right, you write the story and I can focus on my final season, because, trust me, Ambar, I do *not* want to be worrying about this shit right now. This is not fun."

She blew out a long breath and tucked some of that wild hair behind her ears. "Fine. I'll clear my own damn name, and my uncle's, and we can then part ways forever?"

That made me smile. "Or we break open a huge scandal and you write something on your blog that is actually newsworthy and helpful."

"Fine, whatever." She played with the loose strings on her shorts and it briefly brought my attention to her legs. They weren't long or toned but her goofy socks amused me. The splattering of colors clashed with my initial impression of her and I lost a little bit of the edge to my voice.

"We need to talk about some ground rules."

She didn't respond, but she made an odd face that I interrupted as *well?*

"First thing—no one knows about this. Not your roommate, not my teammates, not your uncle. No one. Understood?" I spoke with a little too much aggression and I forced my face to relax so I wouldn't startle her. It was a character flaw, getting *too* into things.

"Then what the hell am I supposed to tell my roommates when they ask why you wanted to talk to me in private?" she asked, cackling at the end. It wasn't an attractive laugh but when she did it, her smile stretched across her face in a pleasing way.

Shit. I didn't think about this part. What would people believe? "We're hooking up?"

"Ha, no." She snorted and adjusted her shorts string again, letting the fabric hang a half an inch lower and flashing a hint of her skin. "No goddamn way we're saying that."

"Project for a class?"

She shook her head and ran her teeth over her bottom lip for a couple of seconds. "We could say I'm doing a featured piece on you with it being your senior year and me needing to build an online portfolio of work. My friends have heard me bitching about it all year, plus, your teammates will buy it after I did that piece on Hilly and Greta."

"Okay, yeah."

"Great. I'll have to do this *and* figure out a real senior project," she mumbled, and a little bit of the light in her eyes dimmed. "Any other ground rules or can you go?"

I ignored her blatant dislike of the situation and shook my head. "We need to set times to meet, preferably that aren't suspect to my teammates. They are nosy as hell and already sensing something is off. Give me your number."

"*Please* give me your number," she replied, tight-lipped.

"Sorry, I'm used to barking out commands on the field. It carries over into life and it's not meant to be rude. *Please* give me your number so we can work out logistics." She rattled off the digits and I quickly sent her a text so she had mine. "You know…you could use this as your senior piece."

"My uncle and I are innocent, so I don't think so."

"Even if you think that, something weird is going on and if we figure it out, that would be a hell of a project. Now, I need to head out, but we'll talk soon."

I didn't wait before taking a step upstairs, but she put her hand on my arm, stopping me.

"Wait!" She jerked her hand back when I turned around and red splotches appeared on the tops of her round cheeks. "How much time do you envision spending on this? What do I need to be doing now?"

"See what you can find out about how you got into college. Any documentation, forms with signature, that sort of thing. In order for us to go forward, we'll need evidence. Let me check my practice schedule and get back to you with some times I have free."

She nodded and jutted her chin out just a little. "I want that picture of names. I'm pretty decent at digging up some information on people and I want to see what I can find on those players you mentioned."

Her determination was clear in the set jaw, the intensity in her dark brown eyes and the slight rise in her voice. Ambar was hooked, but I needed to make one more point clear for this to work. "You have to swear you will not hide *any* information that comes up. If I find out you're protecting your uncle, I will do everything I can to ruin you. And trust me, there is a lot of ammunition there."

She recoiled and a fire entered her eyes. "That won't be a problem because you're wrong, Jeff. And I cannot wait to see the look on your face when I prove it to you."

Chapter Four

Ambar

I didn't miss the hangovers, that was for sure. My roommates groaned and slid around the couches like blobs and the pathetic sight of them made me smile. Laney and Marissa were wonderful women who I support with every grain of my being, but a small part of me was envious of their life.

Last year, I'd witnessed Laney talk herself out of a speeding ticket. Sophomore year? She'd had four fake IDs and had managed to not get written up for distributing them to younger girls. The year before that, she'd convinced the RA to not report the alcohol in her dorm room.

I'd drawn the short straw with my freshman roommate and gotten caught up in a drug scandal and put on probation. Then it'd been academic probation. *And that is still my reputation.*

Jeff Maddow's disgusted facial expression from three days ago told me all I needed to know. I was just the druggie freshman girl who went wild in college. *That's why he thinks I don't deserve to be at this school.*

I'm gonna show him, that beautiful rat bastard.

"Ambaaaaar. Could you bring me some coffee and I'll love you for the rest of my life?" Marissa whined and flipped from her right to her left side. She grimaced and paled, and I grabbed a small trash can and placed it in front of her. "Why do you look so normal?"

"I didn't drink last night."

"I think I killed all my brain cells and forgot."

"You might be right," I said, laughing.

"Did I dance on a bar with some guy with a face tattoo?"

"Absolutely. I only took three pictures."

"Kill me. I told myself I was growing up this semester. I'm going to be a grown-ass adult soon."

"You can still dance on bars when you're an adult, Issa."

"How do you remain friends with us if you don't drink anymore? I can't stand myself sometimes but being around us sober is the pits, girl."

"I love you both. Plus, I learned I don't have to drink to have fun. I know that makes me sound old and wise, but shit, it took a long time to discover that."

"I'm not there yet. Don't tell my parents."

I snorted, feeling a spark of pride in my decision to not drink for four months. While my junior year hadn't been as eventful as the wild freshman year, there had been one too many nights of stupid mistakes and morning regrets. I'd hit a low point when my advisor had said I was one grade away from being kicked out of school and that had been the day I'd decided to clean up my act. That meant no more partying, blowing off classes or hooking up with guys who were too drunk to *really* see me.

That had been my rock bottom and I was slowly pulling myself up from that with a small step every day. *Today's step?* Figure out the real reason I'd gotten into this school, because ever since Jeff had thrown that accusation, it had registered in the most insecure part of me, wedging itself into every thought until it consumed me. *I'm average.*

It wouldn't be *totally* insane if it were true. I wasn't an exemplary student. I hadn't been the star of anything in high school or involved in so many clubs my resume was three pages long with eight letters of recommendation. Even my parents had expressed their doubts at me applying to one of the best schools in our state. *'Don't aim so high, Ambar—that way the disappointment won't be as strong.'*

Well, three and a half years later, I'm going to graduate with a better GPA than I had in high school. So take that, haters.

"I'll make some coffee, but then I'm going to hunker down in my room to get some research done."

"Ah, *research*." Laney dragged the word out for five syllables, making her pitch go two octaves too high. "About our filthy hot and single neighbor."

"Our out-of-my-league neighbor, that is," I added, ballparking the measurement of coffee grinds to make a full pot. My dad called it laziness that I didn't get a scoop and measure exactly the right amount—I called it just fine. No one had complained about my brewing abilities yet.

"Ambar, Jeff Maddow is *not* out of your league," Marissa mumbled. "You would actually have to *try* something to actually be shot down from him, and we all know you haven't."

Ah, yes. My lack of confidence in dating. A common topic in our household.

"I banned talking about my dating life until February. Off limits." I leaned against the counter and sighed at the folder of dating apps in my phone. My roommates had made me download them after a disastrous fling that had left me feeling used and smaller than dirt and I hadn't logged into them. It was a form of punishment. There had to be the right catchphrase to be interesting, and the profile pictures had to be classy but sexy.

I had never been called classy or sexy in my entire life. But that was neither here nor there. I had bigger things to worry about than my lack of happily-ever-afters. A scandal that might or might not involve me and my Uncle Martin. *That* took precedence.

"Let me know if you're dying or something, but I'll be busy for a couple of hours."

They didn't respond and I brought coffee in my favorite mug up to my room. Research phase had begun. *How I got into school.*

It took an hour or so to find all the old materials saved in the cloud—four years ago seemed way longer than I cared to admit. But I found it all saved in a folder. At least I'd been organized online at eighteen.

It seemed normal. I'd filled out an application, sent my transcripts, written an essay—I thought—and hit Submit. Then I'd gotten a letter saying I was in wait, got called in for an interview and got accepted. *None of that seems fishy…yet.*

Who did I interview with? I started making notes containing the names of people who'd been involved. The dean of admissions, the academic advisors for those declaring communication majors and a graduate of the school, *Dean Sanders.* God, that name was familiar. A couple of searches later, nothing popped up and I let out a frustrated sigh.

I'd have to circle back to this process. Next item on the list—internet stalking Max Miller, Cooper Killian and Dillon Cage. Maybe something would magically appear or stand out. *Because I want to reach out to Jeff?*

Don't be an idiot.

"Gah!" I shook my head, refocusing, and got to work. Social media kept more information than we'd care to admit and teenagers weren't the brightest when it came to privacy setups. Dillon and Max might have their account private, but their friends' weren't and *bam*. I was in, seeing their posts.

Interesting that they're still at the school, living life and not showing any signs of an injury. Jeff had been right about that. Dillon liked girls. Lots of them. In every picture he was shirtless with a different chick on his arm and that was something I could use. I jotted the information down. It was officially the note-gathering stage of the search and while my skin tingled with an almost electric excitement at uncovering a truth, my gut tightened. Each oddity meant that Jeff accusations could have merit.

Only one way to find out.

Create account? Yes, please.

It took less than ten minutes for me doctor a photo of myself that looked somewhat sexy—I included a lot of cleavage—and hid my identity. Hit following on a hundred people, got some auto-follows back, and took a chance.

SportsDiva: I've heard a lot about you, Dillon. Can I ask you a question?

Dillon: Name it, baby, only if I can ask you a question.

SportsDiva: I was told you got a spot on the baseball team. I'm really bendy for athletes…

Dillon: I like bendy.

Oh god, boys were idiots.

Dillon: I was a sports recruit during my freshman year but played too hard and got injured. Are you good at taking care of people in bed?

SportsDiva: Oh yeah.

Okay, now I was out of my league. How did I get more information from him and remain sexy? Shit. I really didn't want to do it… I didn't. But I accepted a little defeat and texted the number Jeff left with me.

Ambar: I need help. Are you free?

Jeff: Yeah, what's up?

Ambar: I'm chatting with one of those kids you think was involved and I started it trying to be sexy and, well… I'm not sure how to proceed in the conversation.

My phone buzzed and I waited two rings before answering. It wasn't nearly enough time to calm my racing heartbeat or get my sweaty palms under control. "Yeah?"

"You're *talking* to him right now? In person? Are you an idiot? We need to be discreet."

"Again, insulting me isn't in your best interest. I created a fake account online, dumbass. It's not in person."

Silence. A loud exhalation. "Oh. Are you at your house?"

Why did I call him again? "Yes, why?"

"I'm coming over."

Then he hung up.

"Shit!" I stood and checked my outfit. If I counted right, I had about thirty seconds to change from the booty shorts and baggy sweatshirt. I was sans makeup and had a coffee stain on the white material, but I didn't have time to change. My account pinged with another message.

Dillon: Diva? I really like your profile picture. I'm still hurting from the injury and I think sending another picture, with less clothes, would make me feel better. Here, I'll send you one as motivation.

*Dillon: *image**

I gasped. He'd just sent me a dick pic. *Oh my god. My first dick pic.* Laughter overwhelmed me and by the time I calmed myself down, a loud knock sounded on my door. *Jeff Maddow.* "Uh, come in?"

He entered the room and three things happened simultaneously. His cologne filled my small room and I breathed in deeply. He noticed. Then he widened his eyes and pointed to the computer. "Is that a dick?"

"Oh yes." I giggled again and had to cover my mouth with my hand. "Our boy Dillon wants me to send a slutty picture. I was thinking about doing the elbow thing to make it look like a butt."

Jeff's face remained perplexed, but slowly, it transformed from the hard, angry expression to one of amusement and my legs turned to noodles. I didn't have to like the guy to be attracted to him and how massive he was standing in my room, three feet away from me. Plus, he wore another Henley shirt, showcasing his toned arm muscles and it was probably a good thing it was the dead of winter. I couldn't promise how I would react to his bare arms.

Shit, his smile is growing.

"Fucking shit." He threw his head back and howled, and didn't ask permission before sliding a wooden chest from the end of my bed next to my computer chair and sat right next to me. "This is hilarious. Have you done the elbow thing before?"

"Not since high school. Dare we try it again?"

"I'll take the shot. Make your arm sexy." His eyes lit up with amusement, the deep gray almost the same color as the sky outside, and it was hard to ignore how my stomach swooped at our nearness. I had to remind myself. *He thinks I'm a part of this scam. That I'm average. He's out of my league.*

I handed him my phone and shoved up the arm of my sweatshirt, making cleavage of my elbow. "Get it?"

"Oh yeah." He laughed again, deep and rich in timbre, and handed me the phone. "Now I'm wondering if any of the pics I got were just arms."

"Doubtful. It's you," I said, tensing at the realization of what I'd said. He didn't comment and I considered it forgotten. "Okay, Dillon, let's play."

I sent the image and he opened it within the second.

Dillon: Great start. I want to see more. Show me those nips, babe.

"Oh my god." I cringed and Jeff had the decency to wince. "Do guys do this? Do you do this? My roommates want me to start Tinder and Bumble but if this is what's waiting for me, I'd rather date myself."

He rubbed the back of his neck and shrugged. "I want to say no…but…yes?"

I closed my eyes and let out a frustrated breath. *He's not perfect. Good. Remember that.*

SportsDiva: We can arrange that but I kinda got a kink for injuries. Tell me about yours. I want to imagine my hands on you.

"Nice. Let's see what he says," Jeff said, encouraging me.

Dillon: I hope we can arrange for that soon. It wasn't bad. Just a rolled ankle.

SportsDiva: Someone as strong and built like you couldn't recover from that?

Dillon: Decided baseball wasn't for me after all. I answered, babe, your turn.

I clicked out the messages and went to his profile, scanning pictures and videos of Dillon doing various things on campus. He was into frisbee golf, keg stands and *oh shit*. There was a video of him dated the fall before from a CrossFit gym. *He's a sophomore now and if he got injured right before this video went up…*

"Interesting, isn't it?" I tapped my pen against my teeth and watched Jeff for a reaction. He bounced his gaze back from my laptop screen to my face a couple of times before he ran his hand along his jaw. His lack of response made me continue. "What's the protocol for injuries? You received a full-ride baseball scholarship, right? If you were to get hurt, they'd rehab you or something—not just let you decide baseball wasn't for you. Wouldn't Dillon lose money?"

"This just gets weirder and weirder."

"How so?"

"His name was on the roster the entire year. We were told it was more serious and they even had him come back and make the announcement to us." He stood, gave me a hard look and said, "This is the second athlete with a fake injury. Fuck. You did good, Ambar."

Chapter Five

Jeff

Ambar's smug grin transformed her face. There was no other way to describe it. Her brown eyes lit up and her pink lips twisted up on the side as if to tell me *no shit.* I shrugged, hoping that conveyed enough of an apology, but she didn't react. She gave me a hard look that had me clearing my throat at her scrutiny. Very few things flustered me but the expression on her face didn't sit well with me. "Why the face?"

"Nothing." She jerked one shoulder down, to appear relaxed, but it didn't fool me. Then she said, "Just got a little thrill knowing you underestimated me."

That made me smile. "I guess I did."

"You *definitely* did, but we don't need to rub it in your face or anything." She scrunched her nose and smiled, the entire expression making her seem cute.

Huh. Ambar Henderson cute? That was a new thought I derailed immediately. "I'm thinking we need to talk to these guys in person—possibly figure out a way to get them to admit this on camera."

She nodded encouragingly and continued to tap the pen against her teeth while I rambled my thoughts aloud. "I mean, if these punks had anything to do with it, they aren't going to want to admit anything, or, they could say we are making it all up."

"I see your point." She sucked her top lip into her mouth and brought her bottom teeth up to bite down on it. It was the least sexy thing I had ever seen, but it brought attention to her full lips. *Have they always been like that?* "What's our goal, here? It would help me if we could brainstorm the purpose. This was just a spur-of-the-moment decision to reach out to him and see if he would chat with a random chick. It clearly worked—I mean, look at his social media footprint. Are we just focusing on the two other baseball players or *anyone* who got in under suspicious circumstances?"

Damn, forward thinking. I should've thought of it. "We need to look for similarities between the athletes across all sports teams."

"You did accuse me of being in on this scheme, Jeff, so there's a possibility the premise of sports wasn't even used," she said, the light dimming a bit in her expression. A dull tightness formed in my chest and I ran my hand over my skin, hoping to rid of the sensation. Okay, maybe I shouldn't have accused her of being involved. *Apologize to her. Just say the words.*

I never got the chance. She clapped her hands and her entire body hummed with excitement. "Jeff…I can use the same premise that I'm using with our friends. *Interviewing for my final project.* I can visit other teams, ask around about any athletes that got injured and never returned. Oh! We can print rosters from freshman year and compare them to now. Unless we want to cover all bases and look into sophomore recruits, too. What do you think?"

That I should've come to you sooner, and not been a dick about it. "Those are great places to start for sure."

"Hell yeah." She did a little shimmy where she shook her shoulders but once she saw me staring at her, she adjusted the hem of her shirt and avoided my gaze. "Uh, sorry. The thrill of proving you wrong and getting to the bottom of this is exhilarating."

That makes one of us. I needed to stick to the plan and not get caught up in the betrayal of my coach and the injustice of Jamie. It was enough to cause my insides to burn. "Should we make a timeline and plan when to check in with each other?"

"Sure." She swiveled in her chair and had her legs crossed over each other, showing off a lot of skin. *It is warm in here.* "I don't mind reaching out to some of the other sports teams to get the ball rolling. I have enough connections to at least see if this is a baseball-specific issue or larger."

"Is it bad I don't want it to just be baseball?"

"So my uncle can take the fall?" she fired back.

I did not mean to say that. It was a thought that should've stayed up in my head for me alone to take to the grave. But it was something in her expression, the thrill of the chase, that had me admit it. This was a better time than ever to admit why. *And maybe not be the asshole she thinks I am.* I took a deep breath and pulled on the neckline of my shirt before saying, "No. Not so your uncle can take the fall. My coach…"

I paused and swallowed down the uncomfortable burn in the back of my throat. "My coach has been a mentor to all of us for years. I respect him with every ounce of my blood but if he's behind this…it would kill me. All of us."

She gave me a pitying look and her gaze moved move from me to a picture frame sitting on the small side table. "How do you think I feel about my uncle?"

"I can sympathize with you on that. I really can, but, Ambar, we both have to accept two people we care about might be involved. It's the harsh reality of this and maybe there will be a miracle that we're both wrong."

She blew out a long breath that sounded like a deep growl and nodded a couple of times to herself. "Yes. I know. I'm considering not showing any bias during this one of my main areas to grow."

"I appreciate that."

She smiled tightly at me just as the door to her room flew open. We both jumped as the tall blonde entered and raised two thin eyebrows at us. She wore a playful smile but then her attention went to the computer screen. "Ambar, Jeff, could you explain the dick pic greeting me right now?"

"Fuck!" Ambar scrambled to shut off the monitor and it took all my strength to not laugh at the situation. Her entire face turned red and I swore I could feel the embarrassment leaving her body and making the room turn ten degrees warmer. "It's not what you think, Laney."

"Hm." She entered the room and threw herself onto Ambar's small bed, making herself quite comfortable. "Well, I'm thinking that you're interviewing Jeff Maddow for your senior piece and you got bold and asked him for a dick pic since we all wanted to know if the rumors were true. Knowing the egos athletes can have, he promptly sent you a picture."

"Why would I send a picture if I could just whip it out right here?"

"Oh, great point, Maddow." She winked at me and I grinned right back at her. She ate it up and tilted her head as she studied Ambar. "Second hypothesis. You signed up for Tinder or Bumble and got matched quickly because you're hot and you got your first dick pic."

"Laney!" Ambar seethed and the tips of her ears turned red. Again, if I didn't feel so bad for her, I would have been roaring with laughter. But then, Ambar's posture straightened and she pointed her finger at Laney. "Okay, fine. You're right. I signed up for Tinder and swiped a bunch of times on some dudes and one sent me this immediately."

Laney winced and leaned her elbows onto her knees. "I should've warned you about entering that world. The dating world is brutal. So many dick pics. I got one last night from a random number who called me Chasity. I don't know why guys send them. No girl is like yes, *that's* the dick to rock my world. Eventually, they all look the same. Right, Jeff? When you get all sorts of tit pics, they blur together I'm sure."

Why am I here right now? Jesus Christ. I said nothing.

But Laney wasn't done. She got up, stretched and gave me an amused look. "This piece she's writing about you will get you a lot of attention. She's a dope-ass writer. But she is new to the whole dating thing and can't spend all her time researching. So be nice and don't be an overinflated athlete and steal all her time."

"Really now?" I goaded Ambar, loving the panic in her eyes. "New?"

"A total dating virgin," Laney added.

"Good. Bye, Laney." Ambar stood and shoved her friend out of the door and leaned her back against it once it was shut. She closed her eyes and sighed, giving me a great view of her legs. The tiny shorts left little to the imagination and for the life of me, I never remembered seeing great legs on her.

Is that a tattoo on her ankle? God, I wanted to know what it was.

"You can go now." She still hadn't opened her eyes. She kept them closed tight and ushered with her hand for me to leave. There were a million things I had to do—go over practice plans, do my part on the investigation, look into law school without my teammates knowing I wanted out of the draft and grocery shopping. But I remained in the uncomfortable office chair and grinned. This was so much better.

"Nah, I'm good here. I want to hear more about this *online dating* thing you're so new at."

"Why did I ever think you were great?" she mumbled, and did not hide her displeasure when she came back to sit in front of me at the desk. "You suck."

"I've heard worse."

She snorted and pointed to the spiral notebook that had some wires escaping from the middle. "Let's just… What do you want to work on? I already said my part."

"We're really not going to talk about what just happened?" I didn't want to drop it.

"I'd rather take this stapler and bang staples into my leg than talk about my *online dating life* with you." She jutted out her chin and even put a hand on her hip.

"Why so defensive about it?"

"Because it is neither here nor there. I don't have time for it, really, but my roommates push it on me. They think I need something besides my blog in my life but these online apps… I'm new to them."

"*And* you're bad at it," I teased, enjoying myself more than I thought.

"Technically, I'm not bad because I haven't really done it. That's like saying you're bad at water polo even though you've never played. You don't know. You could be the Lebron James of water polo-ists. I could be the Lebron of online dating but I would need to sign up in order to know for sure."

Good lord. I couldn't stop myself from smiling at her manic expression but also her words. That was a lot to digest. "You could be the Lebron of dating apps. Just gotta try it, Henderson."

"Yeah. *Okay*. I'm ending this awkward conversation right now." She stopped moving around so much and met my gaze, this time full of determination. "You look into rosters from freshman year and compare them to now and see if anything jumps out. I'll reach out to my connections and see if I can't meet up with some of them and get some info. Let's meet next weekend, same time."

"Are you kicking me out, Henderson?"

"Yes. You've seen me embarrassed more than enough." She crossed her arms and crossed her right leg over her left, giving me a quick peek at her tattoo again. "If anything comes up before Sunday, just let me know."

Damn, she really wants me gone. Why does this feel weird? "Next week it is." I didn't stand up to leave, though. I tried to think of something to say, to prolong this conversation for some reason, though I couldn't think why. Ambar continued to watch me with an odd expression and when I was about to say something, she opened her mouth.

"Are you expecting me to walk you out? Is that why you're not getting up? Because I'm not going to do that no matter how popular or good-looking you are."

I barked out a laugh and finally stood. “Glad to know you think I’m good-looking.”

“Not news to you, Jeff. Don’t act shocked. You’re hot. An asshole, but hot. Now get out.”

Chapter Six

Ambar

It was a sad reality to accept that the thought of a scandal happening at our school was more exciting than any of my classes. Three days into the second week, I had homework that I didn't want to do and a missed call from my mom. It was a ten-minute walk back to the house and the perfect amount of time to have the awkward but brief conversation that would eventually have to happen. It was like picking between two wounds—want a dull continuous pain or a sharp stab? Both would bring me disappointment and put a cloud of doubt around me that would take a day or two to lose. *But she's my mom.*

Doesn't mean she can't make me feel like shit.

I took a deep breath and called her back. It would be better than avoiding her… The one time I'd tried, she'd turned my brothers against me and it had been catastrophic during the holidays. *Maybe she won't answer…*

"Hello, Ambar."

"Hey, Mom. What's up?"

"Just checking in to see how my only daughter is doing. Am I not allowed to call you?"

Don't take the bait. Don't. "Of course you can."

"I should think so. Now, Martin mentioned sending you another package, trying to showcase how he is a better human than I am. What did he send you so I can send him the money? The nerve he has sending you gifts and not your brothers… Having favorites serves no purpose."

Yeah, like you don't favor the boys in everything. "He just sent me some notepads for class, a college sweatshirt and hot chocolate."

"If you need supplies and clothes, you need to ask me or your father. And I thought you were dieting? How does hot chocolate fit into that?"

My jaw hurt from how hard I gritted my teeth together. Yes, I had ten pounds that wouldn't go away and she never let me forget it. "My roommates love hot chocolate."

"Mm. Well, share it with them."

Deep breath in and out. "Will do. Hey, I gotta run. I see a professor I need to catch up with."

"Glad to see you take the initiative in something. Talk soon, Ambar."

It didn't matter how many layers I wore—the chill ran bone-deep and the small pieces of self-confidence I built each week were torn down. It took a two-minute phone call to destroy my progress and my eyes tingled.

I am never enough to my mom.

My brothers are her babies.

I am too chubby, too crass, too lazy, too unremarkable to be her daughter.

Hannah Henderson is a knock-out and the fact that I'm not one disappoints her every day.

It pissed her off that her brother favored me over the boys and I hadn't even mentioned the gift cards, cash or the new watch that had come in the package. She would flip her shit and insult me to make herself feel better. It didn't matter how many times Laney and Marissa talked to me about her narcissism, it never stopped the hurt.

God, I wanted to say to hell with being sober and have a drink.

Ambar: Are either of you free? Need a distraction.

Marissa: Talk to your mom again?

Ambar: Straight to the usuals. Weight, laziness, my uncle.

Laney: I'm free in twenty minutes. What you need, girl?

Ambar: Heading to the Lion. I'm getting a strong-ass coffee.

Laney: Be there soon.

Marissa: Stuck in class for another two hours but I'll text you after.

Gratitude the size of an elephant filled my lungs at the support of my friends. We all had our own shit, but it felt worse when it was my own family. The feeling would last a couple of days and by the time I'd work it out of my system, she'd call again and the cycle repeated.

Fuck. *Why did I give up alcohol again?*

I walked faster to the bar, hoping to warm myself up and to distract me from the urge to order three whiskeys and down them. The urge scared me because one wouldn't be enough and soon, I'd be in a pity party that would make me feel like shit about myself for a week. I was better than that. Better than her insults.

"Hey, Henderson, it's been a while. How ya been?" Rocco, the bouncer, grinned at me and I leaned into him for a hug on the patio entrance.

"Hanging in there."

"That's all we can do. Have a good night."

I used to think it was cool I knew the bouncers at all the bars but really, it was because I went out four nights a week. We weren't friends. Sure, they would help me out if I needed it, but I partied a lot and that was how they knew me. *That's how Jeff sees me.*

Woah, okay, brain, settle down.

I removed my large winter hat and ran my fingers through my hair, shaking all thoughts of him out of my head. Another person accusing me of being a piece of shit? *Not today.* My guards were up. I wasn't responsible for people's opinions of me and I needed to remember that. I chose a wooden booth in the back of the bar, not right in the center but a great spot for people watching. Old me would've chosen the bar for quicker access—the current me liked the distance.

"Hey, girl, want a coffee?"

"You're a goddamn angel, Greta."

She pursed her lips. "I know."

It made me laugh and a small bit of envy went through me at her confidence. She was so sure of herself, who she was and what she liked that she dominated a room. It also helped because she was one of the most selfless people I knew. "It's been a while, how you been?"

"Dealing with Aaron and the upcoming draft, graduation and finding a job that could be thousands of miles away from where he ends up. So, you know, nothing really." She shrugged, but her smile didn't reach her eyes.

"Damn, that's a lot."

"It's what it is. We knew this from day one, so it's not a surprise. Gotta admit, it's harder than I thought it would be. I can't show weakness, or he'll lose it."

And I'm worried about petty shit with my mom. My worries paled in comparison and I hoped I gave her an empathetic smile. "I have no doubt you two will make it work. Might be messy, but you'll get there."

The dark look left her face and her signature toothy smile came back. "I knew I liked you. Let me grab that drink for you."

That left me alone at the booth just as Aaron Hill and Jeff Maddow walked in. It was stupid how my pulse sped up at the mere sight of Jeff. His fitted jacket and jeans showcased how strong he was and while I was without a doubt attracted to him, I'd lost a little bit of my crush. He'd already pegged me for someone I was trying not to be and I wasn't about to try and change his mind. No boy was worth that.

Shit. He looked my way.

I adjusted my hair to cover my face and pulled out my phone to check…the weather or something, but the heavy footsteps forced me to look up. Jeff had a killer smile, one that made me feel like he was laughing at me rather than with me, and I hated the insecurity plaguing me. *Is my denim shirt too tight?* I reached to my side to make sure it was tucked into my black jeans and sighed when it was still intact. He still hadn't said anything so I tilted my head. "Hey?"

"Have you always had hair this long?" He gestured to my curly black hair spilling down my chest, past my boobs, and I nodded. "Huh. Never noticed."

"Not sure why you would." *What else was I supposed to say? This is so awkward. Speak. Say something.* "Grabbing a beer with Aaron?"

"Yup. We had a bitch of a hitting session and need a beer to recover." He stepped closer and looked over his shoulder before a serious expression crossed his face. "I brought up Max to our hitting coach today, to see if he remembered him—"

"Henderson," Hilly greeted me. He often did that, just my last name. I nodded to him and he took that as an invitation to sit down in the bench across from me. "Care if we join you?"

"Laney's joining me soon but sure."

"Thanks. I like sitting in booths that are almost full so people don't feel entitled to join us, you know? This goddamn draft is hovering over us. Jeff is the only one not freaking out about it."

Jeff's only response was a wrinkle between his eyebrows. I didn't scoot farther inside, hoping he'd get the hint to sit with Aaron, but he didn't. He plopped down next to me, our legs briefly touching before I repositioned myself. "Mind if I sit here?"

"You didn't give me a choice," I mumbled, not meeting his eyes. I wanted to hear the rest of his story, but there would be no way until Aaron left us. He'd made that part clear—making sure no one would ever find out about the investigation…definitely not his teammates. "The draft has to be exciting, though, right? Terrifying, I'm sure, but how exciting you all get to be a part of it. Thousands of players never get that chance."

"I don't mean to sound ungrateful," Aaron said, rubbing his hands over his eyes, but as soon as he looked up, his entire face softened into a sickly-sweet expression. "Hey, G."

"Ronnie," Greta replied just as she set down my steaming cup of coffee. She moved to sit on his lap for a second and the entire thing caused an unwelcome pang near my heart. It wasn't jealousy. I remembered what they'd gone through and why. It was…a longing for something that might never be mine.

"Fighting a hangover or something?" Jeff asked, pointing to the white mug with a large chip on the side. "Or are you one of those people who can drink coffee any hour?"

"I'm not hungover, no. Coffee is my choice of drink when I want to relax."

"Doesn't work like that. You should have a beer."

"I'm good." I gave a tight smile, hoping he'd drop it, but Greta and Aaron's conversation stopped and she chimed in.

"It's admirable to stop drinking for a bit. It'd probably do us all good to cleanse the binge-drinking from our system. Lord knows I could." She giggled at the end and abruptly stood up. "Shit, my boss is looking for me. I gotta get back."

Aaron watched her walk away with a pining in his eyes and it felt so intimate that it almost felt wrong observing it. *Will anyone look at me that way?*

"The beer doesn't bother you, does it?" Aaron asked and did his best to hide his glass from view. It was a futile but appreciated attempt.

"Today was a bit rough, so it's hard, but nothing I can't handle."

"Wait. Hold up. You're saying you don't drink? I've seen you do a keg stand for a full minute wearing a dress, Ambar," Jeff said, further solidifying his impression of me. "I call bullshit on you *not* drinking."

My face burned red and I did my best to look confident. I straightened my shoulders and looked him head-on. "I don't drink *anymore*."

"Yeah, dude. She stopped in the fall. She's been over to our parties and sober…you're dense sometimes, man." Aaron took a sip of beer and the reasons why Jeff and I weren't friends were like flashing neon lights. I needed to steer clear of people who made me feel bad about myself, not spend more time around them, and the thought of walking away from the investigation crossed my mind.

But what if he's right? The injuries are suspicious.

I sipped the hot brew and tried to think of any comeback that would work. Anything to make him feel bad. But my brain didn't work like that. I'd think of the perfect zinger in four hours when it didn't matter. The embarrassment of that being the old me was enough to have my neck burn for an hour.

"Hm," was all Jeff said.

Like the bright shining star she was, Laney waltzed into the bar and distracted me from the shame of Jeff's intense stare. "Laney!" I shouted at her.

She grinned at my booth mates and took her time talking with people as she walked over. Then, she lifted a finger telling us to wait a minute and went to the bar. *Damn it.* Guess I had to suffer in the awkward silence longer.

"Ah, shit." Aaron narrowed his eyes toward the bar and took off, mumbling something along the lines of his sister. Jeff met my eyes and jutted his chin toward the pretty blonde getting hit on by a group of dudes.

"That's his sister, Kenzie."

"Yeah, I've met her a couple of times. When she was living in your room last year, actually."

He made a face and laughed. "My room still has lingering girl smell in there."

"Good. Boys stink."

He turned his torso all the way to face me so our faces were just a foot apart and an amused, playful expression crossed his face. "Oh, really?"

"Yes. I have two brothers. They are gross."

The playfulness left and the line between his eyebrows returned. "Older or younger brothers?"

"Both older."

"They didn't go to school here?"

"Nope." *They got to go to the private college in our hometown and live in a beautiful rented house that they trashed.* "They stay in our hometown about three hours away."

"Hm."

I chose the silence to take another sip of coffee, feeling Jeff's stare on my face. This scrutiny was new—yeah, I'd liked the wrong kind of attention my first three years in college, but having Jeff study me was nerve-wracking. *He's probably finding something wrong with me.*

"Listen, before they get back, our hitting coach didn't remember any of them. This man is like a steel-tank of memories, so this is really fucking weird."

"None of the three who were injured?"

"Correct," he said, lowering his voice and moving even closer to me. "That means these three punks were on the team but were injured before ever meeting the hitting coach? That seems shady as hell."

Definitely shady as hell. "When you first signed, what was your experience? Did you meet the hitting coach before the season started?"

He frowned and ran his large hand over his jaw, not distracting me whatsoever. Then he said, "I came out and visited the school a handful of times to make sure it was the right fit. Met the head coach and admired the hell out of him. He introduced me to his coaching staff—yes, the hitting coach was there because he intimidated me."

"Are you sure there's no way he just forgot? He could've met the kid once, right? He wouldn't remember a single name when he works with hundreds of players."

He groaned. "I get what you're saying, but three different guys that were on the team? That's not a coincidence."

"You're probably right." I blew out a breath and tried to figure out what the right steps were. "Damn."

"I'll ask him how involved he is with the recruitment process."

"Would that raise the alarm? What if he's in on it?"

"Christ, I hadn't thought of that." Jeff ran his fingers through his hair, messing up the style he had, and a part of me felt bad for him. These were men he admired, looked up to, and worked with…and they could be involved in something huge?

Woah, woah. He blames me and Martin. Don't forget.

I chewed on the side of my lip and grabbed a pen from my purse to jot down notes on the back of a napkin. If I didn't write my thoughts, I'd lose them and Jeff leaned his shoulder into mine to see what I was writing. His body heat was hard to ignore but I succeeded for a couple of minutes.

1. *What is the sports recruitment process? Is there a guide or rulebook we could read?*
2. *Who is safe to talk to about it?*
3. *How can we talk to those three kids without suspicion?*
4. *Follow the money.*

I tapped my pen on the table when it hit me. The quickest way to find trends. "Jeff."

"What?"

"There's a list of all freshmen who were recruited and received spots this past year for each sport. Being a blogger makes it perfect for me to reach out to them asking about their experience, their background. That sorta thing. *A profile of athletes.* I could even stalk online to see who signed for this fall and reach out to them for a showcase or something."

"Brilliant. Yes. I'll schedule it, hype it up like it's a big deal to get interviewed."

"Cool," I said, just as Laney and Aaron returned to the table. Laney sat across from me and wiggled her eyebrows, looking between Jeff and me.

"You two look awful cozy. Things…seem to be heating up, huh?"

Chapter Seven

Jeff

"Not *again,*" Ambar said between clenched teeth. Her roommate had a wild look on her face and I didn't care for the interest Aaron had in our conversation.

"Heating up?" Aaron said with an eager look. "What's this about?"

Ambar snorted and I slid her a look. *I guess this is in the open now.* "She's writing a piece on me for her big project."

"Ambar is the best at what she does, so you're lucky, Jeff, but she should be spending her time trying out these dating apps for her final semester of senior year, not using all her time starting at your face. I don't even care that you happen to be the best-looking baseball guy on the team—"

"Excuse me, that is a bold statement," Aaron interrupted. He always cared about his looks and he took personal offense to the Laney's comment.

"Sorry, Hilly. I meant *single* guy on the team. It's not fair to consider you, Zade or Tanner when you're so into your ladies. It'd be a different conversation if you weren't..."

Aaron gave a firm nod and I couldn't help but laugh. This wasn't the dumbest conversation I've had but it was up there. All hopes of everyone forgetting the topic were squashed when Aaron directed his attention back to Ambar. "So, trying out the dating world, huh? How's it going so far?"

"Great?"

"That was a question, babe," Laney said, and leaned her head onto the palm of her hand, showcasing her blonde hair. "My girl here hasn't had a date in years and is finally trying some dating apps that are more than hook-ups."

I snuck a look at Ambar and covered my smile with my hand. Her entire face was red, but she looked at us head-on. It was an endearing combination. "Dating is overrated," I added, but all three of them stared daggers at me. "What? Girls either date me to say they slept with someone on the baseball team or lie about that being their intention."

"You would actually have to do it to know, dude." Aaron lifted his beer to mine and slid his gaze to Greta. *Right. I left for one summer and came back to couples everywhere. Hand holding, dinners, date-nights, movies and muffled sounds from their bedrooms.*

I pulled on the collar of my shirt and downed half my beer. It wasn't like I was a total asshole...there just hadn't been anyone who caught my interest for more than a day or two. I was preparing to defend myself when Ambar chimed in.

"Didn't think I'd ever say this, but I agree with Jeff. *Dating* is overrated. If you want to hook up, just do it, or if you want to get dinner, just eat. The game of it doesn't appeal to me."

"Girl, you haven't had any decent guys, that's why."

"Well, *that* I know."

The girls laughed and I was going to ask Ambar more about the decent guy comment when Laney motioned for them to leave the booth. "Are you both heading out?"

"Yeah," Ambar responded. "Can you let me out?"

"Sure." I slid out of the wooden booth and couldn't describe the odd annoyance forming in my mind. Did I want to hang out with her? No. But did I want them to leave? Also no.

What the fuck?

Once out of the booth, she stared up at me and it was the first time I'd noticed how long her eyelashes were. They were dark and landed on her cheek when she blinked. *Huh.* "I'll be reaching out to you then for more questions."

"Great."

She smiled, not a real one, and took off with Laney. But not before I watched Laney throw her arm around Ambar's shoulders and say, "You doing any better? I'm sorry it happened again."

I didn't get to hear her response and something like worry took root. I wanted to know why Laney was sorry. *What happened?*

"You decide on an agent yet?"

Baseball. Draft. The future. Again.

I forced my attention away from Ambar and back to Aaron. The determined look on his face was all I'd seen recently. The tightness, the worry and the desperation. Every couple of days it was the same conversation.

Agent.

Press.

Season.

"I haven't yet."

"Coach has met with me a couple of times for some guidance on how to decide and my parents have been as much help as they can, but it feels so heavy. I've heard of horror stories of choosing the wrong one. I know they make money off us, but picking the right one… Do I want a shark? A dealmaker? Or someone who will be like family for my entire career?"

The muscles in my neck tensed and I finished the rest of my beer, buying myself some more seconds of silence. "Trust your instincts, Hilly. Our focus should be playing the best we can this season. If we do that, then the rest will be easier."

"That's what Coach was saying, too. I'm just worried about losing it all." He spoke quieter, just above a whisper, and guilt consumed me. My friend needed support and I was being difficult because of my indecisiveness. I was better than that.

"I can see why you would worry about that, but, dude, you have a huge support system around you that won't let you. Greta, your sister, us… Won't happen."

"The signs are the same, though. The anxieties and thoughts that spiral out of control." His eyes were wild and it reminded me of his sophomore year, the year he went on a bender and did a lot of stupid shit that could've ruined his career. It was just his reaction to life's circumstances and while he'd made a lot of steps to be better, I would hate to see him go back to all that.

"Hilly. What has been your goal for your entire life?"

"Play in the majors."

"How close are you to reaching the first step of it?"

He sighed and the worry on his face disappeared. "Final season."

"This is it. Play your heart out. We all stayed and are getting degrees so we have backup plans, and we never know when an injury can happen and knock us out of the game. So play your fucking heart out this season, man. It'll be the last time the four of us play together and I don't know about you, but that's motivating for me."

"Fuck. I never thought about that." He frowned and held out his fist. I bumped mine against his and he grinned. "When did you become the wise one? I thought it was Zade, but you're the parent now."

"Playing abroad taught me a lot."

Like how I don't like the lifestyle.

Like how the egos are hard to handle.

Like how being away from my friends and family was too much.

"Plus, I still have control over my balls, unlike the rest of you…"

"Fuck off," he replied, laughing at what I assumed was how right I was. But the stress was gone on his face and I shoved my own worries down. Aaron would break if he thought our coach had anything to do with a scandal that would blow up the news.

"Let's get another drink and bother Greta."

"Sounds like my kinda night."

* * * *

Okay. Time to do some work. Ambar had done most of it so far and it bothered me. I was never the kid who did the least in a group project and a week in, my contributions were shit. *Rosters. Other teams. New players on the team.*

Brandon. Hotshot hitter and outfielder, recorded as having a full-ride scholarship to the school. Probably wouldn't start this season but had potential next year after we'd lose four seniors. I scanned my phone for his number and almost cheered when I found it.

Jeff: Hey—you up for an interview with a campus blogger about your scholarship? It'll get your name out there and she's good.

Brandon: Maddow! Dude. Hell yeah.

It was too easy.

Jeff: You free tomorrow?

Brandon: I can be. Just name the time and place. Thanks for letting me know, dude. I appreciate it.

Boom. Interview set up. Now to find a time for Ambar.

Jeff: Brandon's in for an interview. Freshman on the team. What time are you free tomorrow?

Ambar: Anytime before noon.

Jeff: Want to meet in the library? They have those private conference rooms.

Ambar: Sure.

Jeff: Do you want to catch up before or after?

Ambar: Let's do after. I don't think you should be there during the interview.

Jeff: Why not?

Ambar: Look, I gotta go. But just set it up for me and we'll talk after.

Well damn. It was all set to go and I didn't want to show up empty-handed. I got to work and couldn't wait to show Ambar what I was looking up.

The next day I found a spot in the library a couple of tables away from the conference room where she and Brandon would meet for an hour. I assumed they'd both arrived and had started since I hadn't gotten a text from either one, but I wasn't going to wait to hear how it went. Not after what I'd found out the night before. My notes were organized by sport, and I had the papers all lined up when laughter caught my attention.

Brandon and Ambar walked out of the conference room and she had the biggest smile on her face—one I had never seen directed at me. Her outfit was different from the ones I was used to seeing her in. This one was a fitted red sweater that showcased the curves she did have—another feature I'd missed all these years.

He had his hand on her shoulder and she leaned into him before they turned to face each other. They talked a little more, him touching her again, before he left her in front of the room. Ambar bit down on her bottom lip and held her closed laptop tighter against her chest as she watched him walk away.

Is she into Brandon?

An uncomfortable burning sensation formed in my stomach and I was glad he'd left. Without thinking, I blurted out her name and said, "Hey."

The almost smitten expression melted off her face when her gaze landed on me, but something else was there. Almost like a spark of excitement in her brown eyes. She waved and nodded her head toward the room she'd just vacated and I swooped up my materials with one motion and met her there within a minute. I was just desperate to share what I found out with her. That was all.

It had nothing to do with Brandon leaving.

"How did it go with Brandon?" I asked, setting my stuff on one side of the table. It was hard to miss the fact two chairs on the same side were turned, practically touching, and the burning sensation moved from my gut to my chest. "From my end, it looked like it went *real* well."

Her ears turned red when she pushed her long hair behind them. "It did go really well."

"You into him?"

For fuck's sake, why did I ask that?

She focused on the clear white tabletop and ran her finger in a line over the edge. "We had a good time talking, that's all." She opened her laptop and gave me a crazy smile. "Want to know what I found out?"

"Hell yeah, but I gotta say, I got some good information last night, too."

"Can't wait. Here, I'll come over there." She moved and sat next to me, bringing with her a light floral smell that wasn't too strong. If anything, it was nice. She moved the screen between us and read from her typed notes.

"The process began senior year with the head coach visiting him in the fall and watching him play. They scheduled a campus visit where he was able to see the stadium, meet some of the players, chat with all the coaches and take some swings in the cages. When he officially signed, the head coach came to

his school for the photos and the dean of athletics handled all the scholarship aspects."

"We have a person then."

"The Dean of Athletics?"

"Yeah, if he's the guy handling all the recruitment, he'd be the guy enabling or helping out my coach." I scratched my chest and swallowed down the anger, knowing he was involved. It was inevitable. There was no way all this shit was happening without his involvement and the sad thing was that each team had a coach that was dipping their hands into illegal funds.

"I asked him about injuries and what happens if someone wants out of their scholarship or sport on the team—he didn't know what happens if he wanted out, but the injury thing caught my attention. He said there is an aggressive rehab policy depending on the severity of the issue."

"Did you bring up Cooper Killian? He's still a freshman this year but hasn't shown up to practice since fall ball drills."

She ran her tongue over her bottom lip and nodded. In that one gesture, confidence rolled off her and filled the room. It was almost… attractive. "I definitely did. He met him twice but admitted he never saw him display any skill. It was tricky, but he didn't suspect anything."

"If you were flirting, he probably missed it. You are a senior taking interest in him."

Her face hardened. "Again, I'm not sure why your opinion of me is so low, but it wasn't flirting that got me my information."

"Then what was it?"

"I wanted him to feel that the questions were about the freshman class talent and how they each stood out on their own. I didn't just mention Cooper. I talked about all the guys in the freshman class. How their skills were, their potential, what they brought to the team. He loved that angle and spilled it all."

"Well damn." *Good move. Maybe I'm the asshole here.*

"Yeah," she fired back. "I'm terrible at flirting and wouldn't even know how to go about it to get information that way."

"I doubt that. You're a chick."

"Being a girl doesn't automatically qualify me to being attractive or flirty enough to get something from them. I learned that a long time ago and instead use questioning to get what I want."

"Another reason your friends are pushing you into dating?"

"To get me out of my funk. Their words, not mine." She pointed back to her screen and took a deep breath. "Moving back to the reason we are here…I didn't get a chance to look into Dean Sanders yet, but if he's involved with every sport—"

"Then there could be countless students involved in this," I finished for her.

"One thing I want to follow up on is about those players who received partial-scholarships. His story sounded pretty standard, similar to what I imagine your experience was. But what about the kids on the team who got some help? Did they still sign and have the coaches come out?"

"I'm not sure, but what's your take on that?"

She crossed one of her legs over the other and twisted her lips to one side of her mouth before she spoke. "It would be easier to go under the radar with all this if they were dealing with partials. Less media, less social media blasts, less of everything. I bet the coaches don't go out for signing. Basically, less people would know about the player, making it easier to cover up."

"Well, last night I found out that there's no evidence as far as the rosters go. Even baseball, there's no evidence of Max, Cooper or Dillon being a part of the team anywhere on the school's website."

"*What*?" she asked, her wide eyes taking up half her face. "None?"

"That I could find."

"Well, fuck me." She made a raspberry with her lips and looked so unlike…Ambar that I smiled. She looked pissed off and disgusted, the same feelings I had been battling with the entire time. A part of me was afraid she was going to back out at the new hurdle, and I needed to come up with a way to get her to stay.

"Look, it'll be tough, but we can still connect some of the dots. Don't throw in the towel now. We know there's something going on." I reached out my hand to put it on her arm, but decided against it when she narrowed her eyes at me.

"I'm not throwing in the towel, Jeff. I'm pissed because that means they are covering their tracks. This will be harder than you or I could've thought." She cleared her throat and dove onto her laptop, typing furiously fast so her fingers blurred as I watched. "Athletes."

"Hm?" I did not follow her thoughts at all, but I was just happy she wasn't directing that angry expression at me anymore.

"We need to focus on the athletes, or fake-athletes. We need to get them to talk because even if they didn't know what was happening, they'll be able to help paint a picture of how." She pulled up a picture of Cooper, the one I remembered from the year before. *The kid I shouldn't have even seen.*

I laughed at the irony and she shot me a look, making me feel the need to explain. "Last year, I only met Max because I was lingering after a fall workout. Max was walking around with one of the assistant coaches, Tee, and he did a quick introduction to him."

"And Max did an announcement that he was injured and not coming back or…?"

"We just heard he wouldn't recover. It happens and none of us really knew about him or of him so it wasn't a big deal."

"Give me five minutes." She didn't wait for me to respond before she dove back onto her laptop. It was hard not to watch her when she stared at her screen and made small movements with her lips as she read the words. *Huh, her lips are pinker today.*

Feeling inadequate, or unhelpful, was a pet peeve of mine and I looked through my notes of all the players that I knew or trusted enough to ask questions to. There was at least one from all the major teams.

She clapped her hands, startling me, and said, "Got it. I have a plan for Max."

"Care to share it?"

"Yes, because I'm going to need your help."

"Name it." *Help her? Hell yeah. She's been doing all the work.*

"Max is in a fraternity and there's a mixer Tuesday night I need to get into."

"You want me to help you get in? Easy enough. Where's it at?"

"More than that," she said, her voice getting weaker. She glanced at the ground and groaned before adding, "I'm going to need help getting sexed up."

Chapter Eight

Ambar

This is the worst idea I've ever had in my entire life.

Help sex me up?

God damn it.

"Girl, why are you pacing our living room?" Marissa asked, peering up from her large textbook full of Post-It notes and highlighted phrases. Tuesdays were her study night, no matter what, and tonight was no exception. "You're making me antsy."

"Sorry. It's nothing. Just Jeff is helping me with the article, you know that, right?"

"Yeah, Laney brought it up. And you have a date tonight?" she asked, not hiding her surprise—or joy—from me. She had a manic smile and she even dropped her pen. "Like, he's taking you on a date or helping you get one?"

"Uh, the second?"

"Have fun. Jeff is a *snack*."

"I'm aware." I still wore black sweatpants and an old *Game of Thrones* T-shirt, but I had shaved my legs, showered and put on my best makeup. Wearing it always made me feel like I was playing dress-up, or trying to be cute when I never would be. My mom used to laugh when I wore lipstick, telling me it wouldn't help, and those feelings never really went away. But I hadn't talked to her since that phone call and I'd built myself up bit by bit. "It's still weird he's helping me. We aren't friends."

"Who cares. He owes you if you're going to write about him." She paused when someone knocked on the door. "That must be him, huh? I can't wait to hear about how this goes."

I smoothed my hair down and made sure I didn't have anything stuck in my teeth before I let him in. It was obnoxious how my body burst with anticipation. He was going to help me dress the part, coach me on what to say and set me free in the bar to get answers from Max. That was it. It wasn't a date with him. *So chill the hell out.* "Hey, Jeff."

"It's fucking cold outside. Damn, let me in," he said, rubbing his hands together over his mouth. It gave me a couple of seconds to study his loose black T-shirt that was extra-long. It showcased his pecs and biceps—my God, they were perfect—and he brushed past me without wearing a coat. "It's supposed to snow tonight, too."

"Great," I replied, already thinking about the outfits I couldn't wear. It was hard to be *sexy* wearing pants. Jeff didn't wait for me to guide him before he headed toward my room and plopped down on my desk chair. "Sure, make yourself comfortable."

"Already am." He grinned widely at me, crossing his arms over his chest and eyeing me up and down. "For starters, those sweatpants are hideous."

"No shit. They are my comfy pants, asshole. I'm not trying to be cute and shit when I'm binge-watching Netflix."

"I was teasing." He lowered his voice and the expression on his face softened. "Are you nervous? You're a bit prickly."

"This was a terrible idea." I let him hear me before I went to my closet and shuffled through my clothes until I found two dresses. "I am not prickly."

"Yes, you are." His voice was way closer to me than I anticipated and I jumped. He stood right behind me. In my closet. His cologne and warmth didn't have far to travel to greet my skin and the nearness to him caused my pulse to race in my ears. "If you don't mind, I'm gonna grab a couple options that catch my eye."

"Uh-huh," was all I managed to say. He reached his right arm over me, placing his other on my shoulder, and he grabbed a blue dress I hadn't worn in years. It was hard to focus when his hands were on me. His large, strong hands that I shouldn't be thinking about.

The investigation. He thinks I'm unremarkable.

"Kinda got a small closet, Ambar." He moved past me, his pecs pressing against my back, before he stood on the other end and took three more items off hangers. "These are a start. Want to try them on?"

I nodded. It was bizarre, seeing him in my small closet, and he grinned before walking out. *Be cool. Try on the outfits. That's it. No pressure.* My pep-talk didn't help and sweat dripped down my back despite the freezing temperatures. Wait—he'd set out short dresses. That was it. No pants or tights.

"Jeff, it's cold outside. These are tiny."

"You've gone out in the cold before. Gotta tough it out."

"Yeah, when I was stupid and four shots in. I had a nice alcohol-induced blanket then." I picked up the silky material I'd bought freshman year. The dress was thin and left little to the imagination—the whole purpose was to catch the attention of guys and hook up with them. Shame and regret washed through me when I remembered myself in my first year. *I've grown since then. I'm not that same girl.*

I closed my eyes, giving myself ten seconds of pity, and when I opened them, Jeff leaned against my doorway with a concerned look. *Is he feeling sorry for me again? Thinking I'm a loser?* My self-doubt annoyed me and I snapped. "What?"

"I'll drop you off at the door so you don't have to be outside, okay?"

"I thought you were going to come in with me?"

"After I park, I will be. It'll be better dropping you off, though. It is cold as shit outside and if you're wearing any of those dresses, you'll be showing a lot of skin." He wiggled his eyebrows up and down and gave me a playful smile.

It was easy to return. "Thank you."

"Yup. Now quit stalling. Try them on."

Okay. It's showtime. I took off my sweats and shirt and slid on the blue dress that had a deep V in the front that went to my belly button. It was one of the perks of not having large breasts—a fact Laney said she was jealous of because I could wear things like this. I always thought it was a deficit but looking at myself in the mirror, there wasn't as much doubt. My bra straps looked tacky, so I removed it and marched from my closet into my bedroom to show Jeff. "Well?"

He looked up from his phone and jerked his head back. "This could work."

"Not too much for a Tuesday night?" I winced and put my hands on my hips. Another nice feature of the dress was the illusion of having an hourglass figure. "I don't think I've been to this bar before."

"You'll get his attention, I guarantee it." He cleared his throat and dragged his gaze from my face to my chest, lingering for a minute, before eyeing my legs. "You look good. Want to try another?"

"S-sure."

Is his voice lower than normal? Does he hate it? Ugh. Enough. I shook my head and went back to my closet, stripping down and trying on a deep red dress that had no back. Another perk of not having to wear a bra. It fitted well, but it didn't make me feel as sexy as the blue dress and Jeff's expression only tightened when I showed him. I fluffed my hair and asked, "Better or worse?"

"It's fine." He ran his hand under his jaw and looked like he'd rather be anywhere else but here. The lines around his eyes were tight and his lips were pressed together hard. *That* was what got me angry. How dare he be impatient or annoyed? I was doing this because of him and I pointed at his chest.

"Listen, I know this isn't how you'd normally spend a night, but we're investigating this together since you accused me of being a part of this whole thing. The *only* reason I'm helping is to clear my uncle's name, so you don't get to act annoyed. I didn't force you to come here and I'm not enjoying a second of this either, okay?" My voice shook a little at the end, but I wasn't sure he noticed.

"Woah, Ambar, I'm not…" He sighed for a good thirty seconds before a look of regret crossed his face. "I'm sorry I gave you that impression."

"I'll just wear the blue one and we can get this over with." I ran back into the closet with my heart beating so fast it was pushing against my ribcage. I wasn't confrontational. I didn't do that, and yet, I said exactly what I wanted and got a high from it. *Go me.* It took a minute to get back into the first dress and find some cute brown booties to pair with it. My favorite floral perfume sat on the shelf and I spritzed it in my cleavage and hair and called it a night. But when I entered my room, Jeff wasn't sitting on the chair. He was leaning over my dresser, looking at some pictures I had there. "Uh, what are you doing?"

"You look so happy in the pictures with Laney and Marissa." He dragged his finger over my favorite photo—the three of us sophomore year covered in mud after it had poured rain on the quad and we'd fallen. It was in my top three favorite memories from college.

"I am happy with them. They're my best friends."

"You don't have any family pictures in here."

"Good observation." *Don't ask about them. Please.* I cleared my throat and asked before he had a chance to talk, "You ready?" I grabbed a swanky black blazer I'd bought for an interview the year before and, while it wasn't considered sexy, it paired well with the dress.

"It's a little early to head there. Plus, we should go over the questions and how you're going to approach him." He remained standing, and even with me in heeled shoes, our height difference was at least a foot. He towered over me but never made me feel unsafe. "What's your line of questioning?"

"First thought was to act like a baseball groupie wanting to get all his information. Dudes love talking about themselves."

"Hell, no." His face twisted into one of disgust, like he'd swallowed a sour lemon whole. "Groupies have a bad rep and will make any sane guy run away as fast as he can." He moved to sit back on the computer chair right next to me.

"But a groupie is easy to forget. I'll just be another chick trying to get close to fame. They are forgettable."

His gaze flicked to the deep cut-out of my dress for a second before he shook his head. "I'm not confident that would work."

"Well I can't use the blog or an interview as a premise. That only works when it feeds the egos and—"

"Like Brandon, hm?"

My face warmed and I gave him a stern look. "Brandon was different than I envisioned. He was humble and kind."

Jeff made a mocking face and said, "Sure."

"You're the worst." I smiled when I said it, but it didn't make it less true. *Huh, this bantering is fun.*

"Okay, new plan. When you were hooking up with guys, what was your game?"

"I was drunk most of the time." *They were too. It was easier that way. Less sting if they said no.*

"Still, you had to say or do something." He smiled and tilted his head to the left a bit. "Did you have a one-liner or a routine or something?"

"No!" I scoffed and tried to remember what I did. "It was more like…buying shots for guys at the bar, or grabbing one by the hand and dragging them to the dance floor. It wasn't talking."

He laughed. "Okay, Ambar. That's *definitely* a move."

"I guess."

"Oh, it is for sure. You wearing that dress and not even speaking before taking someone to the dance floor is big-dick energy. Well done." He gave me another appreciative grin and it took me a second for me to digest his words.

You wearing that dress.

He thinks I look good. Oh my god.

Concentrate. Investigation.

I cleared my throat and recapped to help refocus the purpose of why we were doing this. "Groupie route is out, blog is a no. What else is left? What do you suggest?" I moved to sit on the edge of my bed and he span the chair so he faced me—scooting closer in the process so he could reach out and touch my leg if he wanted. *But why would he want that?*

"I think you build up his ego. Mention how strong he is, how it's a shame he wasn't on the team, and see what he does. Feel him out."

"What if..." An idea struck me. A brilliant one. I stood up and snapped my fingers. "Get this. I'm going to tell him I heard he knew a guy. I have a sister back home who needs to come here. I'll say I'm from money and just need a number."

Jeff's forehead furrowed. "No."

"Why the hell not?"

"You're not putting yourself in danger. I won't allow that." His entire demeanor changed. Gone was the laid-back, almost arrogant baseball player. Instead, he looked ready to pounce and every muscle on his face tensed. "If he suspects anything and reports back to my coach or your uncle, it could be bad, Ambar. We really don't know how deep or involved this goes. We need to stay under the radar."

"I'll use a fake name. Hold on—Laney has some extensions I could put in my hair to disguise myself more." I yanked open my door and called to my roommate. She appeared from her bedroom and whistled.

"*Dayum,* mama. It's been a minute since you've shown off your figure. You look amazing. You help pick that out, Jeff?"

He grunted his response, but I didn't lose my momentum just to chastise him for being a grumpy-ass. "Can I borrow your dark extensions?"

"Oh, for sure!" She shoved me into her room and said, "You can follow if you want, Jeff, or you can watch from the hallway. Your choice. But we are going to gossip while I put them in."

"What kind of gossip?"

He followed us into the room. Laney pushed me onto her vanity chair and laughed. "Who is she going on a date with tonight?"

"He set me up with one of his teammates, Brandon."

"Is he hot?"

"God, yes."

"Are you wearing panties?"

"No. I can't with the cut of the dress."

Jeff dropped something hard onto the ground and we both jerked at the sudden noise. "Sorry," he mumbled. Laney grabbed the clips from her hair accessory drawer and parted my hair with a small comb. "You know, I'm not really into athletes. I think it's a selfish thing. Like, I understand their Dedication to a team and sport, but I'm a girl who likes a lot of attention."

I snorted. "At least you admit it upfront."

"It's the only reason I haven't asked Hilly to set me up with someone."

"Well, I'm glad Jeff set up a date for me. I don't mind the Dedication, actually. I need my alone time and with him having baseball…it would give us space."

Jeff's gaze met mine in the mirror and he had an unreadable expression. It wasn't interest or anything, but it wasn't bad. It was like he was studying me. I made a silly face at him and enjoyed how his eyes softened. "What do you think, Jeff? If you're dating and a girl has a problem with baseball, what do you do?"

"Uh, we wouldn't be dating if she had a problem with baseball. It's a huge part of my life."

"Fair enough," I said, enjoying the added length to my hair. It still looked like me but it was enough to not make me recognizable if Max was tipsy. "Do you have red lipstick, or something bold I could wear?"

"I love this confident Ambar. Seriously, where has she been? Yes! I have blues and reds and oranges. What do you think, Jeff? What would make these full lips pop more?" She reached out and squeezed my cheeks to my lips came together in a highly unattractive angle, but Jeff laughed and the sound comforted me.

"Red is always good."

"Boom. Here you go." She handed me a green tube of lipstick and patted my head. "I cannot wait to hear about it, girl. I'm proud of you."

And the guilt arrives full force. "Thanks."

"Now apply this shit and go!"

I did and felt a stir of excitement when I stared at my reflection. *I look happy.* Jeff jutted his chin toward the hallway and we walked to the front door together. "Is your car here?"

"No, I'll go get it." But he made no move to leave. We stood facing each other, our bodies close enough to touch, and he reached out with his thumb and brushed it against my skin—right next to my mouth. He swiped up. "You had a little color there."

"Oh, thank you." I flushed with embarrassment, but he hadn't removed his finger. It remained on my face, the small amount of contact causing my legs to feel like clouds, weightless and fluffy. Then, he added the rest of his fingers to my chin and lifted my face up while he studied every part of it. My breath got stuck in the back of my throat at the way he was looking at me and it took all my effort to not fall to the floor when he said, "We have one flaw in our plan. You are not someone he's going to forget."

Then he let go and walked outside.

The winter air hit me and thank God for that because that was the most intimate thing I had ever experienced. *What the fuck?*

Chapter Nine

Jeff

Max was a douchebag. Disgust rolled through me as I observed him and how he talked to girls. The slicked-back hair and constant roaming hands were enough reasons to dislike him, but to see him go from one chick to another, dismissing them when he reached a certain point had me clenching my pint of beer. Ambar hadn't made a move yet in the past hour and I was minutes away from calling the entire thing off. I took another drink and met her gaze over the edge of the glass. She arched her eyebrows and tilted her head toward him. *Is this her way of finally getting to work?*

I gave her a curt nod and rubbed my jaw. The muscles had hurt the past two hours I had been in her presence and I had no idea why. *Probably all that talk about Brandon.*

Or the fact she isn't wearing panties.

It's Ambar…she's not hot… Is she?

Oh fuck. She took the blazer off and set it on the back of a bar stool. Her cherry-red lips stood out against her skin and a shot of heat went below my waist at the thought of them. It didn't help how the cold showcased a slight outline of her perky nipples in the dress...hell, did she go braless too?

There wasn't enough beer in the world to watch this, yet I remained frozen to my seat. She sauntered up to Max and it amazed me how she transformed herself. She stood with confidence and oozed sex appeal. My neighbor who'd done drugs freshman year, who'd given up drinking and wore rainbow socks looked hot as hell and it was really messing me up.

Max noticed her as she leaned over the bar, letting the front of her dress hang forward, damn well giving everyone in the bar a glance at her cleavage, and a dull pounding began in the base of my head.

He reached out and placed a hand on her arm, caressing her skin, and she giggled. It sounded so fake, but he responded to it. He pulled her closer to him and she let him. Her long black hair flowed over her shoulder and the creep pushed a lock of it back behind her ear. *Kill me – that move is old as hell.*

"Another beer, please," I croaked out. One was not going to be enough to watch this shitshow. By the time the bartender had replaced my drink, Ambar stood on the footrails of the stool and leaned over the bar with two fingers in the air to get the bartender's attention. It gave me and all the hot-blooded people around us the perfect view of her ass.

Has she always had one that curvy? My god, my mouth watered staring at her and I forced myself to look away. *I can't get a goddamn boner in a bar, for fuck's sake.* A different bartender—a young guy who stared at Ambar like she was his own personal dream—handed her four shots of clear liquid and she blew him an air kiss.

This wasn't part of the plan we talked about. She was going to build his ego and comment on his physique, trying to get him to admit he played baseball. We never talked about getting drinks and—wait... *Isn't she supposed to be sober?*

Rage wasn't enough of a word.

This is the Ambar I thought I knew.

She threw back two of the shots and slid her arms around Max. He held on to her and let his hand linger just above her ass. I couldn't take it. I chugged the rest of my beer and threw a twenty on the bar, unsure if I needed to punch a wall or abandon our plan. If I couldn't trust her to do her part of the investigation, then we had no business working together again.

With one more glance toward her, I fisted my keys and made my way out of the bar. Fuck, I was pissed. She'd lied about being sober, she'd gone off-script and she was going to fuck up the entire thing. For what? Some douche? *This is why I have trust issues.*

Shame on me for believing she changed.

I passed a couple on the way out and the girl fell to the ground, laughing in a drunken stupor, and the guy helped her up, promising her he'd get her home. The freezing-cold air whipped across my face as I got a block down from the bar. It was almost like a slap of reality. *She's with some asshole she doesn't know. She needs to be safe.*

While my anger hadn't dissipated, guilt wove its way in, making me hate my actions even more. I didn't abandon people because I was pissed, especially not women. *Most definitely not drunk ones.*

I jogged back to the bar and was ushered in quickly when I showed the stamp on the back of my hand. I scanned the area where they'd been ten minutes ago and it was empty. *Fuck.* My stomach dropped at all the possibilities of what could've happened. *If she's too drunk, he could… No, don't think that.*

"Another round, babe?" the bartender asked, but I shook my head. "Suit yourself. The dance floor opened up so I'll be in there if you want another."

Dance floor.

The loud stereo hadn't even registered with me but now I followed the sounds and flashing lights. Ambar had said she used to get guys to dance. It was her go-to move. That goddamn blue dress stood out in the sea of people and the relief at finding her shocked me. My entire body relaxed and my heart went back to its normal pace of beating, but once I settled down, the anger returned. It had already been two hours and we'd never discussed if it were to run long. But just as I thought of ways to grab her and get the hell out of there, she looked up mid-grind and winked at me.

What the fuck does this mean?

She spun around to face Max, leaned real close to him and whispered something in his ear before walking away from the dance floor. Her expression was wild. Some of her hair stuck to her temples from the sweat, her large brown eyes glowed and those damn lips were curved up in a huge smile. We didn't talk when she walked by me, like we'd planned, and I waited a couple of seconds before following her out of the bar. She grabbed her jacket and once we were outside, we matched strides.

She looked so confident and smug and when I opened my mouth to say something, she shook her head and put a finger to my lips. "Nope. Not yet."

"What the fuck—"

"I said, not yet. Come on, it's cold as shit." She looped her arm through mine and dragged me down the street despite the fact I outweighed her. My blood still boiled at being played, but I didn't get a whiff of alcohol from her breath. If anything, she smelled good.

She still lied about drinking even if she smells good.

I unlocked the car and she jumped into the passenger seat and held her hands near the heat vents. She looked freezing, but I swallowed any protective thoughts of her. Not before I had my say. "Look—"

"I got it." She grinned wildly. It was a scary look on her face and not flattering the way her eyes doubled in size and her smile was exaggerated. She held up a plain white business card with a phone number on it. "He didn't give me a name because he didn't know it, but this is the number his parents called to get everything in motion. He heard about it from a buddy. We have a lead, Jeff. We have a goddamn lead!"

I had a whiplash of emotions to the point a headache exploded at the base of my skull. "You got a number."

"Yes! It's probably unlisted, but this is huge. I'm not sure how we can call it to make it untraceable, but it would be a huge lead for us to have a legit number."

"You got this from Max at the bar?"

"I'm not sure where you got confused. You were there, right?" A line formed between her eyebrows and she slid me an incredulous look. "I tried our first plan but it wasn't going to work unless I let him go farther with me than I wanted."

"You took shots."

"Is that why you look so goddamn cranky?" She laughed and shook her head like I'd told her the sky was purple, not blue. "I prearranged a plan with the cute bartender. Told him to get me water, my date vodka, and I gave him a big tip. If I was going to give up on my break from drinking, it certainly wouldn't be with vodka or that clown. It'd be an aged whiskey and with friends."

She didn't drink. She planned ahead. Shame filled my entire body and I tightened my grip on the steering wheel. "So you got a number."

"Jesus, Jeff, *yes*. Max was super into sharing his wealthy-white-boy secrets. Sure, the shots loosened him up and the dancing was a bit of overkill, but he revealed a lot." She rubbed her hands together and blew hot air into her fingers, reminding me that I should probably start the car and get her home.

I pulled out of the spot, lost in my own thoughts of shock and regret, and couldn't figure out what to say. I snuck a glance at her and if she was worried about my strange behavior, it didn't show. She had a smile on her face and a lightness to her eyes as she leaned back against the headrest and relaxed.

It made me feel worse. My muscles tightened and I pressed down on the gas harder, desperate to drop her off so I could be alone. *She didn't do a damn thing wrong and I'm being an asshole.*

"You look deep in thought. Do you want to come in and we can add the new information to our notes?" she asked once I pulled into her driveway. She had that blissful look on her face again and the selfish part of me wanted to say no. It was the clear hope and excitement she had that had me nodding. "Sweet! I can make hot chocolate but fair warning, I'm going to change back into my sexy sweatpants."

I followed her into the house without saying much and made the decision then and there to trust her. She clearly wasn't the same girl I remembered from freshman year. Ambar had matured and who was I to judge someone from how they'd acted three years ago?

I snorted, thinking about my roommates. They'd all been assholes and womanizers before they settled down.

I never judged them or second-guessed every decision they made…and I owed Ambar that courtesy too. With my new resolve in place, my chest felt lighter than it had in weeks. "You did really good tonight, Ambar."

She stopped in her tracks in the middle of the kitchen and faced me. She had one of her eyebrows arched and pursed her lips. "It is nice to be acknowledged for my hard work. Thank you."

Her eyes were a little too big for her face and remnants of the red lipstick showcased how full her mouth was and suddenly, it wasn't so cold. "I saw you order the shots and drink them and well… I almost bolted."

She blinked slowly, realization dawning on her face, and her previous smile disappeared. "You still don't trust me, do you?"

"I do now." I closed the distance between us and placed my hands on each of her petite shoulders. "It took me a bit but I do. I won't assume the worst anymore. You deserve that from me and I'm sorry it took so long."

She shrugged and instead of looking at my face, she focused on the floor as red splotches appeared on her face. Then, she met my gaze. "I can't force you to like me and I'm not going to try and prove to you I'm not who you think. But I appreciate you being honest, and having an element of trust between us is a good thing."

She thinks I don't like her? I wanted to explain myself or ask why she thought that, but she moved away from me and reached up to a tall cabinet. The motion showcased her legs and the thin material of her dress shifted up. I gulped, unable to look away from her skin. It wasn't until she grunted that I looked up. "Do you need help getting mugs?"

"Yes, please. My leggy roommates forget I'm a shrimp."

"You are kinda shrimpy."

"I'm five-four, thank you very much," she replied, attempting to make a disgruntled face that made her more adorable. I gave her a placating smile and took two mugs off the top shelf with ease. "Ugh, show-off."

"Height has its benefits."

She rolled her eyes and made us both mugs of hot chocolate before motioning to the stairs. "Let's go up there to talk."

"After you," I said, overdramatizing my gesture with my hand. It made her smile and that was the whole point. *I like making her smile now? Okay, weird.*

We got into her small room and another wave of heat went through me when she shrugged off her blazer and waltzed around her room in that goddamn blue dress. It hugged every part of her and I could imagine how smooth her bare skin was. She removed her shoes and took out the extension she'd put in and gave me a sheepish look. "Sorry, this is odd for you, huh?"

"What? Watching a girl undress? No. Not really."

She blushed a darker shade of red and mumbled something under her breath and I regretted saying it. I backtracked, hoping to get her to relax again. "Shit, I meant, it's not weird watching you take out parts of your hair."

"Oh. I meant… I meant hanging out with me in my room on a Tuesday night. I realize it's about the investigation but if you'd rather meet up tomorrow, we can."

"No, I'm free tonight."

"Okay." She moved from her bed to the closet and shut the door. A wave of disappointment hit me at not seeing her in that dress and it surprised me. *Am I attracted to Ambar?*

She came out in sweatpants and a baggy plaid shirt that almost slid off her shoulder.

Okay, maybe it was just the dress.

"Do you know anything about tracing a call or text from an unknown number?" She sat on the wooden chest I'd used the last time I was here and pulled up her laptop. "It would be amazing to figure out who owned it or at least get a location. Like the crime shows!"

I chuckled. "Probably not gonna be able to trace it ourselves. Sorry to burst your bubble. Now, tell me what else you found out."

"Right! You were so quiet in the car I didn't get to blab it all." She set her computer onto the bed and gestured wildly with her hands the entire time she spoke. "He never had a signing day in high school—just an unofficial visit where he only met two of the coaches. He couldn't remember who because this guy with the number was there that day, too. I played up the fact my sister had no athletic ability but was super flexible and he said talk to this guy and he'll find the sport that makes the most sense."

"That makes the most sense?"

"Yeah. He said that this guy will make it work as long as the body type is similar enough for people to believe. He even went on to say he wanted to go for football but this dude said no because he wasn't strong enough. This guy is smart."

"Jesus." I rubbed my forehead with my hand, already getting a light headache.

"I told him my sister is real skinny and pretended to be worried about her finding a team. Max assured me there are multiple opportunities to get her in. I just gotta give this guy a call."

"Well fuck. It's more than just baseball."

"Yup." She met my eyes with such a solemn expression that my muscles tensed. "This is bigger than I thought, Jeff, and a part of me is worried we're going to piss off the wrong people."

Chapter Ten

Ambar

I'd never given a shit who I passed on the quad leaving classes before, but now I constantly was on the lookout. It was stupid because wealthy people paying their way into college didn't stand out, did they?

Is it the girl with the red coat? Or the dude in the parka? Or the one carrying a coffee?

Is there a look that says 'I bought my way into school'?

Someone screamed from the other end of the quad, making me jump. God, I needed to get it together. My heart raced like I'd run two miles rather than just taking an easy stroll just as Brandon's familiar face appeared in front of me. His jolly energy was a lot to take and he practically sang. "Hey, you, how's it going?"

"Hi, Brandon." My mood instantly lifted and I felt silly for being so paranoid. It was not as if anyone knew we were looking into this whole scandal thing and I needed to play it cool. Brandon was a part of the web of lies I had built surrounding this and I had to keep that cover. "Thank you again for meeting me for the interview."

"It was no hardship spending time with you." He gave me such a genuine smile, my insides warmed and I blushed. He had such a boy-next-door look to him with his khaki pants and navy coat. I'd bet ten dollars he wore a polo underneath, too. "I was hoping we could get together again soon."

He means for another interview, not…like that. I shook my head a little to clear that line of thought and replied, "Of course. I have some follow-up questions for you."

He chuckled and responded with such a warm tone. "I'd like to take you on a date, Ambar. I want that to be very clear."

Oh.

Oh my.

"With me?"

"Yes." He cleared his throat and took a step closer to me. "I know I'm younger, but I think we could have a really good time."

"I think we would—"

"Ambar, girl, you are not gonna believe what I just heard!" Laney interrupted and threw her arm around me without a clue she disturbed Brandon asking me out. My words got stuck in the back of my throat at how awkward I felt and I couldn't do anything to stop it. She spun her attention on him. "Hey there. I'm Laney."

"Uh, Brandon," he muttered, and I had never felt so embarrassed in my life. I met his eyes and hoped I gave him a sympathetic smile. His equally disconcerted look snapped me to the present and I could speak again.

"This is my crazy roommate. Sorry for her interruption, but she doesn't know better."

"Oh god, I'm such an asshole. I'm sorry." She removed her arm and took a step back with a look of regret on her face. "Just punch me in the gut if I do this again."

Brandon looked horrified and I had to laugh. "Will do."

"So how do you know my girl, Ambar?" she asked him, going into full best-friend mode.

"She interviewed me for an article on athletes and I asked her out."

"Bold. Damn. I love it." She made an absurd face at me that was a combination of eyebrow wiggling and pursing her lips. Then her expression changed to inquisitive. "Wait—is this the same article you're writing on Maddow?"

"You're writing something about Maddow?" Brandon asked, a little hurt in his voice.

Panic spread through my body within seconds. All the lies were overlapping and I had to figure out how to connect them to two major pieces that were unrelated. Shit. *Shit.* "I'm thinking my senior piece will be about baseball athletes and he suggested I interview you to get a different perspective."

He didn't look like he bought it, so I added with just as much truth as it was placating him, "It wasn't supposed to be more than a few questions, but I enjoyed talking to you so much I kept going. That sounds unprofessional but—"

"I dig it," he interrupted, looking cheerful again. "You have my number, Ambar. Let me know your answer." He gave me a smoldering look, one that had me squirming, and I blushed. He winked, and left me with my roommate.

"He's got game for being young and he was in to you. Girlfriend. Like, I felt second-hand vibes just from being near you. He's cute. Way to go." She hit her hip against mine and changed her look to a more serious one. "I am sorry I interrupted like that. It was a dick move."

"Don't worry, it's probably best. I don't think I can balance working on all this and dating right now. So it would be easier to tell him that over text than in person."

"You are *not* saying no to that cutie. Ambar. Live a little, girl." Her phone went off and she cursed. "I gotta go. Goddamn group projects can kiss my ass."

She left just as loudly as she'd entered and I used the couple of minutes before my next class to gather my thoughts. Too much was going on in my head between Jeff, my uncle, the *articles* I was supposed to be writing and the real senior project I needed to start working on if I wanted to graduate on time. Coffee.

That was what I needed. Coffee.

My Thursday afternoon class didn't take attendance and if I was little late, it wouldn't make a difference so I chose a swanky coffee shop located right off the main strip. They had the best drip coffee and just the thought of it made me warmer. I adjusted my scarf to cover my face and made the trek there in ten minutes. There were only a couple of people ahead of me in line and I made a plan of how to start balancing my spiraling semester. Priorities, sorted by high and low needs, and dividing my time based on the need. If that meant less time with Jeff, then so be it.

Even if the thought of not seeing him didn't please me.

"Next!" the barista yelled, and I placed my order and moved to the counter. It was ready within two minutes and I brought the cup to my lips with a heavy sigh. It tasted like caramel heaven with the added creamer and my mom's nagging voice about unnecessary sugar didn't even cross my mind. *Progress.* Even if it was as minor as enjoying a sugary drink, I didn't feel bad about it and that notion had me smiling.

But the joy didn't last long. It was during the second sip that two things happened.

The first—Jeff walked into the coffee shop, looking way too handsome for his own good. Like, the jawline alone was distracting enough let alone pairing it with his long eyelashes and gray eyes.

The second—Max stood in the same line and stared at me with a confused look on his face…like he was trying to remember where he knew me from. His mouth formed an *oh* shape, as if he was going to say Olivia…the name I'd told him.

Everything would be blown. The story, my cover, all of it, if he recognized me That was the entire point of dressing up—to be just another girl flirting in a bar.

Shit.

How do I escape this? Should I run out? Pretend I don't see him? Throw my coffee in his face? A ploy…something to throw him off my scent. That's it.

Without thinking a second longer, I marched past Max and up to Jeff. "Hey, baby. I missed you."

He didn't have time to react before I threw my free arm around his neck and dragged his face down to mine. His lips were cold and hard, not unlike his reluctance to trust me. In all the ways I'd secretly fantasized about kissing Jeff, none of them were like this, stiff and awkward in a coffee shop. It was three seconds of agonizing embarrassment before something shifted. Awareness fluttered in my lower abdomen when he placed his hands on my hips, drawing me closer to him.

His lips weren't hard anymore. His entire body softened against me and he *kissed* me.

Like, a holy-shit,-my-crush-likes-me type of kiss. He opened his mouth slightly and teased mine with his tongue, sending a bolt of attraction through me that had my thoughts getting fuzzy. He tasted like mint and smelled like fresh air—a combination lethal enough to make me forget why we were kissing.

But it didn't matter in those seconds where our mouths were connected and his hands were on me. I felt that kiss all the way down to my cold toes and I curled them in my boots when he slid his tongue deeper into my mouth. It wasn't until I groaned that he stopped. When he broke our connection, it was a rush of overwhelming realization that we were in public and the kiss wasn't real.

He stared down at me with his gray eyes swirling with just as many confusing emotions as I had. "Wh…hey?"

My throat was clogged with words I wanted to say, but the force of that kiss made me speechless. Instead, I grabbed his gloved hand and dragged him out of the coffee shop and onto the sidewalk. "Max was in there and he recognized me from Tuesday. I panicked."

"Your plan was to kiss the hell out of me instead?" he asked, an amused grin forming on his face. His lips were a little red and it brought me an insane amount of pride to know I was the reason why. "Tell me how *that* plan helped."

"To throw him off. If I was involved with someone, then I wouldn't have been all over him."

Jeff made a face like he didn't believe me and the weight of what we just did hit me. "People don't like watching couples kissing and I figured if I did that, he would be less suspicious than if I ran out of there when he said my name."

"He knew who you were?" Concern laced his voice and the goofy smile he wore disappeared. "I don't like that."

"He knew my fake name."

"What did you tell him?"

"Olivia."

He tilted his head to the side and smirked. "You could pull off being an Olivia."

"Thanks, but that's beside the point." I felt flustered. Like my coat was too tight and my hair was in my face even though it was pulled back into a high ponytail. "It was an undercover kiss. I don't regret it because—"

Max walked out of the doors. My heart rate spiked and I didn't think. Yanking Jeff's collar, I connected our mouths for the second time and he didn't need to warm up. He circled his arms around me and overwhelmed me with all of him. His cologne, his mixture of hard muscles and soft lips and how, despite his size, I felt safe.

He bit down on my bottom lip, pulling back enough to make me open my eyes. When I did, he was staring right at me, and I had never been so turned on in my life. He knew his way around the bedroom, that was clear, but too soon, the kiss broke apart. "Did you just want another taste or was it for *cover* again?"

I shoved his shoulder with my free hand and hoped he couldn't see how it trembled. "He walked out and looked my way."

"Uh-huh."

"Trust me, that was the only reason I kissed you."

"I think you liked it the first time and wanted more. No need to be embarrassed. It happens." He looked way too smug and my temper flared.

"If I wanted to kiss you, I would, Jeff Maddow. I did it for a specific reason and that was the *only* reason." I pointed my finger at his chest and hated how hot I was. The wind-chill was below freezing, but it didn't matter.

"Okay."

"I'm serious." I narrowed my eyes and spoke in my deepest voice.

"I said okay."

"Yeah, but you said it all smug and shit." His grin kept growing. "See? You're sick. You're enjoying this."

"It wasn't unpleasant."

"*Jesus,* it was a good kiss. You can admit it." *What is my life? Why are we talking about a kiss?*

"So you did like it."

"I'm not… We aren't… I need to go." I let out a long sigh and got about ten steps away from him before he joined me. I ignored him. Surely, he'd leave if I remained silent.

He didn't say anything either and the silence grew from a couple of seconds to minutes, and soon enough, we were on the main quad and heading toward the communications building. When I got to the door, I broke. "Fine. You win. I don't even know what we are competing about, but you win. Happy?"

He smiled, held the door open for me and ushered me in. "I am happy right now. Thank you for asking."

"Why are guys so annoying?"

"I think it's in our DNA. I can't be certain, but I think there're enough studies done to prove it."

I rolled my eyes but made no motions to head to class that already started. "I'm sorry if I crossed some boundary kissing you. I didn't ask and I hope it doesn't make things weird between us. So let's just…forget about it, okay?"

"Not sure if I can, Ambar."

Damn it. "It won't happen again, if that's what you're worried about."

He bit down on his lip and ran his tongue over the spot—the mere gesture had my breathing coming out heavier and my reaction to him was embarrassing. "It wasn't a kiss a guy could forget. So you've got it completely wrong. I'm worried it *won't* happen again."

He let my awkward silence last for five seconds before he grinned. "Have a nice class. Let's catch up later."

What the fuck did he mean?

Chapter Eleven

Jeff

"Damn, Maddow. Something's got you all revved up," Hill said as we finished up in the batting cages two days later. "You're hitting way better than your average. No offense."

"None taken." I picked up one bucket of balls, he grabbed the other and we started putting the equipment away. "I felt good today."

"I'll fucking say. You mad about something?"

Just the fact I think Coach is involved in something illegal that affects student athletes all across campus. Oh, or the fact I keep thinking about the kiss with Ambar and how I've gone without hooking up with someone.

"Nah, just amped."

"Well, whatever it is, keep it up. Honestly, I thought something was bothering you, but you just kicked ass so I won't pester you."

I didn't respond and instead nodded to the coach I worked with the most. Allen had spent ten years playing catcher in the minors and had great insight for me to help with calling pitches and while I dreaded making the decision to not continue after college, I still ached to learn as much as I could. "Hey, Allen, you got something you want to work on. Before we head out?"

"Not today. Coach was looking for you, though, if you have a few minutes to stop by his office."

Don't react. Keep your face the same. "Sure, I'll head there now."

"Come prepared to work on blocks more Monday. Rest tomorrow, but I want Coach Tee working with you. It's going to suck losing you next year, man. We need to train these young'uns."

"That we do," I responded, proud my voice remained even and didn't give him a clue of the panic raging in my chest. He clapped my shoulder in a familiar gesture and left me alone with nothing to do besides go talk to Coach. *Be cool.* My pep talk didn't do shit to calm my erratic heartbeat or stop my palms from sweating. Each step closer to his small office felt like a punch to the gut. *What does he want to talk about? Does he know I'm asking around? Does he know I know?*

Jesus, this is fucked. I rubbed my temples and straightened to my full height once I arrived at his door. How many times had I come in here and talked to him about stuff? He provided advice and life guidance whenever we needed it and did his involvement taint all the lessons he taught us? I gritted my teeth together, causing a sharp pain in my jaw, and I forced myself to count to ten to relax. Then I knocked. "It's Maddow."

"Jeff. Come in."

With one last gulp of air, I entered his office and immediately looked for anything that would give me a clue. There wasn't anyone else in there with us, nor was there a red flag or flashing light that would tell me to get out. It was just him sitting at his weathered chair with an expression that I could never figure out if was happiness or confusion. It was the way his eyebrows were curved. It gave him the impression he was uncertain all the time. I wiped my palms on my shorts and sat down on the chair in front of him. "Allen said you wanted to see me."

"Why are you so damn stiff? Word is you're kicking ass in the cages." He shuffled some papers around on the desk and I made sure to never once glance down at them. He paused, frowned and spoke in a concerned tone. "Something's up with you."

Fuck. He knows. He fucking knows. "Nerves for the season, Coach. That's all."

"No. I've watched you for four years, Jeff, I know your mannerisms." He set the papers down and gave me his full attention: arms on the desk, dark eyes narrowed at me and the damn toothpick sticking out of his mouth. "Is it your parents? Someone on the team?"

I blamed the fear of him finding out the truth about the investigation for the reason I blurted out, "I don't know if I want to get drafted."

His only reaction was shifting the toothpick from the left side of his mouth to the right. "That bothers you?"

"Shouldn't it? I've dedicated my entire life to the sport and I might want out. There are other options that excite me and the thought of going a different path… Shit. It's like throwing away all the blood, sweat and tears me and my parents have put into it."

He grunted and leaned back onto his squeaky office chair and crossed his arms over his barrel chest. "You have talent, Maddow. I'll be clear with you. You could be one of the greats if you went that route. You have the brains and the physical ability to be an elite catcher, but if your heart isn't there, then you walk. That life is not something you can do half-ass."

"I know." I put my head in my hands and felt a huge weight lifted off my shoulders. *This* was who my coach was. He was man to talk me off the ledge. A small twinge of guilt crept up, but I pushed it away. *This will get him off my scent.* "When I played overseas last summer, I hated being away from everyone. Friends, family, my style of life…it was miserable. I made friends on the team, but it wasn't the same and I'm not someone desperate for the paycheck."

"You'll get drafted, but it'll be up to you if you accept. I gotta say, son, it seems you already have your mind made up, but you need to convince yourself it's okay."

God damn, he's right.

"I'm afraid of disappointing my parents and teammates."

He scoffed. "If I know this team, they'll support any decision you make. And your future is up to you. If you don't mind me asking, what do you want to do?"

It's now or never. Tell him the truth. "Look into law school."

He digested the information for a full minute before his face broke out into a smile. It was so rare to see it on his face I blinked to make sure it really happened. "Damn, you'll make a hell of a lawyer."

"Thanks, Coach."

"That's what I'm here for. This stays between us, so don't worry about it getting out."

Relief coursed through my veins followed by guilt when he added, "And you're sure there's nothing else you want to tell me?"

He doesn't mean…that, right? I tensed for a couple of seconds before settling on the burden eating me up. "Not continuing has been on my mind since I came back last summer. I didn't realize it was showing through my mannerisms."

"Coaches see more than you think." He cleared his throat and went back to his normal expression. "I was just checking in with you so head on out and enjoy your day off tomorrow."

"Thank you. You too."

"The wife wants to go furniture shopping. There is no day off with that shit."

His comment made me laugh and I walked out of the office in a totally different mood than I entered, but one comment stuck with me.

Coaches see more than you think.

Was it a threat or a hint?

While I hadn't talked to Ambar since our kiss, she'd crossed my mind more than I liked. I shouldn't be thinking about trying to come up with something involved in the investigation just so I could text her. I wasn't that guy and we weren't even friends…right?

Fuck, I didn't think about shit like this. I had enough to worry about. Plus, I wanted a couple of hours to research law schools and the best programs to study for the LSAT away from the house. While it felt great to tell my coach, I was not ready to tell my teammates. We vibed so well with a shared goal, and throwing a wrench into that before the season was the last thing I wanted to do. Away from any of my teammates was the best option.

There was a pizza place that served gelato and coffee off campus that I'd found two years ago when my parents had visited and I grabbed my laptop and promised my roommates I'd meet up with them later. Time alone, away from *everything,* sounded great and I could afford to eat at least three slices of pizza after running two miles that morning.

Content with my decision, I drove to the parlor and didn't think about my coach, Ambar or the investigation once. But that changed when I walked in and found Ambar sitting at a table with a middle-aged man. The man I knew to be Martin Rhett. *Why didn't she tell me about this?*

I clenched my fists against my sides at the quick onset of anger, then I dismissed it. I'd chosen to trust her and maybe she was going to tell me about it after. Without drawing attention to myself, I selected a table far enough away where she wouldn't see me but I could observe them without being creepy.

First thing I noticed was that she smiled often with him. She never looked down at the ground like I saw her do a lot nor did she look tense. She was completely relaxed and I had to admit, I liked this version of her. She had her long curly hair down around her shoulders and the bright red sweater she wore looked great on her. It matched her lips and our kiss from Thursday replayed in my head.

Passionate. She kissed with so much energy I was dying to do it again. *That* should terrify me, but it was Ambar so it wasn't like we were going to do anything more, right?

She glanced in my direction and I quickly put my head down. *Shit.* She saw me.

My phone buzzed two seconds later.

Ambar: Be honest, are you spying on me?

Jeff: Wasn't my intention.

Ambar: Wasn't a no, either.

Jeff: Were you going to tell me you were meeting with your uncle?

Ambar: Wow, our kiss must've really messed with your brain. Pretty sure you said you trust me now.

Was…Ambar flirting? Damn, but I found I kinda like it.

Jeff: That kiss did mess with me. I think we should do it again.

Ambar: I imagine this is how you get all your women. You tell them what you want and they oblige.

Jeff: Need I remind you, Ambar, you kissed me.

Jeff: Twice.

Ambar: To. Cover. Our. Asses.

Ambar: Only. Reason.

Jeff: Bull. Shit.

Ambar: Whatever. We'll talk later, okay?

I didn't reply but I had a huge grin on my face when I saw her blush from across the restaurant. She met my gaze for a second—her uncle also turning in my direction—so I forced my attention onto the menu. Despite what Ambar said, my gut told me Martin Rhett would be the one who answered the inconspicuous phone number. Why else would his name be on *any* sheet of paper in my coach's office? And, why did Cooper Killian know him when there was no reason to?

I have to show the others his picture. The thought of going behind Ambar's back didn't feel great and caused an uncomfortable rock in my gut, but if she wanted to clear his name for real, it was the right move. Now, the question was to tell her about it or just do it? I made a list of five people I wanted to ask about Martin Rhett and saved it on my laptop. My goal was to work on law-school stuff, not the investigation, but it was hard to focus with Ambar and her uncle being in the same vicinity. My attention drifted toward them every few minutes and each time, a different question popped into my mind. Were they close? Why did she look so happy with him? What did they talk about?

Are they in this together?

No. I refused to believe that small doubt because of how intrigued she was with the investigation. And I had to admit she had put more work into it than I had and why would she do that if she was involved in the scam we were looking into?

I let out a frustrated sigh at my lack of discipline. It was no use and I closed my laptop and accepted defeat. Ambar and her uncle remained in their seats and she didn't look my way once when I walked out of the pizza place. Having drinks with my teammates and not thinking about her was the only plan to get my distracted mind on track…and it had nothing to do with the incessant need to text her. She said she'd reach out later and that would have to do.

Chapter Twelve

Ambar

Music blared across the hockey house, the loud bass shaking the walls enough for a couple of things to fall off onto the floor. The living room smelled like stale beer and cologne—a typical college party scent I knew well. My red cup was filled with soda and I bobbed from side to side as Marissa and Laney were in an intense conversation with one of the hockey guys. Instead of moping around about the weight of *everything* going on, they'd dragged me out to a party and I hated to admit I liked being around people. Even if I wasn't engaging with them, it was better than being alone with my thoughts.

Like how I was betraying my uncle and lying to everyone else.

Enough. I shook my head and smiled at the burly guy joining the conversation. Timothy "Teets" Thomas was the human equivalent of Bigfoot and we'd become fast friends freshman year. "Teets. My dude."

"Henderson." He wrapped me in a hug and I got blasted with his unique scent of laundry and musk. "Haven't seen you around lately."

"I've taken a sabbatical from partying. Had to get my head on straight." I shrugged, unashamed of admitting it. He'd witnessed my demise countless times and withheld judgment, so it wasn't rude for him to nod in understanding. "How's your season going?"

"Rough. We got a tough schedule and were plagued with some injuries that could set us behind." He frowned and the gesture made all his facial hair morph into an upside-down U.

His use of the word 'injuries' was like a car alarm going off in my head. I stood a little straighter and leaned closer to him. "Can I ask an odd question?"

He raised his eyebrows so much they disappeared into his crazy hairline. "You have my interest."

"You've been on the team all four years, right?"

"Correct."

"Have you had many players get injured and not return? I'm not talking about a couple weeks out or just starters. Any players that stopped showing up one day."

He thought about it for a couple seconds before his eyes widened. "You know…there might've been a kid my freshman or sophomore year. Can't remember the tool's name, but he was a dick. Didn't mesh with any of us and couldn't play worth shit." He scratched his chest with his large hand and tilted his head. "Why are you asking?"

"You know me, always asking questions for some blog post." I tried to make light of it, but he didn't buy it for a second.

"Henderson, you're a shit liar and you always undersell your intelligence. I remember our speech and debate class together freshman year. You ask hard questions that are rarely without meaning." He lowered his face so his mouth was inches from my ear, but my reaction was nothing like when Jeff got close to me. "If something is going on, you can trust me, okay?"

"I've missed you. We need to catch up more often."

He laughed and gave me a half-hug. "While I agree, you're avoiding my question and it's probably for a reason. I'll let it slide right now, but seriously, you can talk to me."

His insistence helped fill the hole I had been carrying around since finding out about everything. His words were sincere and I did trust him. It was just easier to keep everyone at a distance *just in case* Uncle Martin was involved.

Because his answers today were shallow.

"You're the best, Teets." I leaned into his hug and he dwarfed me. But while I looked around the room, a familiar pair of beautiful gray eyes was staring right at me. And they did not seem happy. "I'll reach out if I need to. How's that?"

"Better." He removed his arm and someone called his name. "Ah, shit. I said no fucking fighting. I gotta check on them. See you later."

He stormed off and I tried to think of a way to escape Jeff approaching me but came up empty. Marissa and Laney were still within arm's reach, but they were coupled up with some guys I knew they were crushing on so that left me on my own. Jeff held a brown beer in his hand and lazily stepped closer to me. I had no reason to look him up and down, but I couldn't stop myself. His body was hard and his fitted jeans and light sweatshirt showcased every bulge and ripple.

Why is my body tingling? Is the heat turned up? Why did I wear a plain green V-neck and jeans?

He scanned my outfit and a slow grin spread across his face. The movement forced me to look at his mouth and heat spread from my face to my core at the memory of our kiss. The one he wanted to do again.

"Thinking about our kiss?"

"N-no," I stuttered and knew my entire face flushed, giving my lie away. "I was admiring your smile."

"Uh-huh." He laughed and left very little room between us. For one split second, I wanted him to put his arm around me, but the thought left as soon as it came. "You know Teets?"

"Yeah, pretty well. We met freshman year."

"He's a dog when it comes to girls." He flattened his lips together and all traces of his previous smile was gone. "You don't want to get involved with someone like that."

"Someone like you, you mean? Flirts with everything and never calls them?" I replied, immensely proud of my immediate comeback. When it came to others, I could be witty and defensive, but when it came to myself, I'd spend hours plotting the perfect response.

Jeff's only reaction was a slight eye roll. "I'm just saying, since you're trying this *dating* thing, he'd be the last place I'd start."

"I'm not really doing the dating thing, Jeff. You know this." I took a deep breath and already was annoyed with him. It was our new routine. Banter, flirt, annoy. "Listen, I think I should get back with my friends." I pointed over my shoulder to Laney and Marissa, but he shook his head.

"You said we'd talk later. It's later." His voice came out deeper than normal, causing me to glance up at him and for the second time that night, I got tingles all the way across my skin at how handsome he was. It made no sense. "I want to hear about your *lunch*."

"We're at a party." I gestured around us and gave him an incredulous look. "Wouldn't you rather get drunk and screw around? We can catch up tomorrow."

"Call me curious, Ambar. Desperately curious." He placed his hand on my lower back and gently nudged me in the direction of the basement. "Ten minutes?"

"Fine." I motioned to my friends I'd be right back and they grinned when they saw Jeff. He just waved and gave a sheepish grin—a grin I never was privy to receiving. It was too carefree and flirty for me to be the recipient. "Ten minutes then I'm back up here. I came here to *not* think about all this for one goddamn night."

The lines around his mouth tightened and he leaned forward. "I know the feeling."

His warm breath hit my exposed neck and I couldn't prevent my shiver. If he saw it, he didn't react, but his grip on my lower back tightened. His hand never left my body as we headed downstairs and through the crowd of people. Clearly we both had been to the hockey house before because he weaved us through the party area and into the backroom that was typically used for hook-ups.

I bet he knows how to give great orgasms. Oh my god, stop it! I blamed the room. *And the fact I haven't had one that wasn't self-induced in months.*

He shut the door and turned the lights on in the room and when I looked at him, I forgot why I didn't like him. His heated gaze felt like a caress on my skin and I hoped he couldn't see how much I started sweating. The only seating options were a hook-up futon, a loveseat or the floor. I chose the loveseat and hid my surprise when Jeff sat down right next to me…so close our thighs touched. "Really? Couldn't sit somewhere else?"

"On the hook-up bed? Nah, I'm good." He leaned into the cushions and took a long swig of the drink. My mouth dried up watching the way his throat moved as he swallowed the liquid and my entire body felt on fire with awareness. Every breath he took, I felt. Every time he shifted on the couch, I wanted him to touch me.

I had to get out of there.

"I'm sure it's at nine minutes now."

"Right," he said, adding a small chuckle at the end of it. "How was lunch with your uncle?"

"It was great."

"You know what I'm asking, Ambar." His gaze flicked from my eyes to my mouth and it lingered there. "What did you two talk about? Did you get any new information?"

I hesitated for a second and Jeff noticed. His features shifted and his anger almost radiated off him. "Ambar…fucking tell me."

"We tend to grab lunch once or twice a month when he's on campus. He always told me it was business meetings with potential clients that brought him to our college town. Never thought anything of it. Not once. Why wouldn't I trust the only person in my family I like?"

His face softened for a second but then he said, "Okay, so?"

"I probed about what type of business he was in and used the ruse that I was confused about my major and graduation. Hell, I *am* confused about my lack of career options, but I tried asking in a way if I could work with him. He derailed the conversation or changed the subject instead of answering. He's never done that in my entire life." *And that's what hurts the most.*

Jeff sighed and finished his drink. He set the bottle on the ground near his feet and gave me a long look. "Thank you for sharing that with me."

"You're welcome."

He stared at my mouth again and said, "I've been thinking…"

"Yeah?" My response came out like a whisper. *Is he going to kiss me? Do I want him to? Yes. Yes I do.*

"We need to show a picture of your uncle to some of these non-athletes. If they recognize him or know him, it would be another huge lead."

No kissing. Uncle Martin. Get a grip. I forced myself to relax and let his words settle. All that goddamn teasing about the kissing messed with me. I cleared my throat and hated how he made sense. "You're probably right."

"I didn't think you'd be up for it, actually."

"If I want to get to the bottom of this, then there is no other choice." My shoulders slumped into the cushion and the motion caused me to lean into Jeff, but instead of immediately trying to remove myself from him, I lingered. He was warm and it wasn't so wrong for me to be comforted for a minute, right?

"We both have people involved in this who will hurt us. Don't forget that."

"True." I closed my eyes and let myself enjoy the warmth for ten more seconds before pushing to get up. "I think it would be better if you went around asking about him. We don't look too much alike, but I don't want to draw any extra attention to the fact he's my uncle. You know?"

"Yeah. I agree." He stood and made a resigned face, like he wasn't finding any joy in doing that part. "I'll see how I can run into this guy this week."

"Cool." I chewed on my bottom lip, unsure how to exit this secret meeting and hating how unsure I felt around Jeff. I was used to knowing my place with people, whether it was favorable or not—I knew and could react based on that. But our relationship was unknown, we weren't really friends but we did share two incredible kisses investigating something illegal. This was unfamiliar ground. "I guess we can get together after you talk to them?"

"Are you in a hurry to get back upstairs?" he asked, his face a new kind of serious.

"Yes?"

"That's a shame." He hummed and walked to stand right in front of me, crowding my personal space. He looked at me through hooded eyes and used a silky voice that almost made me moan. "I want to even the score."

"Hm?" *The score? What score?* His proximity sent my body haywire and he knew it. He brought his hands to each side of my collarbone and drew me to him.

"You've kissed me twice now. It's my turn."

That was my only warning before his warm lips touched mine, carefully and gently teasing me with a controlled restraint I couldn't match. He took his time, tasting me at a frustrating speed that caused a moan to escape my throat. That changed the pace and he slammed me into the wall. He moaned into my mouth, "Christ, Ambar."

In one swift motion, he lifted me off the ground, placed my legs around his waist and ground into me. This kiss was a claim, one to ruin anyone else who dared to put their lips on mine, and I rode it out. The way he gripped my skin with a ferocious passion and sucked my tongue deep into his mouth had my nipples straining against my thin lace bra. When he let me take a breath, he noticed and gave me a wolfish grin. "I have one more left."

"Make it count then," I said, shocked at my crassness. Something about him drove me wild and he liked my answer. He pressed his hips into me, holding me against the wall, and used his free hands to trace the outline of my nipples over my shirt. I hissed at the pleasure and he pinched the pebbled tips. His breathing was just as heavy as mine and knowing it was mutual was an aphrodisiac itself. "Suck them."

A wild look crossed his face and he used one hand to lift my arms up over my head and the other to lift my thin shirt. He removed it from me and stared at the black bralette Laney had bought me for my birthday with the promise of *driving guys crazy* and I had to report back it was a success. Jeff's jaw became slack and his nostrils flared when he dragged his fingers down the center of my small cleavage. He slowly trailed them over my exposed skin, not quite touching where I desperately wanted him to, but the slow game somehow made it better when he finally snuck his hands under the material. He cupped a breast in each hand and kneaded them, using his thumbs to flick my nipples.

"You're so responsive. What will you do if I put my mouth on them, Ambar? Will you buck against me or moan loud enough for anyone to hear?" he asked in the huskiest voice I had ever heard. He didn't give me time to answer before placing his mouth around the pink tip and sucked it into his warm mouth. The sensation was electric and I gasped when he bit down and played with the tip between his teeth.

"Oh my god," I moaned. He hummed against my skin and moved to the other, repeating the same process. I never once thought about how chubby I looked, or if he thought I was ugly, or how silly I looked naked. I couldn't think like that when he looked at me the way he did, intense and like I was a goddamn buffet. "Jeff..."

His only response was teasing my sensitive breasts more and kissing up my chest, over my jawline and back to my mouth. He groaned my name and gripped the back of my head. "I don't know what you're doing to me."

I didn't get a chance to respond. Someone banged on the door. "I need the room. It's been long enough."

That snapped me back to reality and when we locked eyes, the lack of regret in his the only thing that made me feel okay. But I didn't do talks after hook-ups. I typically never saw the guy again and embarrassment and uncertainty hit me. I wanted nothing more than to run home to figure out my next move. "We should go."

"Uh-huh," he said, but made no move to put my shirt back on or leave. "Don't go shy on me, Ambar. You enjoyed that just as much as I did."

Do I admit it? Deny it? Pretend it didn't happen? What's the protocol for this?

"We're even now, right?" I asked weakly, and Jeff did not like that.

"They can fucking wait." He jutted his chin toward the door before lowering his face and giving me a hard look. "Are you okay?"

I did not expect him to ask me that. The thoughtfulness in it had my throat closing and I nodded while I scrambled to put my shirt on. He set me back on the ground and sighed. "Ambar, you won't look at me and I'm worried I crossed some line."

"You didn't. No." I turned to leave but gave him one more look over my shoulder. "I enjoyed it. Just got carried away."

"I'll let you go now, but we need to talk about this. We *will* talk about this soon."

Chapter Thirteen

Jeff

Between actually researching potential law schools, cleaning the house, gruesome practices and attempting to get something done for the investigation, I hadn't found time to talk to Ambar in three days. I thought about it—in the showers or when I couldn't fall asleep at night—but couldn't figure out how to start a conversation unless it involved new information. And to get something new, I had to find Dillon the Dick Pic Sender and question him about Martin Rhett.

Dillon posted a ton of shit online and none of it seemed to be about classes. *Figures.* I didn't understand college students who didn't take their classes seriously. They were paying money to attend…why wouldn't they try? Shaking off my irrational annoyance at their choices, I continued my research on how I could casually run into him and how to bring up Martin. It wasn't like I could walk up to him and show him a picture without explanation. *Hey, man, know who this is? Yeah? Okay, cool, thanks.* That sure wouldn't raise suspicion at all.

Okay, I needed to find this dude before I could even think of what to say. I was going to step three before steps one and two were even done. *Idiot.* A small part of me wanted to ask Ambar how she would do it. She had been beyond resourceful getting information from people and she would know how to find Dillon. I span my pencil in my hand, hoping for inspiration to kick in. A couple of minutes went by, then more, and I sighed, defeated at my lack of creativity.

Fuck it. I was asking Ambar.

Jeff: How would you go about finding the habits of a person online?

Ambar: Are you taking up stalking now?

Jeff: I don't have enough going on, obviously, so yes.

Jeff: No. I'm stuck on how to run into Dick Pic Dillon casually.

Ambar: LOL. Find a bar he likes to go to, hang out there, act like you recognize him.

Jeff: And ask him if he knows your uncle?

Ambar: Oh, probably not. Hmm, not sure. You could say you're looking for him, or trying to find him to help a friend, or…

Jeff: I wish you were the one doing it, you're better on the spot than me.

Ambar: I accept the compliment but I'm not doing it. You're on your own. Let me know when it's done.

Okay then. I was on my own.

Dillon… Most of his posts were from The Hound or Big Sal's—notorious bars for frat guys—and he constantly posted about Tootin' Tuesdays where he went for dollar beers. It wasn't where I would picture someone like him going, but it would work. *Perfect.* I'd head there and question him. *Somehow.* I closed my computer, pocketed my phone and took the stairs two at a time to end up near the front door.

Zade and Tanner saw me put on my jacket and Tanner asked, "You heading out, man?"

"Yeah, thought I'd try Tootin' Tuesdays." *Don't join me, please.*

Tanner's eyes lit up and he jumped from the couch. *Shit.* "Dude, I'm coming. I need some beers after my shit of a day. Wanna come, Zade? It'd almost be like old times."

"Nah, Callie's coming over. Her internship moved to other sports, so she's been busier than normal." He shrugged and always had the same soft expression on his face when he talked about his girlfriend of almost three years. His hard eyes—ones I feared when he was on the mound—went all gooey and he had this dumbass smile on his face. I didn't relate, or even try to, when they all talked about their chicks. The rest of the guys were all like that in the house and while I dug their girlfriends, it could be a lot.

"That cool I'm coming?" Tanner asked but I couldn't figure out a way to say no. What other reason could I give for why I was going to a bar…alone? I nodded and said bye to Zade as we headed out of the door. Tanner waited until we got to the driveway before he said, "Kenzie wanted a night out with her roommates and I wasn't about to sit around with Zade pining after Callie. He's a sucker."

"You're just as bad, dude."

He shrugged with a huge smile. "I know."

I hit him on the shoulder as he laughed at himself and we walked in comfortable silence for a few minutes before arriving at the bar. This was where it got tricky—I had to find a way to talk to Dillon without Tanner realizing anything and without drawing any unwanted attention. Tanner would know immediately if I did anything out of character. He was annoyingly perceptive.

Cool, no big deal. I can do this. Tanner waved at some folks and I froze, waiting to see if they would call him over to their table…but they did not. I tried not to show my disappointment when he put his hand on my shoulder. "I'll get the first round, buddy. For two bucks, I'm game."

"Thanks." I used his absence to look around for Dillon and couldn't find him anywhere. His picture was pulled up on my phone and I glanced down, memorizing his face and ridiculous haircut. It wasn't a large bar. If anything, it was kind of small and grungy for attracting such a preppy crowd. He should stand out amongst all the people here dressed in dark clothes and plaid. A few people glanced at me when we walked in with recognition on their face but it wasn't like walking into The Lion or another sports bar on campus. This was a dive, hole-in-the-wall Tootin' Tuesdays.

"Here you go, my friend. Cheers!" Tanner handed me my drink and we each took a long swig before plopping down on two bar stools. "It feels like yesterday when we arrived fresh-faced and anxious as fuck to start playing ball. We were wild those first few years, huh?"

I barked out a laugh. "Yeah, we were."

"Can't say I regret it. Honestly, the past three and a half years have been the best. Playing ball, hanging out and living with you guys. The longest we've been apart was when you left last summer. I know you don't talk about it a lot, but, man, how was it *really* playing overseas for three months?" He set his mug on the bar-top and while his face looked relaxed, his shoulders were tense. It was a common occurrence for any one of the guys to stress out about *the future* and while their tension was fueled by something different than mine, I could still relate.

"Parts of it were hard, I won't lie to you. The curfew, the range of maturity levels of the players and their recklessness, and the demanding schedule were tough." I scanned the crowd again to see if Dillon had arrived and felt bad about my straying attention when Tanner frowned. "If I have a shit day here, I can come back to the house and no one will mention it. You'll offer me a beer and we'll kick it. Over there, if you have a shit game, no one talks to you. There's no family aspect and while that could be because I was a newb, it sucked. Felt like an island instead of a team."

Tanner winced for a second and masked his worried face with a forced smile. "I'm nervous about the lifestyle. Don't get me wrong, I'm stoked to get drafted and to finally get to live out my dream. But I do good with routine and everything is so unknown. The minors could be a long journey of different cities, the worry of never getting the call up. If I think about it too much, I start to sweat. Plus, this thing with Kenzie might be somewhat new and I want it to last with her. It's never been like this for me…thinking about someone else *and* baseball. Does that make me sound sappy as fuck?"

I forgot about my secret plan for a second and reached out to put my hand on his shoulder. "You know what you want. There is nothing sappy about that. I gotta say though, it was hard as hell being away from everyone. I had to battle time zones and international costs, but it was eye-opening." *Just tell him. Tell him your doubts.*

He flinched and rubbed his temples with his fingers. "Do you think a relationship can survive that?"

His question made me pause. *I can't tell him no.* "Tanner, you two will figure it out. Guys maintained relationships when I was playing over there. Sure, some were pricks and cheated and slept around but others, nah. They made the choice to stay faithful. You'll be the same, man."

"I've been looking forward and working so hard for this final season, I'm forgetting to enjoy it with all this fucking worrying. I'm going to get gray hair at twenty-two."

I barked out a laugh. "We should focus on this final season together and play our assess off. We need to enjoy every second of it. Every dumb joke Allen makes, or life lesson Coach gives us—hell, even all the stupid shit Aaron says during games. That's the shit I'm gonna miss. The brotherhood on the field."

"I'll drink to that." He held up his mug and we clinked glasses. He spilled a bit and leaned forward to grab napkins and I used the extra seconds to search the crowd again. "Who you looking for?"

"Just checking out the crowd."

"Need a hook-up? Thought you had enough girls available to you when you wanted."

"I have options, which makes me sound like a total dick, but they aren't really holding my interest."

"I told you the one-and-done shit gets old."

I laughed. *Yeah, if I could finish what I started with Ambar... Woah, don't go there.* "The monogamy thing hasn't worked for me."

"You and Ambar have been hanging out a lot." He made a stupid face of intrigue and added, "She's cool."

Apparently I never got that memo. Why does everyone say that? "She's writing an article about me for her senior project. We've gotten together a couple of times for questions. It's nothing more than that, really."

"Is it the same article Brandon was going on about the other day? He's got it bad for her. Told him there was no way in hell a senior would go for him but the kid's got balls and asked her out."

I tightened my grip around the beer bottle. "Brandon asked Ambar out?"

"Yeah, he was going on about how she singled him out for an interview and some of the older guys knew who she was and it helped his ego. Damn kid has talent, but these egos… I swear. Were we that bad when we were freshmen?"

"She said yes to him?"

He was about to answer before he stopped and ran his hand over his jaw. "You got a thing for Ambar, man?"

"No. I don't." I took another drink and ignored the pinching in my throat at my blatant attempt of lying to myself. "She's…not my type."

"Didn't know you had a type, man. No offense." He smirked and glanced down at his phone with a frown. "My brothers are texting me. Hold on a second."

I gladly gave him space and used the time to search for Dillon and figure out the best approach to make it clear I did not have a thing for Ambar. Yeah, that kiss had blown my goddamn mind and the way her body reacted when I touched her… *Shit.* I didn't need to get turned on in a bar. Okay, fine, I was into exploring whatever the fuck was going on between us physically, but that was it. I ran my hand over my face and when I opened my eyes, Dillon stood three stools away from us. *Fuck. Think.*

Tanner held up his phone and offered a quick apology before heading outside and I couldn't have been happier. This was it. My time to get some info. I finished my beer and waved at the bartender to order another. Dillon glanced in my direction and I nodded at him. "Hey, you gotta second?"

He looked real confused and glanced at his friends before scooting down one stool. I knew he recognized me. He had the familiar widening eyes and little nod to himself. I wasn't one to let local fame mess with my head, but I was photographed and on numerous campus billboards. If I was ever going to use my clout beyond getting easy hook-ups, this was it. "Dillon Cage, right?"

"Yeah. What's up, man?"

"Just ordered a couple beers. One's for you if you can help me out." I flicked my gaze to his friends and they all watched us, eager for something. They dressed in a typical frat guy uniform of khakis, polos and a sweater, boat shoes and the same smug and eager expression on their face. "You guys heading out after this?"

"There's a huge party at Gio's."

"Oh shit, that's right. I forgot they did that in January." My mind went to the year before, where I'd had a hell of a time doing shots with some international chicks. I'd given the bouncer their names and they'd showed me all night how thankful they were. *Shit! The list! An in!* I looked at him over my mug, hoping I didn't come across weirdly excited. "You all on the list?"

"There's a list?" His face blanched and damn, I had my ticket. *Go me!*

"Yeah. They broke some codes two years ago and had to limit the number of people and no offense, dude, they are letting chicks in over you."

"Fuck!" He hit his fist on the bar and I swooped in.

"I need you to answer three questions for me and if you do, I'll get you in." I knew the bouncers at Gio's really well and would promise them whatever I had to get this information. "What do you say?"

Dillon scanned my face, his own expression full of doubt, before he said, "You can *really* get us in?"

"Dude, yeah." I took another drink and asked the first question. "You played on the baseball team for a little bit a couple of years ago, right? I thought I heard that."

"I didn't play, but I was on it for like a fucking second." He made an annoyed face and glanced at his watch.

"What happened?"

"Is this the second question?"

Oh, he's a smartass. "No, it's a follow-up. Don't be a dick."

"I'm answering your questions, Maddow. Remember that." Dillon narrowed his beady eyes and puffed out his chest.

Seeing as I'd faced players who wouldn't hesitate to pitch a fastball at my body to send a message, this punk ass was the furthest thing from a threat. "I can get you and your boys off any list as fast as I can get you on them. Now explain what happened."

"Fuck," he whined and ran a hand over his face like I'd told him all the beer in the world was gone. "I got injured and was told not to report back. Didn't want that life anyway with all the restraints." He glanced at his friends and back to me with a light-red blush creeping up his neck. "Where is this coming from?"

"Did you get to meet the entire coaching staff?"

He rubbed his forehead and shook his head. "No. Just...a couple of them. I can't remember their names."

"If I showed you a picture of one, would you recognize him?"

"I don't fucking know. Maybe? Why do you care?"

I didn't respond. Instead, I opened my phone and pulled up a picture of Martin Rhett and showed him. "Him."

"Yeah...I remember him. He was one of the guys who met me and my dad when I arrived to campus." He looked at his watch and sighed. "Is that it? Can you get me on the list?"

"Sure." I sent a quick text to the guys I knew at Gio's and showed him. "You and your crew should be good."

"Hell yeah!" He didn't say anything else before returning to his group and the excitement of finding out information had me buzzing with a high I hadn't experienced before. It wasn't the same as hitting a walk-off to win a game. It was different. I needed to tell Ambar.

Shit.

Ambar. Her uncle.

I paid for the second beers and met Tanner outside the bar just as he got off the phone. "Hey man, I gotta head out. That cool?"

"No worries. I was about to say the same thing."

Perfect.

I didn't even think about texting Ambar before knocking on the door in a frenzy of enthusiasm and dread. *We have a second confirmed lead. Martin is posing as a coach.* The cold air whipped around me and I hit the door harder. It was only nine so it wasn't like I was too late or anything. It took another minute before the knob twisted and Ambar opened the door with a surprised look on her face.

"Jeff. What the hell?"

"I gotta fill you in."

She ushered me in but stopped me with a hand to my chest. She motioned to the living room with her chin and I followed her gaze. I counted at least six other people on their couches and I felt bad. "Five minutes. That's it," I whispered and she nodded. We didn't have to go through the room with everyone to head upstairs and she didn't say anything to the group. *Is Brandon there?*

Woah… Okay, errant thought.

I followed her up the stairs and tried not to stare at her tight black leggings and how they hugged her ass. She wore a large sweatshirt that hung off her bare shoulder and suddenly I wanted more than five minutes with her.

She ushered me into her room and closed her bedroom door, leaning against it with a wary expression. "What happened?"

I paced her room and focused on the information, not the tingle of desire coursing through my body at how good she smelled. "I talked to Dillon and he confirmed your uncle was one of the *coaches* who met him when he got to campus."

Color left her face and she closed her eyes for a few seconds before meeting mine. There was a sadness to them, but it wasn't as much as I thought there would be. "How did you get him to confess?"

"Bribes. He wanted in to a party and I guaranteed it if he answered three questions. The dude was a prick who cared more about partying than about my prying. To tell you the truth, he'll probably kill any brain cells drinking than remember our conversation tonight."

She snorted and adjusted her hair—causing her sweatshirt to lift and exposing the soft skin of her midriff. Blood surged south and I had to clear my throat to get the lust out of my voice. "I'm sorry."

She shrugged and let out the deepest sigh, looking at the floor with the posture of someone who'd given up hope. I had seen that body language a million times on the field after strike outs and instead of cheering her up with a high-five or an ass slap, I figured she would want something different.

I walked over to her and wrapped my arms around her shoulders, waiting until she relaxed against me. She leaned into my hug and I rested my chin on the top of her head. She fitted against me well, but I shut that part of my brain off and focused on her. I would never admit it to her, but her insistence that her uncle was innocent had me hoping that maybe he was and we'd figure out someone else involved in all this. But it wasn't happening. While my coach was a mentor, he wasn't a family member I had known my entire life and it still tore me up thinking he was involved in something like this. *Poor Ambar.*

I didn't have to ask her what she was thinking. She spoke on her own in muffled voice with her face pressed against my chest. "He took me here when I was a freshman to do my interview with the dean. I've always known I'm average—my family doesn't let me forget it—but knowing he might've *bought* or lied my way into this school is killing me."

Those words were like a fist reaching into my chest and squeezing around my heart, causing a continuous dull pain in there, and I had no idea how to stop it. *What does this mean?*

Chapter Fourteen

Ambar

The news should've surprised me more than it did, but the hurt still was enough to render me completely vulnerable to Jeff—the one person who I didn't want to admit my faults to. But he held me tight against him and ran his hand up and down my back in such a comforting way I let myself be weak for a minute. Okay, maybe two. It felt nice to have strong arms around me offering support and I wish it could've lasted longer. One more squeeze and one more whiff of his cologne then I broke our hug apart. "Thanks. I needed that."

"Do you need another one?"

His offer made me smile. "I'm good."

He still stood close to me, close enough our noses were inches apart, and he looked at me with…tenderness? That made no sense. "I don't know how deep or what role he played, but there's a chance he's not the mastermind behind this. We need more information before anything is confirmed."

"Yeah, you're right, but with his half-answers Saturday and this kid recognizing him, it seems naive to defend him anymore." I sucked my lip into my mouth and embraced the disappointment. It was the karma of my life, punishing me for making poor decisions all those years ago. The one family member who had my back was involved in something shady and had probably involved me. If I thought about it too hard, I'd break down and retreat into a dark mindset, not unlike the one I got every time my mom talked to me. Jeff stared at me with his intense and beautiful gray eyes and my knees almost trembled at the attention. When was the last time any guy had ever looked at me like that?

Never. That's when. "Look, I should probably get back downstairs."

He nodded for a second but put one hand on my shoulder, gently brushing his thumb back and forth on my exposed skin. My insides turned into a flurry of butterflies at the contact and I barely heard what he said.

"Wait, what?"

He smiled, showcasing one perfect dimple, and repeated, "Do you want to go over next steps for the investigation or anything? I know you like plans. Or if you want to hang out up here and talk about anything else, I don't mind."

I ran my fingers through my hair and weighed my options. Watching rom-coms with my roommates and some friends was *not* on my agenda with my mindset and knowing Laney, she'd want to gab about it and I wasn't in the mood. But...she'd have a lot of questions if I was up here with Jeff alone all night. "It would look suspicious if we hung out up here the rest of the night, wouldn't it?"

"I really don't care." He shrugged and gave me another warm look. It was so similar to the warm looks I'd observed others receiving but never me. *Wait—is it pity?* "I feel responsible for being the bearer of bad news so it kinda feels like my responsibility to make sure you're okay."

Definitely pity.

I shrugged his hand off my shoulder. "Don't feel guilty. Honestly, I think I want to be alone right now." I moved to my dresser and started picking up some necklaces I'd left out and shoving them into drawers. After I'd tidied up about five, I moved on to my desk. He remained in the same position when I glanced over, but his face had transformed into an expression I hadn't seen on him. His eyebrows were drawn together so deeply they almost looked connected in the middle and his jaw had tightened so hard that I saw each movement he made with his teeth. He turned and faced me.

"Trust me, being alone sucks sometimes." He twisted his mouth into a grimace and moved to sit down on the wooden chest at the end of my bed. He was so tall that he still almost matched my height. "You knew I played baseball overseas last summer, right?"

His voice changed into a different, undemanding tone. It was soft and vulnerable...and dangerously like honey. That got my attention. "Yeah, that's when Kenzie lived in the baseball house."

I moved to sit on the edge of my bed, sitting criss-cross and leaning against the wall. His posture changed from the confident guy I knew well to one less confident... I would even go as far to say defeated. "Why do you bring that up?"

"I don't talk about it much to anyone but it kinda sucked." He laughed, but not with humor, and leaned over the bed railing to rest his head on his arms. "I had never felt so alone in my life. It was practices and games constantly and when there were off days, everyone on the team had family or friends to hang out with. I had no one. My off days were spent in hotel rooms watching stupid TV."

"I thought you loved it over there."

"That's what I said to people." He sighed and his breath had a hint of beer on it. "I was goddamn lucky to get the opportunity to play in Japan for three months and earn some money doing it. I couldn't complain about it, right? That would make me sound foolish and entitled. *Hey, the guy who got offered the spot is a whiner* doesn't have a good look."

"You can be grateful for something and still not enjoy every aspect of it. There's nothing wrong with that."

"Damn, I'm sorry." He had an odd look cross his face before he stood. "I wanted to stay to comfort you, not talking about me. Fuck, sorry."

"No, it's okay." *Maybe I don't want to be alone anymore.* "Tell me more about your time over there. It's distracting me from my own thoughts."

"Are you sure? I feel like such an ass right now." He pinched the bridge of his nose and really did look like he felt bad.

"I'm sure." I patted the bed next to me and waited. He struggled with his decision because he looked at the door, then my face, then my bed before he moved to join me. His body weight shifted me so I fell into him but neither one of us made a move to readjust our position. "What aspects of the experience did you like?"

He hummed for a second before saying, "The coaches had a different approach to offense than I was used to playing. It taught me a lot about pitch selection and being aggressive. My hitting has been the best in off-season since I've gotten back."

"That's good. Definitely going to help you in a month when you guys start your season. What else did you like?"

"I got to try new food."

"That's always exciting," I teased, earning a small smile from him. But it seemed off and I reached out to touch his arm to offer some form of comfort, but I paused. We weren't there. We didn't offer each other comfort.

But he gave you a hug when you needed it. I touched his arm with my hand and kept it there when he continued talking.

"I imagined playing in the majors being like how it is now, like a brotherhood. A family. It hit me when I was abroad that my heart isn't in it, like my roommates. It could take years before making it. Years of living with host-families, struggling, traveling on busses, not knowing if the call will ever come." He exhaled and slowly tilted his head to look at me and the amount of turmoil and uncertainty in his eyes had me suck in a breath.

"You don't want that life," I said, nodding as his words pieced together. "That's what has you feeling so guilty."

"I don't have the guts to tell my teammates or my parents. It's shameful." He leaned his head back against the wall, producing a loud thud. "I've given almost seventeen years of my life to baseball and now I'm not sure I want it. How fucked up am I?"

I waved my hands in the air, making big circles as I talked, hoping that would somehow help my get my point across. "The amount of time you spend on something shouldn't determine if you walk away from it or not. We have our whole lives ahead of us to work. It drives me insane when I think that we have to have our shit figured out at twenty years old. We're still growing up, making mistakes, learning, all of that." I brushed my hair out of my face and took a deep breath, filling my lungs with air since I didn't pause in my rant. "I have no idea what I want to do after graduation and it terrifies me. Everyone else has a plan or a career path to guide them."

He let out something of a chuckle. "Well, I don't really have a plan either. A goal, yeah, but nothing concrete."

"Yeah, what's that?"

"Law school."

"Damn." I took my time studying his facial expression and felt the pang of jealousy at the determination there. Even with his uncertainty of his future, he still had options and the talent to back up the aspirations. My voice came out more strangled than normal, but I still meant it when I said, "Good for you. I can see it."

He brushed off my comment and tilted his head slightly to the side. "What about you? You graduate in May. What's next?"

I made a helpless face at him, moving my mouth without anything coming out for a couple of seconds before making a raspberry sound with my lips. "Psh, uh, I've been kind of hoping something pops up this semester, because I have no idea. I'm not skilled at anything particularly but I enjoyed the blog at one point until it became forced. The posts became trivial and—"

"Not skilled?" he asked in an incredulous tone. "Ambar, you've been incredible during this investigation. Your ability to get people talking, the way you ask questions. Are you kidding me? You'd make a hell of an investigative journalist." He laughed and nudged my shoulder with his. "You wouldn't believe how much I was stressing and trying to figure out how to get Dillon to talk. I was a fucking mess and wanted to ask you the entire time. But you, you think on your feet."

His words were like a warm embrace, wrapping around me and filling me with something I wasn't used to, my pride. My height grew two inches as my posture straightened. Just a flicker of confidence transformed my mind and it was almost embarrassing. *Incredible. A hell of an investigator. Me!*

Both my cheeks burned at the declarations he threw out without realizing how much they meant to me. I had to look away from him, toward the direction of the small window, and it took a good ten seconds to collect myself. *If he sees me cry…* My nose made a whistling sound when I sucked in a deep breath and the awkward noise was the perfect distraction to knock me out of my emotional moment. I cleared my throat and hoped my voice sounded normal. "Thanks for saying that."

"Well, I meant it. Took me a bit to learn that about you but it's pretty obvious." He shrugged and reached out, putting his hand on my knee, patting it twice. "You know…I do recall reading one of your posts ranting about eighteen-year-olds having to make decisions that can affect the rest of their lives. I scoffed when I read it because I was one of those over-confident kids who thought he knew everything about his future. You were right."

"You read my post?"

His face flushed just enough for me to notice and he took his time before replying, "Well, yeah. I had to read all your shit to see if you were writing subliminal messages hiding the truth of what was going on."

"Yeah, that's plausible," I deadpanned, earning a smile from him. Seeing him so relaxed sitting less than six inches away from me, in my bedroom caused a swooping sensation to form in the pit of my stomach. My gaze dropped to the curve of his lips and lingered longer than appropriate. He smiled and I glanced up to see him staring at my mouth with something like hunger on his handsome face. The air shifted as the spark between us grew. My pulse sped up the longer I stared at his mouth and I had to squeeze my thighs together as my attraction to him burned. I wanted to make a move, to press my mouth against his and confirm the last two times hadn't just been my imagination, but I couldn't. *What if he rejects me?*

"Ambar…you're looking at me and giving me certain signs. I need you to say what you want right now." His voice was gruff and restrained, as if his control held on by only a thread. It thrilled me and I replayed the words I'd said at the party.

"I was admiring your smile."

He closed his eyes and groaned. "We still haven't talked about what happened that night."

"Do we need to?"

He took his time shifting his weight on the bed, moving closer to me and causing me to lie on my back with his large frame leaning over me. I was beneath Jeff Maddow. I couldn't believe it and I didn't want it to stop. His breath came out fast and it thrilled me to see his chest heaving. "You tell me. If I kiss you again, are you going to go shy on me after?"

He dipped his head low enough to run his nose along the length of my jaw, teasing my earlobe with his teeth and biting down. "We can do this all night if you want."

Can I do it? Hook up with someone I'm going to see again in daylight? With someone who knows me? My throat hurt at my indecision, but then he pressed his lips against my neck and I bucked underneath him. My words sounded like a needy whine when I said, "Yes, yes. Let's."

"Let's what? I need you to be very clear," he mumbled against the sensitive skin beneath my ear. It sent a ripple of shivers straight to my toes and I arched my back to get closer to him. Each time his lips touched my skin, my brain cells disappeared. Lust took control.

That was the only reason I said, "Let's do this all night, Jeff."

Chapter Fifteen

Jeff

Thank Christ.

I ground against her, loving the fuck out of the way she squirmed underneath me, and a desperate, almost animalistic need to find out what else she liked took over. *What would she do if I snuck my hand beneath the tight waistband of her tights? What sounds would she make if I slipped my fingers inside her?*

I sucked the skin just above her collarbone and bit down, wanting it to sting a little bit, but I didn't stop there. She tasted so damn good and I trailed farther down, over the bare shoulder that had distracted me the second she opened the door. She moved her hands to grip the edge of my shirt and fisted the material in her hands, forcing it up my body and over my head. What type of gentleman would I be if I didn't oblige her demand?

I quickly repositioned to remove my shirt and tossed it on the ground. Her eyes glazed over with desire and she licked her lips when she reached up and traced my pecs. "God, your muscles are insane."

"I like your hands on me," I growled, when she trailed her dainty fingers downward toward the uncomfortable tent in my pants. Her touch promised pleasure, but I wasn't done exploring her. Not even a little bit. *Shit – she dipped into my pants.* I placed my hands on hers, stopping her movements and watching the flash of hurt cross her eyes. *What the hell?* "Hey, do you know why I'm stopping you?"

"No?" she said, more like a question, and red splotches started forming on her face. Her intense gaze moved from my face to my shoulder and something like anger lit me up inside. *Why is she so unsure in the bedroom when she's so passionate?*

"Because, Ambar, I'm selfish. I've been thinking about your body for days and want to spend time tasting you. I won't last long if you put your hand on my dick." I paused, letting her digest my words, and it took a bit before her gaze landed back on mine. Without breaking eye contact, I straddled her and slipped my hands under her sweatshirt and slid the soft material over her head. *"Jesus."*

She wore her tight black pants and the tiniest sheer bra with nothing but thin straps. It gave me the hottest vision of her small tits pushing against the fabric, her dusky rose nipples pebbled and begging for attention. I took one between my thumb and pointer, pinching it and teasing it. She moaned and her eyes fluttered when I added my second hand, taking my time pleasuring her.

For some goddamn reason, I hated her uncertainty about her own sexuality and wanted her to know how attractive she was. I pulled with both of my hands and stared at each pebbled tip. "You have perfect nipples."

"My boobs are small," she said in just above a whisper. She never opened her eyes when I dipped down and pushed the fabric to the side to suck one hard into my mouth. The other one fit into my hand and I caressed it, switching back and forth between them with my mouth. I flicked my tongue against one and blew on it and waited.

"Look at me," I demanded. Her chest heaved with each shaky breath, but she finally met my eyes and I held her gaze when I brought my mouth down on her again. "They are fucking perfect for sucking. Watch me."

I bit down, pulled up and let it go, leaving evidence of my saliva on her chest. "Do you like it when I do that?"

"Yes." She puffed her chest out and ran her own hands over them. "No one's told me I had good nipples before."

"Then they are idiots." I pressed a kiss right in the center of her chest, where there lacked cleavage, but it wasn't any less attractive than girls with huge racks. I could cup a breast in each hand and drive her crazy with my fingers while I licked down her soft stomach. "Your skin tastes fucking good. It doesn't make sense."

She giggled and put her hands in my hair. "No one's ever said that either."

"You need to sleep with better guys." I paused and looked up, ignoring the foreign feeling in my gut when I said it. But when I looked at her expression, she had a smug grin. "What?"

"What do you think I'm doing right now?"

"Oh, you think we're going to fuck tonight?" I teased, enjoying the hell out of her shock. "What if I just want to eat you out all night? Would you say no?"

Her lips trembled and nothing but a small gasp left her lips. *Good.* I wiggled my eyebrows at her and continued my perusal of her exposed skin until I reached her pants. It took a lot of effort to not rip them off her, but I managed to take my time sliding them off her legs and leaving her in a plain black thong. There was a small patch of moisture showing on the outside and I grinned at her, tracing it with my finger. "Are you wet for me?"

She slammed her eyes shut and nodded.

"No going shy." I moved up to her face and cupped the back of her head. "Ambar, we agreed, no getting bashful."

Her dark brown eyes held something like worry and confusion and it zapped the urgency from me. *Why is she afraid?* "Hey…we can stop."

She sighed and tilted her head into my hand, hiding her face. "I feel like an idiot."

"Why? Were you enjoying yourself?" *Think about her, not your dick right now.*

She kept staring everywhere besides my face and spoke in a monotone voice. "Look, I really haven't ever hooked up with someone sober…or with the lights on."

She what…? "Do you want the lights off?"

She reached for a sheet to cover her chest and turned away from me. "No. Well, yeah, but it's not that. It's uh…god, this is embarrassing."

Never in my life had I been in this situation. My own insecurities rushed to the front of my mind. Was I not pleasing her enough or was I misreading her reactions? But small pieces of what she shared with me clicked together. "You've hooked up with a lot of guys, right?"

"Yes…as you have with plenty of girls." This time there was fire in her voice and I was glad to hear it.

"Not judging you, just trying to figure out what's going through your head. Why pull back with me?"

"Because, Jeff." She huffed and gave me a wounded look, like she accepted defeat and was about to surrender. "It was easier to sleep with guys who I didn't know, wouldn't see again, and with the alcohol flowing to ease the sting if they turned me down. The lights were always off to hide the unattractive stuff and with you…so open and vocal, I'm out of my element."

I opened my mouth to respond but nothing came out. She must've taken that as an insult and moved from the bed to grab her sweatshirt and put it on in a rush. "I'm pathetic, I know. You now know almost all my bad parts. Great. Just…" She rubbed her hands over her face and let her arms fall to the side. "Can you leave or at least say something?"

"We can go slow." I moved so my legs hung over the side of her bed. "Because there is no way I'm going to be able to forget this."

Her mouth dropped open. "You're wanting to…hook up again?"

"Yes." I stood and put my hands on her shoulders. Her gaze dropped to the bulge in my jeans, but she averted her attention to my face when I said, "We both have a lot going on right now—my final season and you and your final project. Throw in this scandal and we essentially have no time. I'm attracted to you and I'm pretty sure you're into me if I was reading your body right." I stopped and waited for her blush and smiled when it appeared. "Neither of us do relationships, hm? I see the perfect solution."

"Repeated hook-ups? You and me?"

"Yes, Ambar." I cupped her chin and tilted her face toward me. "If it makes you feel better, this is new for me, too." I pressed a quick kiss on her lips and gave her what I hoped was a reassuring smile. "Until we finish this investigation, we can work together *and* have some fun."

"Naked fun?"

"Now you're getting it." I didn't want to leave and go back to an empty house with my dick still throbbing in my pants, but from everything I knew about Ambar, she needed some space. That was something I could do for her. "Want to meet up tomorrow at my place after classes to come up with a plan for next steps? You can let me know if you're in."

She thought about it for a couple of seconds before nodding. She wore no makeup yet had perfectly clear and soft skin. I rubbed my thumbs over her always blushing cheeks and laughed at myself. *When have I ever thought about how soft a girl's face was before? How about never.* I forced myself to focus and tilted my head. "I need a verbal answer, Henderson."

The use of her last name made her smile. "Yes. I'll come over tomorrow."

"Can't wait." I dropped my hands and found my shirt. It wasn't until I was about to walk out of the door that I remembered what I shared with her. While I trusted her, it was still difficult for me to remember she wasn't going to sell me out. "What I told you tonight…about the future, no one else knows."

"Thank you for sharing it with me. It'll stay here."

"I know." I gave her another smile and found myself stupidly excited about what tomorrow would bring. "See you later then."

* * * *

The next day, my phone buzzed in my hand on the walk back from my final class and when I glanced down,

I expected to see something from Ambar. *If she's backing out, I swear I'll lose my mind.* Instead, I froze in place.

UNKNOWN: Let it go. Stop asking questions.

A dull ringing began in my ears, like someone had hit Mute on a high-frequency TV, and all my blood rushed to my head. *Holy shit. Shit. Someone knows.* My neck tingled and I whipped my gaze around the neighborhood. Was I going to find someone staring at me with binoculars? No. But it felt like someone had eyes on me and it creeped me the hell out. Who had access to my number? *A lot of chicks…any one of them could've sold you out.*

"Dude, what the fuck?" Aaron yelled from twenty steps ahead of me. "Why did you stop?"

"Sorry," I mumbled and shoved my phone in my pocket. "Read something weird."

"Did you see the headline about the student busted for thousands of dollars' worth of drugs in their dorm? They raided the old building on the south quad yesterday. One of the freshmen on the team lived next to him."

"That's crazy." I tried to act normal, and not like a bounty was on my head. Aaron gave me a weird look and I caught up to him for the final block. He was insightful at reading people and if I didn't chill the fuck out, he'd start asking questions I didn't want to answer. "Drugs, you said?"

"Yeah, like hard-core shit." He kicked a rock from the middle of the sidewalk and it bounced into someone's yard. "Sampson said he's banned from his dorm for a couple nights until they search the walls between their rooms. How wild is that?"

"It has to be making the news, right?"

"Probably. Our school doesn't have scandalous shit like that happen. Just cowardly blog posts accusing athletes of being drug-addicted whores," he said bitterly, referencing the summer before his junior year.

"Don't be bitter. You and Greta got together because of that and you were a real piece of shit before her."

He shoved my shoulder with a grin. "Dick."

"Just being honest." I laughed at his dumbass expression, but it was short-lived when I thought about the scandal that was definitely going on at our school. *And someone found out I'm involved.*

We approached the driveway and Aaron rushed to the door. "I'm sick of this fucking winter already. It better be quick because I'm not trying to pull a muscle playing in these temps."

"Midwest winters can last until April."

"I swear, if I get drafted somewhere butt-ass cold, I know it'll be karma for all my idiot shit sophomore year."

I laughed because he was right. He held the door for me and I tried to discreetly look around our block for anything that stood out. A person, a telescope, someone in a car staring at me, but it all looked bleak and normal.

"You hanging around the house tonight? I think all the girls are coming over for dinner if you want to hang with us."

Couple-world again. Blah. "I might eat with you guys, but I'm working on a project with Ambar."

"Ah, Henderson." He smiled and raised his brows at me. "Don't hurt her, man. She's got it bad for you."

Wait…what the fuck did he say? "What?"

"Dude, haven't you noticed her the past three years? She blushes every goddamn time you're in the room. I told her to make a move once and I thought she was going to throw up." He tossed his bag onto the bottom of the stairs and plopped down onto the couch, not realizing at all that I remained fully dressed in my winter coat by the door. "I don't get why she would be into you...you're a real ass most of the time."

"Who's a real ass?" Zade asked, strolling into the living room from the kitchen with food hanging from his mouth. The dude ate more than anyone I knew, but he was a beast on the mound.

"Jeff."

"Yeah, I agree." Zade looked amused and smug.

I snapped out of my momentary paralysis and flipped them both off. They laughed but let the topic go. I was torn. Part of me wanted to ask more about the bomb Aaron had dropped on me but I didn't want to bring attention to it. *She has it bad for me? Three years?*

Does this change anything?

"I'm gonna head upstairs to get started on some homework," I said, not waiting for their reply. It was an unspoken rule in the house that if we had schoolwork, no one gave anyone shit for doing it. It was one of many reasons why I loved these guys like brothers and I didn't feel the slightest regret for lying to them. My mind was completely occupied with two things and while the threatening text should have been my only priority, I couldn't stop thinking about Ambar.

I started typing out a text to her but had to erase it three times. *What the fuck is happening?*

Jeff: Come on over when you can. I'm home the rest of the night.

Jeff: Something huge happened today.

Ambar: What was it?

Jeff: It's a better conversation to have in person.

I told myself it was true—someone had my number and I didn't want to risk anyone seeing my text to her—but my gut knew she would come over faster with the promise of information.

But if she's into me, why wouldn't she want to come over?

Or why stop us from hooking up?

Why do I care?

"God damn it." I rubbed my palms over my eyes and hated the uncertainty and unease at the entire situation. It changed nothing. Not the way I saw her, not how I would act, not how much I wanted her. There. That decided it. Nothing would change and I found my normal swagger when I texted her again.

Jeff: I haven't stopped thinking about your body. Please say yes.

Ambar: I'll be over in thirty minutes—in class still.

Chapter Sixteen

Ambar

"Nice work on your sports, media and culture piece, Ms. Henderson. Your writing has a certain edge to it that I haven't seen in a while. It's refreshing." Professor Madsen gave me a curt nod—her notorious sign of approval—and moved on to the student after me. My insides wriggled and swelled at her compliment. Maybe I'd been feeling down more than normal, because that simple statement combined with Jeff's compliment caused me to smile so hard it hurt my face.

"Your theme of media bias was spot-on. Kinda jealous I didn't think of it myself." Kayla Crawford, a fellow senior who had been in most of my classes all four years, was the third person to give me a compliment. The world had to be ending. That was the only explanation.

"Thanks," I mumbled, trying to hide the aggressive blush taking over my face. "I guess I've always been into sports."

"Well it shows and I'm only like eighty percent proud and twenty percent angry at you…give or take twenty."

I laughed and buttoned up my long red winter coat. The wind was freezing and I wasn't looking forward to the walk home. *But you're going straight to Jeff's and you know it.* My fingers shook with either nerves or adrenaline when I slipped on my gloves and said goodbye to Kayla. Jeff's unanswered text remained at the front of my mind. Could I do this? Hook up with him…sober…and still work with him?

Was that a semi-relationship? *No. It's partners-in-an-investigation-with-benefits.* My skin tingled when I thought about his mouth on me the night before…the way he'd brought my body to life and been so vocal about it. *It's never been like that before with anyone.*

It could be fun to explore that with him. *My campus crush wants to sleep with me repeatedly.* I would be a fool to say no. *God, I wish I could talk to Laney about this. This is her territory, not mine.* I had nothing to lose by doing this. It wasn't like I would fall for him. He thought me average and unremarkable. *But he's changed his tune.*

I groaned and bent my head down to walk faster. This was one of the times I wished I could invent a button that would stop all thoughts. I was always in my head, second-guessing or doubting everything and just once, I wish I could let my body decide for me. *That's why you drank and slept with random guys. It was primal.*

God, I wanted a beer.

My heeled boots clicked on the sidewalk and, instead of letting my mind wonder about sleeping with Jeff, I thought about the investigation the rest of the way. How would I go about reporting it if we broke it open? Who would be the target, the face of the scandal? The coach or my uncle? The players or the university? If I did write up about it, what would be the goal? To expose them all?

What's the new information Jeff has?

That was the question I repeated and focused on as I walked right by our house and to the baseball one. This was the first time I'd visited Jeff in his domain and I wasn't sure if I should call, text or knock. It was too cold to wait around so I rang the doorbell and pulled my coat tighter against my chest. I hated wearing tights and a dress most of the time, but it had been required for my presentation and the cold seeped into my legs.

"Hey, Henderson," Aaron said, ushering me inside. "What's going on?"

"Is Jeff here?" I asked, suddenly unsure. Zade and Tanner sat on the couch and smiled at me in greeting, but I got the feeling they were all laughing at me. *Like they know the deal Jeff proposed to me.* "I'm supposed to meet up with him for my final project about athletes and how sports affect their education." *Wow, I'm good at lying on the fly.*

"He's upstairs, but I'm a little pissed you chose him to write about. Any one of us would've been better options. We're all more interesting."

His attitude made me laugh and it was easy to relax around him. "I won't disagree with you there."

"At least you admit it. If you need better people to interview, let us know."

"Yeah, I take way better photos than Maddow," Zade chimed in. I was about to reply with a sarcastic comment when Jeff stormed down the stairs and leveled his intense stare at me. His gaze dropped from my face to my legs and he jutted his chin upstairs.

"Wanna get to work?"

"Nice to see you, too," I mumbled and gave the rest of the guys a weak smile. "Maybe I will change the focus of the article onto you three."

"You know where we live. The invitation is always open," Zade said with a wink. Jeff cleared his throat and each step I took closer to him, it felt like lead appeared in my shoes. Nerves, excitement, doubt and lust merged into a lethal combination and I wasn't sure if I wanted to strip down or run away. *Focus on the information.*

"These clowns get loud so I figured we can work upstairs." He put his hand on my lower back and gently nudged me to head up. I held on to the railing and paused when I got to the top. "My room is on the left."

It's like I've never been in a dude's bedroom before. I have, multiple times. The first thing that struck me was how clean his room was. The bed was made, the floor spotless, his entire desk organized and he even had curtains. "Damn, you're clean."

"Yeah." He shut the door with a soft click, solidifying it was just the two of us now in his small room. "I'm covered in dirt when I'm behind the plate so when I come home, I need my area to be the opposite."

"Interesting. I never would've pegged you for a clean freak," I joked, finding it significantly easier than talking about the big what-if between us. He chuckled and reached out to place a hand on my shoulder.

"Want me to hang up your coat?"

"Oh shit. I forgot I was wearing one. Sure." I undid each button and felt his stare on me. He gave nothing away besides rubbing his lips together and I handed him the red jacket, leaving me in my very fitting professional black dress. It hugged all my curves and made me feel powerful—hence for the presentation—but the way his gaze roamed my body had me fidgeting. It was easy to invent all the negative things he could be thinking about me, but there was a heat to his eyes. *Maybe I do look good?*

"Why do you look so nice?" He hung up my coat on a hook on the back of his closet door.

"I had a presentation for one of my classes." I eyed the options to sit down and wished I'd gone home to change into sweats first. There was no real ladylike way to sit on a bed in pantyhose. "We get graded on professional appearance and this is one of my three power outfits."

"I'll say. The sheer things you're wearing on your legs are distracting. I'd say that's powerful."

My face warmed, but Jeff didn't waste a second before reaching out and placing his on my sides. "You're maddening."

"Me?" My voice came out throaty and flirty when he slid his large hands up and started massaging my neck. It felt really goddamn good and I closed my eyes.

"Yes, you." His voice dropped to a dangerously low tone. "Have you thought about it?"

"The investigation?" I responded, damn well ignoring the intent of his question. He responded with a growl and moved his hands to my chin, using his thumb to trace my bottom lip.

"You're toying with me, Ambar, and I'm having a hard time being a gentleman right now. I want nothing more than to rip this dress off you and finish what we started last night but before I can, I need you to say yes."

"Investigators-with-benefits?"

"I don't give a fuck what you call it. I just want to make you feel good and be inside you."

A whimper escaped from the back of my throat and my gaze snapped open to see his amused expression. He heard it and knew I was seconds away from caving. But then lifted the veil of worry I wore. "We'll go as slow or as fast as you want but, Ambar, we both know how explosive it would be between us."

"Okay."

His answering grin sent a thrill through me. "Turn around. I want to take this dress off you, but I don't want to damage it."

I obeyed and trembled when he slowly undid the zipper from my neck to just above my ass. He grazed my spine with one of his fingers, causing me to shiver, and I bit down on my lip to prevent any unwarranted sounds. The material slid to the floor and, in broad daylight, I stood in Jeff Maddow's room in a black bralette, boy-shorts and pantyhose. But instead of being insecure and nervous, I felt alive.

He stood behind me, running his mouth over my neck while his fingers teased my already hard nipples. "Mm, you taste just as good as I remember."

"Really?" My voice shook when he spread my legs wider with his own. It left me completely exposed and I gasped when he reached between my thighs and teased the outside of my panties.

"I wonder if you'll taste just as good down there. I'd really like to find out, Ambar." He pinched my nipples hard, relaxing his grip before doing it again, and I moaned at the pleasure of it. "But first, I'd like to suck on your pretty tits for a while."

My entire body shook with need when he picked me up like I was nothing and placed me onto his bed—not with my head on his pillow though. My legs hung over the side, giving him the perfect angle to kneel between my thighs. He removed the bralette with ease and gave me a scorching stare before swirling my nipple in his warm mouth.

"I love this," I moaned. "Never enjoyed it before...*oh!*" He sucked it hard and used his free hands to slide my pantyhose down my legs, over my feet and onto the floor.

"It's probably fucked up," he said, kissing down my body, stopping just at the lace of my panties. "But pushing you outside your comfort zone is fucking hot."

"Not fucked up," I moaned, gripping his perfectly styled hair. He was too clean-cut and I wanted him messy...like me. He traced the outside of my panties, right over my clit, and gave a throaty laugh when I jumped at how good it felt.

"Feeling okay?" He stood a little to lean over my naked torso, his eyebrows drawn together. "No regrets?"

"No." The back of my throat got tight at the concern in his voice. It was too personal, too kind and the errant *what if this goes badly* thoughts started to intrude so I reached out to his hand and moved it between my legs. "Touch me."

His eyes lit up and he sprung to action. He went back on his knees, caressing my chest, nipples and thighs before sliding my panties off and inserting one finger into me. "Christ, you're ready for me."

"Yes." I squirmed on his bed at the continuous in and outward motion of his finger. He added a second and flicked his tongue against my swollen clit. "Oh my god."

He combined the two actions, changing between sucking and swirling his tongue on me, humming as he pressed down hard with his mouth. He curled his fingers and increased his pace, the familiar tightening of my muscles starting as a slow burn formed in my core. I was so close, seconds away from the release I desperately needed. The only sounds were my whimpered cries and the wetness of his tongue lashing against me before my orgasm hit me full force, the pleasure spreading through each limb, causing his name to escape my lips in a moan. "*Jeff,* yes!"

"Fuck," he grunted, pressing down on my stomach as I bucked against his face. He let me ride it out before pressing one more kiss on my swollen lips. "That was…hot."

I kept my eyes closed when I tried to catch my breath, but Jeff didn't let me rest long. He reached up toward my breasts again, caressing them while slowly tracing my inner thighs with his tongue. *Thank God he has such long arms.* "A-again?"

"Ambar. Your body is begging for another release."

I glanced down to find his gray eyes dilated and entranced with my bare pussy. "I've only ever had two back-to-back orgasms, but it took a lot of work."

"Interesting." He dragged his tongue past my entrance, up over my clit, over my soft chubby middle and to my chest. Then he moved me so my head rested on his pillow and he quickly removed his shirt. *Good god, his chest is perfection.* "Should we make a bet?"

"A bet?" I mumbled almost incoherently. He moved his hands up and down my legs, massaging and tickling my skin as though he had all the time in the world.

"Yes, a bet." He leaned forward so our lips were inches apart and I could smell my own sex on his breath—not something that should be sexy but damn, it was. "If I can get you to orgasm again, then you can wear real stockings and keep them on when I fuck you next time."

The crassness of his words, the desire in his voice and the mention of *next time* caused an unrecognizable urge through my blood. I wanted to do that and more with Jeff. "Deal."

"Good girl." He put one foot on the ground to balance himself and removed his jeans and boxers before leaning over to open the drawer of his nightstand. The muscles in his ass clenched and I was mesmerized by the hard-earned ripples across his back. Jeff wasn't a meathead who was born huge. All his angles were built from hours of work and I had a wave of appreciation for those gym days. He turned around with a condom on his hand and I got my first glimpse of Jeff Maddow in all his naked glory.

"My god…" I trailed off as my mouth became dry. He was better than any image my mind could've conjured and I wanted to taste him head to toe. His cock pressed against his abs and the thought of orgasming a second time didn't seem so far-fetched. I licked my lips, entranced with the way he slid the condom over his dick.

"Not today, Ambar. Someday, I want your lips around my cock, but I want to bury myself inside you." He kneeled on the bed and ran a hand down the length of my body. "Flip over."

Unsure, I pushed up onto my arms to move, but he gripped my waist and flipped me with an impatient grunt. "You have an incredible ass and I'm a selfish man. Can I take you from behind, Ambar? Would you like that?"

"Y-yes," I stuttered, hyperaware of every touch. He lifted my hips so I was on all fours and he gripped my ass cheeks, squeezing them and spreading them apart. "What are you—"

"I'm an ass man and yours is making me weak. Fuck," he cursed, grinding his cock into the space between them. Then he moved to the right angle and slid into me, patiently letting me stretch for him. "Ambar, *Jesus*."

My breath came out hitched and whiney when he slowly moved in and out, gripping my ass to the point of pain, and I arched my back, giving him deeper access. He moaned and slammed into me. Our bodies hitting each other was the sexiest sound and I pressed my face into his pillow to prevent any loud screams. It smelled so much like his clean scent it sent a wave of arousal to me and a faint tingling sensation formed in between my thighs.

"You feel incredible, god." He leaned forward so his sweaty chest leaned against my back. He reached around and found my clit. "I need you to scream my name when you come a second time. Can you do that?"

"Mm-hm." A ringing began in my ears with each thrust and when he started swirling his thumb, I swore I was going to burst. "Oh, I'm close."

"Thatta girl. Grind against my hand with my cock deep inside you. I want to feel you tremble as I fuck you."

His words did it. The orgasm burst at the base of my body, almost like an electric shock, as pleasure surged through me. I cried his name, losing all dignity and rationale when he pumped into me harder. "Yes, Jeff!"

Waves of pleasure spread from my core, through my veins, and into my mind where all thoughts blurred together. But he didn't stop—he tightened his grip on me and his entire body tensed before he groaned, thrusting a final time. "*Christ,* Ambar."

He slid out of me and ran a hand down my back. "I'm going to clean up real quick. You okay?"

"I can't move," I said, my face still buried in his pillow. He chuckled and patted my ass twice before his footsteps carried toward the bathroom. That left me alone for a minute and all the typical reasons for why I should freak out didn't arrive. If anything…I felt alive. Satisfied and alive and nothing was going to ruin that.

Chapter Seventeen

Jeff

Ambar hadn't moved an inch from her face-down position and her incredible ass remained in clear view. The sight had me smiling like an idiot and I put on some loose sweats before sitting on the edge of the bed. "Are you alive?"

"Maybe?"

"This is doing wonders for my ego, by the way." I patted her ass and loved how it wiggled. It was so full and I made plans to spend way more time on it next time. *Because there will be a next time, soon.* "I didn't hurt you, did I?"

"No." She pushed herself up onto her elbows with the groan of someone three times her age, and she slid me a coy look. It was a sight to see—Ambar Henderson naked in my bed with her perfect small tits, crazy sex hair and bite marks on her chest from me. She saw the direction of my stare and red splotches appeared over her neck and face. "I guess I'll go put my dress back on."

"Do the bite marks bother you?" I traced one around her pink nipple and I considered it a good sign when she shivered at my touch.

"No. I really enjoyed getting them. More than I thought." She looked at the ground and hurried around the room to pick up her dress. She frowned at it before sighing.

"If you want something more comfortable, I can give you a sweatshirt or a T-shirt." I stood and opened my dresser drawer, pulling out a long-sleeved shirt. "You want to borrow it?"

"For a little, yeah. I can't walk downstairs in *that*. They'll all know." Her eyes got wide and I shrugged off her comment.

"They'll mind their business."

"If you say so." She took the shirt from me and slipped it over her head, not bothering with her bra, and I found the thought of her chest bare against my clothes real appealing. "Wow. It's been a while since I slept with anyone and damn, I forgot how wobbly my legs can get."

"Excuse me, I blame your *two* orgasms for the weak legs." I gave her a pointed look and she rolled her eyes. "Are you denying it? We had a bet, Henderson."

"Yeah, yeah, whatever. You want me to wear stockings." She stepped into her cute little boy-shorts and jumped back onto the bed and moved the covers so they were over her legs. "Shit… is this cool? Do you want me to sit at your desk when we talk about the investigation or…?"

"Stay there. It's warmer." I ignored her uncertainty and grabbed my phone and notepad with all the information I had. "Move over though. I'm joining you."

She scooted so she was against the headboard and wall, letting me have the edge, and it struck me how odd it was to *not* have the urge to get her the hell out of there. Most of the time I either rushed to get home, or, I'd make some excuse for them to leave. I think maybe once…or twice I'd hung around longer than an hour. It wasn't because I was an asshole. There was just nothing to talk about.

She looked at me expectantly and made her eyes get all big. "Tell me the news, Jeff! While I know what we just did was fun, I really did come over because you said you had news to share."

"It was more than *just* fun," I teased. "But check out the last text I got." I handed her my phone and waited as she scrolled to find the one I was referring to. It took about thirty seconds before she gasped.

"What the hell? Someone threatened you? When did this happen?" She threw my device onto the foot of the bed and gave me a panicked look. "We were careful."

"I know. It freaked me out, too. I got it this afternoon. I haven't done anything with it besides read it. It's not like we can trace an unknown number."

She had a thoughtful look and ran her fingers over the collar of my shirt before saying, "It means we're getting closer. Someone's worried."

"I thought the same thing." *Do I tell her I'm freaked out? Act cool about it?*

She did what I dubbed her *thinking* face—where she had half her lip sucked into her mouth and one of her eyebrows raised—and I swore I could hear the wheels spinning in her brain. "How easy would it be to find your number?"

A dull twinge of embarrassment hit me when I admitted, "Not hard. A lot of girls have my number and anyone could've gotten it from them."

She didn't look put off. If anything, she nodded, then clapped her hands in excitement. "Duh! The entire baseball coaching staff has access to your information. They had to block the number just in case someone recognized it. I would bet thousands of dollars it came from them. It would be weird to have a grown man ask a college girl for your number. *That* would draw attention."

Again, she thought differently than I did and I was impressed. "It makes more sense and solidifies my coach being involved, even though it sucks."

"Are you worried?" She scrunched her nose and her eyes softened on the sides. "I'm freaked out and it wasn't even sent to me. Fuck! Do you think…do you think my uncle knows I'm involved?" Her voice rose an octave and her words blurred together as she exclaimed them in a hurry. I didn't even think about it before putting my hand on her knee.

"It was sent to me. You have no reason to be worried." I squeezed her leg and let it linger for a second before saying, "If anything, I'm glad it was my number. I can handle anything thrown my way and that can help keep attention off you—the person who's going to write this article and expose all these assholes."

"I don't know, Jeff. This seems so much more real now. People know you're asking around." She rubbed the center of her forehead with two fingers and grabbed my notebook from my hand. "We need to wrap this thing up as fast as we can. If anyone of them knows someone's onto their actions, they could start taking actions to cover their tracks."

She flipped the page and started jotting down a timeline and I leaned closer to her so I could see what she was writing.

-Athletes involved
-Coaches/administration involved
-Martin Rhett
-Where is the money?
-Sports involved

"I'm going to start drafting an outline." She bit down on the end of my pen and starting chewing before she realized it and stopped. "Shit, I'm sorry. This is yours. It's a habit."

"Not worried about it." I scanned her list and something was missing. I couldn't figure out what and while I understood her motivation to get a head start, the fear of someone catching us wasn't enough to get ahead of ourselves. "I know the text freaked us both out, but I don't want to rush this. We both have people who matter to us involved in this and we can't half-ass it."

"I understand." She narrowed her eyes at me and tapped the pen against her teeth, not biting it this time. "We've focused on baseball the majority of our questions. We need to switch it up."

"Agreed."

She let out a sigh and shook her head. "Photos. Documents. Evidence. We can speculate as much as we want but for anyone to take this accusation seriously, we need some hard evidence."

"There's no fucking way we'll get our hands on that." I balled my fist and hit the side of my bed in frustration. "Shit, I never thought about the lack of that. Who's going to believe two college kids?"

She made a dismissive sound with her tongue and grinned real wide. "Evidence can be as simple as rosters from previous years that proves that some names on these lists don't have a shred of evidence they played the sport in high school. Max assured me that my fake sister didn't need to have any athletic experience. Said that these guys have all the tools to cover it up. I'll have to check my notes I wrote down after I got home that night, but he said something along the lines of never touching a baseball in his life, but this *dude* could make it happen."

"Okay," I responded, nodding more to myself than her. That's more manageable. We don't only need proof of payments or anything serious."

"We'd never get access unless we…" She tapped that pen against her front teeth again and had a crazy gleam in her eye. "Unless we got access to your coach's or my uncle's phone. We could search emails with the names of the guys we know."

"We can't chance that, Ambar. It's too risky." The thought of trying to sneak through my coach's phone was so fucked up. I couldn't risk it—not with my scholarship and the season. The weight of letting my team down was too strong. "There's no way I could pull that off. I'm sorry."

"Don't feel bad. I could probably do it the next time I see my uncle but there's no guarantee either I'll find anything we could use or he won't catch on. I've admired my uncle most of my life for his quick wit and how he handles my mom. He's intelligent and if he really is a huge part of this scandal, well, he'll make sure he's covering every track."

"Not *every* one. Look how much we know."

We shared a brief look of pride, I'd like to think. These assholes were taking real sports on athletic teams away from people who needed them, like Jaime Smith, and we were uncovering small pieces that hopefully added up to their exposure. Ambar leaned back against the headboard and closed her eyes. "I'm going to have to talk to my uncle at some point about all of this, but I want to make sure we have every angle we can think of… Have you thought about what happens when your coach finds out?"

Have I?

"No. But I need to start thinking about it, soon."

I avoided it at all costs and the thought of confronting him had my gut filling with acid. There could possibly be an investigation, suspension, our final season on the team without our coach. *Can I do that to the rest of the guys? What will they do if they know I had a part in it?* The uncertainty and anger crept into the momentary content I had exploring Ambar's body. It was the same rage I'd had when I had stormed to her house and accused her of having a part in it all. It struck me I'd never officially apologized for it. She had proven herself countless times since then and a ball of shame took shape in my gut. *I'm just a pathetic glass case of emotion, aren't I?*

"Ambar," I said, pulling her attention away from wherever she escaped in her mind. "I'm sorry I accused you of being a part of this entire thing. You clearly aren't and I don't have any excuse."

"Thank you for saying it." She gave me a half-smile, her full lips curving up on one side of her cute face. "It's crazy that was only a couple of weeks ago."

I could've agreed with her, changed the subject, kissed her, hell, I could've done any of those but instead, I asked, "Do you forgive me?"

"Hm," she said, twisting her lips to the other side of her mouth. "Maybe. Answer one question for me."

"Anything." The need for her to forgive was essential and I had no idea why. Her saying maybe wasn't enough. "Ask me anything."

"Be honest, okay? Why did you jump so quickly to the conclusion I had some part in it?" She dropped her gaze to a piece of fuzz on my bed and picked at it with her fingers.

Her shoulders slumped and she guarded her face—as though she expected my answer before I said it. I felt like the world's biggest asshole when I thought about why it had been so easy to blame her and point all my anger at her. Was it because it was easier than accepting the truth? "Look, I judged you without knowing you and that's all on me. We had a class together freshman year and you skipped all the time, then the whole drug thing spread pretty fast among the freshmen. It was easier for me to blame you the second I learned Martin Rhett was your uncle."

"Yeah," she mumbled, still not looking at me. The pressure in my chest built to the point of pain and I hated how defeated she looked.

"I'm in the wrong here, not you. You don't get to be sad when I'm the asshole. Okay? You're incredible and I'm pissed at myself I didn't get to know you sooner." I waited for her to smile or show some sign of relief at my words, but nothing came. I reached for her chin and tilted her face up to mine. Her large eyes held a little sadness and something I couldn't decipher. "You are fucking awesome and I hate that it took me this long to figure it out."

She smiled shyly and a spark returned to her eyes. "Well, thanks."

"You're welcome. Stand up for yourself sometimes, Henderson. I'm appreciative that you gave me a chance after I was such a dick." *Is it because she has it bad for me? Could that be a reason? Do I want her to have a thing for me?*

Woah. Not the time for those thoughts when Ambar clearly had a confidence issue that I'd played a part in sustaining. *Support her. Be her friend.*

She let out a small chuckle and pointed her finger at my chest. "The only reason I gave you a chance was to prove you wrong. I'm untalented at anything athletic but apparently I'm super-competitive. You made me so mad that day, I wanted to punch or kick you." She trailed off and gave me a dorky smile that showcased all her teeth. "And to think I had a huge crush on you."

Had?

Past tense?

"Have, you mean?"

"Had," she fired back with a teasing glint in her eye. "You ruined the illusion of Jeff Maddow that day you told me I was unremarkable."

"Fuck. I'm sorry—"

"You're forgiven now." She patted my face this time and slid out of the bed, moving to put on her tights. "Plus, after sleeping with you, I know I wasn't missing anything."

"You take that back." I jumped from the bed and within a second had my arms around her, preventing her from leaving. "Are you trying to rile me up right now? Because it's working. I'm competitive too, babe, and I will show you what you were missing."

Her answer was to lean into me and have her lips linger an inch away from mine. "I need to head out, but rain check."

Chapter Eighteen

Ambar

Mom: Are you coming home to visit for spring break?

Ambar: Not sure, still a ways away.

Mom: We need to know if we can give your bed away to your brothers' friends.

Ambar: It depends if I get all my schoolwork done. Don't let them sleep in my bed. I don't trust them. They are gross.

Mom: Calm down. I need to know in a week or I'll let them use your room.

I fell back onto my bed in a sigh of pity for myself. It seemed unfair to complain about my family when I hadn't wanted for anything growing up, especially when so many others suffered real complications. But it didn't take the sting away when my mom chose my brothers over me every chance she got. *Maybe I won't go home.*

The thought of not returning to my parents' house during the summer seemed more and more likely. I didn't have a job lined up for a lot of savings, but I made decent money with the blog to rent a shitty one-bedroom for another year. *Freelance writing, social media kits, affiliate tags and basic graphic design.* I could do any of those things to support myself until I figured out… oh, the rest of my life. *No big deal.*

What would Jeff think?

I bolted up at the thought of asking him for his opinion. It came out of nowhere, but it wasn't unwelcome. Our friend-investigator-ship had changed at some point and I was still reeling with how to deal with the modification. I trusted him with the investigation, no question there. Did I trust him with talking about real shit?

Yeah, I think I do.

It had been two days since I'd left his house and while we'd texted a handful of times, I wouldn't mind seeing him again. *Can I just text him asking to hang out?* I cringed. The thought of texting Jeff Maddow to hang out seemed unreal…not likely and I dismissed the idea. The only logical explanation was to get more information. Schoolwork had piled up and I wasn't pretending to be an A or a B student, but I hadn't liked falling behind on assignments ever since I'd faced probation. My classes took priority so I finished my most pressing assignments before moving on to the investigation. I had to flip through my journal and review my notes on who I should follow up with to get some insight. I scanned my notes and grinned when I saw Teets underlined twice.

Hockey.

A potential for another sports team to be affected by the whole ordeal.

Ambar: Teets. You in town today? I want to buy you a beer.

Teets: Goddamn, Henderson, that's bold. I'm in.

Ambar: Lion, four?

Teets: I'll take the biggest one they got.

Score! I made a fist and raised it in the air, feeling stupid for reacting that way alone. Screw it. Teets would hopefully have some answers that would give us more information. *And give me a reason to meet up with Jeff.*

My skin tingled if I closed my eyes and pictured his hand—and tongue—on me and while I had fantasized about him before, it didn't compare to the real thing. My body buzzed with anticipation and I shot up to get ready. If I was going to smooth-talk Teets for answers and hook up with Jeff after, I wanted to look good. I got out of bed and called downstairs. "Laney?"

"What'up, mama?" She was a genius and never had class on Fridays so she often partied on Thursdays and slept all day to get ready for another round.

"I'm meeting an old friend for a drink and have the potential for a hook-up later. Help me look good."

She appeared at the bottom of the stairs with a wicked smile and stormed up to my room. "*Please* say it's with Jeff. Please."

Don't blush. Don't blush. "Why would you want that?"

"Because you spend alone time with him and you've had a crush on him for years. He's hot as shit and probably an animal in bed." She pushed her way into my bedroom and went straight to the closet. She glanced over her shoulder at me and gasped. "Shut the fuck up. You *have* hooked up with him."

"W-what?" *Shit. Shit!*

"Your face gives you away, babe." She wiggled her eyebrows and leaned against the doorframe with an impatient look. "If you don't spill the details, I will kill you."

"Okay, fine. We've kinda hooked up twice."

"And?"

"It was…amazing." My face burned like a roaring fire, but relief also coursed through my blood. *Someone knows. I can talk to her now about it.* "It will probably happen again."

"Thank god! I called it." She smacked her palm against the wall and gave me a proud look. "He was coming over here too often for someone not into you. Plus, I saw him give you heated looks."

"We're not dating though," I said way too fast. "Just hooking up until my project is done. That's all."

"I'm glad you're putting yourself out there and not using alcohol to feel bold." She went straight the core of my issue and moved to place her hands on my shoulders. "I love you something fierce, Ambar, but this is a good move to help build the confidence your mom shattered. You are a catch for anyone and once you start believing it, you'll see a change."

My eyes stung a little and my mom's text from earlier had me asking, "Are you going anywhere over spring break?"

"Hell no. I'm broke from student loans and will probably spend the entire time binge-watching *Housewives*. Why, are you? Is your sexy uncle going to pay for a trip for you?"

A weight formed in my throat when I shook my head. "No, he's not. I might stay here with you then. We can get into shenanigans."

"Hell yeah, girl." She cupped my face and tilted her head dangerously close to mine. "Now, let's pick out some sexy shit to blow Jeff's mind."

* * * *

My hair was down in loose curls that framed my face. I wore my favorite black jeans paired with heeled boots and a low-cut black blouse that flirted with showing my tits, but since I wasn't gifted there, Laney assured me I could pull it off. She let me borrow her dark-red lipstick and gave me the sexiest smoky-eyed look I would never be able to do myself. If I had a confidence meter, it would read at the highest level. *Damn it feels good. Do people feel like this every single day?*

The Lion was packed for a Friday afternoon, but there wasn't much else to do in the dead of winter on campus. If students weren't at the library studying, they were at one of the campus bars. It was just what we did. I nodded to the bouncer and walked in, looking for Teets' unmistakable frame. His man-bun gave him away. I bopped it with my hand as my greeting.

"Henderson, you look fucking good." He pulled me into a hug and I welcomed the warm embrace. The walk had chilled me down to my bones and his natural warmth helped ease the pain. He smelled like nature and musk and I imagined him living in the woods. The image had me chuckle and my mood lifted even more.

"Thank you. I appreciate you coming." I sat across from him and Kenzie Hill walked up to our table with an adorable smile.

"Hi, y'all. What can I get you? Coffee, Ambar?"

"Yes, please. And the tallest amber ale you have for this behemoth."

She nodded and took off, leaving Teets to grin at me. "What?"

"You just look cute and shit. Makes me happy. You were a bit sulky sophomore year. Wore black a lot and always had a pout. Happy Ambar is beautiful."

My blush came and went like it always did and I waited for Kenzie to return with our drinks before I lowered my voice. While a part of me wanted to analyze his compliment and ask more questions, I pushed the urge away. I was here for a mission. "Do you remember our conversation from the party last weekend?"

"I do." He took a huge swig and left a beer mustache on his already very long one. "Figured something's brewing and I meant what I said. I'll help anyway I can."

"Bottom line is that kids are getting athletic spots on teams without *ever* playing the sport."

"Fuck." He groaned and leaned back against the booth, causing it to creak under his weight. "You think it's happening with the hockey team?"

"I think it's happening with a variety of sports, but I can only confirm one so far." I eyed the people around our booth and continued, "This shit is messed up, so I trust you to keep this between us."

"Of course." He took another long swig, almost finishing half of the massive mug. "You asked me about injuries and disappearing players. I kept thinking about this guy who was a total dick and why he rubbed me the wrong way. I was grinding for a captain spot and this little fucker glided around without doing any work. Connor Long."

"You're sure that's his name?"

"Thought about him more than I'd like since last week. Asked some of the other guys if they remembered him and they all said the same thing. Entitled, untalented and no loss to our team. No one could remember details on how he left the team, but the consistent theme was a bullshit injury. We all figured he wasn't tough enough to make it and used it as an excuse. It's not entirely uncommon for guys to walk away after an injury. Kids come in from small schools thinking they're hot shit and learn real quick they don't have what it takes. This kid didn't at all."

I jotted down some notes in my journal and moved on to the next question. "What about your coaches? Have they been the same the past three, four years?"

"You know…no. Our head coach has been around for decades, but the supporting staff changed two years ago." He scratched his chest and frowned. "I don't recall anything weird happening the last two years, either."

"Do you remember the coaching staff names?"

He mentioned about four of them and I wrote them down, none of them standing out, which led me to another question. "Do you know the name Martin Rhett?"

"Can't say the name rings a bell."

Relief. "It's this guy." I held up a picture of him on my phone and hated how my entire body tensed waiting for his answer. It wasn't like my uncle was innocent in all of this, but to have him have a minor role would be the best-case scenario at this point.

Teets squinted at it for a few seconds before snapping his fingers. "I've seen him around the rink."

My voice shook. "Are you sure?"

"Yes. It was last year. He wore a leather jacket and a fancy-ass watch that reflected the lights. I remember because I was getting ripped into from one of our support coaches when he walked in. Mark was pissed at the interruption and barked at him to get the hell out." He closed his eyes in thought and I cringed at the array of scars scattered on his face. "This dude with the watch said something about the offer expiring and Mark looked furious. He dismissed me and I got the hell out of there. I played like shit that game and was so caught up in my own drama I didn't really think about how weird that was until now."

"And you haven't seen him since then?"

"Mark? I see him every day."

"No, Martin Rhett."

"Correct. I haven't seen him since then and I wouldn't dare ask Mark about it." His face relaxed and he leaned closer to me over the table. "Is this Martin dude the one involved in whatever this thing is?"

"It's looking more and more like it." This was definitely something to add to our ongoing list of shady behaviors. "Is there anything else you can think of that relates to this?"

"Don't think so, Henderson. But hey, whatever it is you're uncovering, be careful. I've never seen Mark that angry that fast and I play hockey. We're a bunch of angry assholes."

I smiled at his attempt to make me feel better. "I'll be careful."

"Is there anything you want me to ask some of the guys? They might remember more than I can. I've taken quite a few hits to the skull."

"Right now, it'd be best to keep quiet." I tapped my pen against the notepad. "Does Connor still go here?"

Teets opened his mouth a couple of times before saying, "You know, I think he does. I saw that bastard's face at a bar a while ago. Didn't give him a second thought, though, until last weekend. He's one of those special kinds of assholes I'm happy to forget."

"That gives me enough information. Thank you."

He finished his drink and gave me a look that said *Well?* "Want to stick around for another one or you need to head out?"

"I should head out but we need to catch up more often." I left a ten on the table and moved to his side of the booth for a hug. "Thank you, really."

"Of course, Henderson. I told you. I got you if you need help." He wrapped his arms tight around me. "Let me know how it ends up."

"Will do."

I waved and quickly grabbed my phone with my heart racing in my neck. *Is this about the new information or about seeing Jeff?*

Ambar: Hey, you free?

Jeff: I can be. What's up?

Ambar: Got some information about the hockey team. Wanna meet up?

Jeff: My place or yours?

Ambar: Yours.

Jeff: You wearing those stockings as we discussed?

My stomach swooped at his insinuation and I typed out a couple of responses before settling on one I felt was flirty and teasing.

Ambar: Double or nothing.

Jeff: Get your ass over here.

Chapter Nineteen

Jeff

"You aren't heading out with us tonight, man?" Tanner asked as he opened his second beer. "Our weekends are limited until the season starts and we all just passed our mandatory drug tests. I think we deserve a beer after having that dude watch me pee in a cup."

I snorted. "Yeah, not a fan of having someone watch me take a piss. But get used to it, man—you'll do that in the majors, too."

"I'm ready for it. But tonight, you down to clown?"

"Nah, I'm hanging out with Ambar for a bit and I might meet up with you."

"Bring her with. The girls are joining us after Kenz gets off her shift."

"I'll mention it to her." I finished the sports drink and tossed it into the recycling bin, anxiously watching the front window for Ambar to arrive. Between practice and homework, I had no time to do any research and her text was like a fucking gift. *I want to see her naked again.* "I'm not in the mood for socializing tonight, you know?"

"I get it. You've seemed a little a down lately." He gave me a long look that made him seem years older than he was and I hated how guilty I felt hiding everything from them. "You sure you're good?"

I tilted my head to the right, cracking my neck to relieve some tension. "Just working through senior-year anxieties, that's all. I'll be fine."

"Get laid. It'll help." He smiled like the chump he was and I fought the urge to roll my eyes. He wasn't wrong in his advice, but it wasn't like I could tell him I planned on doing just that as soon as Ambar got her ass over here. "I'm showering and meeting up with some of the other guys in an hour. Let me know if you join. Despite what the other two say, I did miss hanging out with you when you were gone."

I nodded, but my muscles were stiff from tension. Practice had been brutal and it hadn't helped that I'd dodged questions the entire time. Coach had cornered me twice to see if I had thought about my decision yet and, while I appreciated his concern, I felt there was something else in his tone. Something like an underlying threat…like he knew what I was doing and wanted me to be aware of it. *Because he might be the one texting me warnings.*

The reminder of our conversation had me looking at my phone. There hadn't been any other texts or warnings but the feeling of being watched hadn't gone away. My guard was up everywhere I went and all the worry caused my muscles to tighten more than normal—a sure way to get injured. *I need to collect myself and get it together.* Our team couldn't afford injuries with the back-up catcher nowhere near ready to start in a month and while my future with baseball was in the air, I wanted to go out on top.

Cleaning helped and I started doing the pile of dishes that had stacked up the last few days. The guys weren't total slobs, but they weren't the best and keeping things in order. They preferred to let stuff get to shit then step in. It caused the sink to form a slight stench and it drove me crazy. It was mindless work and the repetition calmed me. Rinse, scrub, set in dishwasher, repeat.

It forced me to relax but after a couple of minutes of the monotonous motion, my mind wandered to the future, my coach, the investigation, telling my teammates, and Ambar. She was the most fun to think about and it was easy to imagine her naked, her black hair spilling out over my pillow and the sounds she made learning all the ways sex could be fun. Anticipation of seeing her had me checking my phone every three seconds and a weight of disappointment filled my chest when she still hadn't arrived when I'd finished the huge stack of dishes.

I gave myself a hard-on. Great.

It wasn't like me to text to see where the hell she was at, but I had the message typed out just as someone knocked on the door. *Thank Christ.* I dove for the door and flung it open, smiling at the sight of her. She was bundled in a large puffy jacket that didn't hide her crazy beautiful hair or her wild eyes that had nothing but mischief in them. "Hey."

"Hey yourself," she replied, pushing past me, shivering. "It's cold as shit outside."

"You came from two houses down. You're made of tougher stuff than that." I moved to take off her coat and hang it up, and when she shimmied out of it, I had to bite back a groan at her shirt. It dipped low. Real low. My mouth watered at the way it hugged her curves and showcased her body. "God damn, Ambar."

She gave me a killer smile, full of confidence and something like swagger, and put her hands on her trim hips. "I came from The Lion, first off, and thank you."

I couldn't stop staring at her. Her hair seemed longer, framing her round face, and her lips were red. *Lips I could imagine sucking me off.* It wasn't enough to look and I closed the distance between us, placing my hand on the base of her neck and running it down her cleavage. My hand was massive compared to her petite body and the stark contrast between our sizes caused a funny, unfamiliar feeling to creep in my chest.

I dug my fingers into her skin, just a little. She sucked in a breath and her eyes heated over—a good fucking sign we were on the same page—and a slight outline of her nipples poked through the thin black shirt. I pinched one with my thumb and pointer and rolled it back and forth between the pads. The littlest groan escaped her lips and she straightened her posture, so I did the same thing with my other hand. "You like when I touch you here, don't you?"

"Yes," she breathed, and I pushed her back against the wall. The fabric was light enough to easily push to the side and her dark pink nipples were exposed, begging to be sucked right in our entryway. "D-don't you want t-to know what I found out?"

I closed my lips around her pointed tip and swirled my tongue around it, not quite able to satisfy my hunger for her. My grip on her waist tightened as I moved to her other breast, biting down and pulling the sensitive part away from her body. My dick twitched when she groaned my name and I wanted her to completely lose control. When I came up to breathe, she said, "Teets had good information."

The mention of another dude's name caught my attention and I snapped my gaze to hers. My voice came out like a growl. "Why are we talking about another guy right now?"

Her chest heaved for two beats before she replied, "The information I got. We met at The Lion."

I didn't like the fact she'd met with Teets while looking as good as she did, but that was way too possessive of a thought and I focused on her. "Are you telling me that you would rather talk about the investigation right now?"

I traced her exposed nipples and dipped my head low so I could run my tongue over her ear. She shivered and I kissed along her jawline. "What will it be? Investigation talk or…?"

She whimpered and I wasn't sure what I expected her to do or say, but it wasn't grabbing my face in her hands and slamming our mouths together. It hurt when our teeth clashed but her desperation and fire set my body alive. I gripped her hair in my hands and met her stroke for stroke as we tasted each other. Her familiar and intoxicating scent drove me wild and I couldn't kiss her hard enough—a completely new and alarming feeling I had never experienced before, but I didn't have time to analyze it when she lifted her legs around my waist and ground into my cock.

"Fuck, Ambar," I said between kisses. "You're gonna kill me."

"Good."

I laughed and pushed into her center, wishing her pants would suddenly disappear, and I decided I couldn't wait to go upstairs. "No one's here."

"Yeah?" she replied, her voice deep and husky. It was a straight shot to my dick and I gripped the edge of her tiny shirt and ripped it over her head. I stared down at her bare torso and spent minutes sucking and licking every part I could. "Didn't know you had a thing for small tits, Jeff."

"Your skin tastes so goddamn good." I used my weight to hold her against the wall and quickly removed my shirt. She helped and dragged her nails down my chest. "*Fuck.*"

"You like that?" She repeated the action and moved her hands down to my belt. She undid it within a minute and when one of her fingers grazed the tip, I bucked. "Are you gonna do me against a wall, Jeff? I've never done that before and I'd like to know how it feels."

Christ. "Do you want that?"

She looked up at me with hooded eyes and nodded. "Yes, please."

We didn't waste any more time. We frantically removed our pants with awkward movements that were fueled by passion and any errant thoughts of how not normal it was for me were left behind. She was hot and ready. For me.

I grabbed a condom from my wallet and handed it to her. "Put it on me."

"Mm," she hummed, and ripped open the package. She held the rubber over my bulging head and used her small fingers to roll it down my shaft. I had to squeeze my eyes shut to avoid embarrassing myself at how good it felt. "You're so hard."

"I know." I grunted and gave her one more long kiss. Then I lifted her up and spread her legs wide. "You fit me so well. Fuck."

She moaned when I slid right into her and every single thing she did sent an electric current through my blood. The way she bit her lip, the way her hair bounced each time I thrust into her or the way she played with her tits as I held us up against the wall. "You're so fucking sexy, Ambar."

Her hazy eyes met mine and I crushed my mouth down on hers as I continued a rhythm of in and out. It felt like heaven and while I wanted to pound into her, I had to make sure she came first. Using one hand to hold her against the wall, I used my other to flick her clit.

"Yes! Oh, I'm so close, Jeff." She bucked against me when I paced my finger movements with my cock. Sweat pooled between our bodies and the musky smell of our sex sent me into overdrive. I quickened my pace as the start of the orgasm formed in the base of my spine. She fell apart, screaming my name and pulling my hair as I thrust a final three times, the explosive pleasure making my ears ring and my legs turn to jelly.

My world spun for a full minute where I wasn't sure who I was or what anything meant—all I knew was my body and mind felt incredible and Ambar's face was there when I closed my eyes.

Our chests heaved in unison when I rested my forehead against hers. I wasn't sure I could walk just yet so I waited longer than I normally did and when I met her gaze, hers was just as unsure and cloudy as mine was. *Is it regret or with pleasure?*

"How's your back?" I croaked out. "Did I hurt you?"

"Oh no. The opposite." She grinned and winced when I slowly pulled out of her. "That felt…wow."

"It did feel wow." I matched her smile and carefully set her down on the floor. It was then I realized we were stark naked not three feet from the front door. I had never lost it like that where anyone could've walked in to see us. "Let me clean up real quick."

I walked to the kitchen and disposed of the condom in the trash and quickly washed my hands. My muscles were no longer tense and my headspace wasn't terrifying to be in. Relief and relaxed were my mood and I had a huge smile on my face when I walked back into the living room. Ambar was ass up in the air, bent down looking for something, and I wished I could take a picture. Her ass was incredible. "If we didn't just fuck against a wall, I would want to really convince you to go doggie-style so I could grab onto your perfect ass."

"Oh." She looked over her shoulder and her face turned bright red. "I can't find my cute thong."

"Don't care why you're on the floor. Keep going." My smile grew and grew when she made a humph sound. I should worry about getting clothes on or helping her, but I made no move. She was too entertaining to watch. She found a thin black string that I'd paid no attention to earlier and slipped it up her legs. She found me staring and dropped her gaze. "You're the cutest thing. We just fucked against a wall and you're worried about me seeing you naked?"

She sucked her damn lip into her mouth and let a self-deprecating laugh. "Still working on the whole be bold and confident part."

"Ambar, you're beautiful." I scoffed and helped get the rest of her clothes onto the top of the couch. Only then did I slip on my boxers and jeans. She had her tight jeans and equally tight shirt stretched across her chest and I almost bit the edge of my knuckle at the picture she made. "Let me get this straight. You wore that to meet up with Teets?"

"Uh, well, no." She wouldn't meet my eyes and I did not like it. I moved around the couch so we were both on the same side and I lifted her chin. Her cheeks were tinged red, again, and suddenly, I needed to know the whole story.

"Why are you blushing right now? Did he hit on you?"

"Teets? No. We're friends. He did mention how good I look, but I think he meant happy. Yeah. He meant happy. Not hitting on me good. No one hits on me, really. Well, I guess Brandon did, but he's younger than me so it really didn't count since it was for an interview," she rambled, not taking a breath between either statement. That caught my attention and I put a hand on her shoulder.

"You tend to talk fast when you're nervous. We're past the point of being nervous around each other so…what is it?"

"I wore this hoping to seduce you, okay?" She put her face in her hands and made a goofy sound. "It sounds silly saying it out loud."

"It worked. You weren't inside the door ten seconds without me touching you." I wiggled my eyebrows at her and jutted my chin to her shirt. "Your shirt about did me in."

She grinned real cute and scrunched her nose at my compliment and I made a promise to myself to compliment her. She cupped her boobs and said, "I didn't realize these little girls had that much power."

"Those with great power come great responsibility."

She snorted at my joke and any unease in the air disappeared. She plopped onto the couch and leaned back with no trace of a blush. "So you wanna hear about how the hockey team is involved?"

Chapter Twenty

Ambar

A week later, I didn't even think twice about texting Jeff to get together. We had *gotten together* three nights since the wall incident and I finally got why people liked sleeping with the same person multiple times. Each experience was different, but comfortable, and a new feeling had started forming in my gut. It was almost a combination of happiness and reassurance, confidence and awareness. Jeff found me attractive—he made that obvious—and having all these new sober sex experiences was teaching me about an entirely different world. I didn't hate it.

Thinking about it all made my smile almost hurt my face, if I was honest with myself. But instead of freaking out or overanalyzing what it meant, I just went with it.

"Barf. Look at you." Laney made a stupid face at me and threw a pillow from our sofa as we lounged around watching *Riverdale*. "One week of getting banged and you're on cloud nine. I'm jealous."

"It's...it's been something." I still had a hard time vocalizing it to Laney, but with each heated look and touch, Jeff was teaching me it was okay to express my sexuality. For the first time in our friendship, I felt as if I could be like Laney. Like I could talk about sex without needing a drink or feeing stupid. "I'm starting to understand why people date the *same* person."

She rolled her eyes, but her face changed to an almost proud one. "Don't mistake my banter for anything more than that. I'm just giving you shit. Seriously, it's about time you learn how awesome sex can be and how with the right person… Oh, baby, it's the best."

"Yeah," I said, smiling to myself thinking about Jeff convincing me to try different positions. It was liberating. "Didn't think I'd be doing this all with Jeff but hey? It's temporary and I'll enjoy it."

"Have you DTRed?"

"Uh, what now?"

"Defined the relationship. Are you just friends with benefits? Are you exclusive?"

My stomach dropped at her question. *Are we exclusive?* That had never seemed like an issue until now. I never thought about him hooking up with other girls, but I guess he could've been. *But he says he doesn't have time.* I frowned and a dull headache formed behind my eyelids. "We agreed to explore this chemistry until I finish my project. That's all."

"Damn, look at how chill you are. You're so nonchalant about it. I admire you. The ambiguity of hook-ups stresses me out. Like, are you only hooking up with each other? Or can you hook up with whoever, but make time for each other? Do you go on dates or just spend time naked? You don't even care if he's out there sleeping with random chicks each night he's not with you. It's why Berkman dumped me sophomore year. He said I was too damn clingy and asked too many questions."

As I digested every word, dread creeped into my brief moment of elation. Talk about mood swings. One second I was smiling like a goon at my sex life and now Laney's words crashed my walls of happiness. She meant well—her intentions were always good for those whom she cared about—but I wasn't sure she understood the massive impact what she'd said had on me. Because if I thought about it, I did care.

"Oh fuck. Babe, I'm so sorry. I talk too much and don't think." She scooted from her spot and moved to sit next to me, getting into my personal space and hugging me tight. "Why are you even friends with me?"

I half-snorted to appease her, but it did nothing to the ball in my stomach. Jeff and I laughed together, joked, brainstormed and talked about the issues in our life. At some point, he'd become a friend and the thought of him sharing all that stuff with someone else somehow lessened what I had with him.

But what do I have with him?

Goddamn Laney. I rubbed my temples and excused myself to my room. Throwing myself into my Saturday blog post would push all thoughts of Jeff to the side—where I was happy to keep all thoughts of him otherwise I'd distract myself into a worry wormhole. I didn't get far, though. My phone buzzed and my heart about leapt into my throat at seeing my uncle's name.

"Hello?" I answered, hoping I sounded normal.

"My favorite. How are you?"

"I've been good." I paused and bit down on my nail at the lack of words. He was so easy to talk to, to ask questions or get guidance from, but now, every cell in my brain told me to not get caught. "How are you?"

"What is this small talk? Your voice sounds off. Do I need to take somebody out?"

Can he really do that?

I forced myself to laugh and hated how fake it sounded. It seemed to work, because he chuckled. "I talked to your mother this week."

"I'm sorry for you," I responded without thinking, and he cackled.

"This is why we have each other. She complained about spring break coming up and not hearing from you. I refused to do any of her bidding and told her there was probably a reason you don't call her."

"Uncle Martin…" I warned, damn well knowing he was causing the rift to grow bigger between us. "Did she get fired up?"

"Oh yes. It was entertaining to say the least. But my reason for bringing that up? I would love to see you over spring break. Maybe you can come visit for a couple days just to get away?"

My heart physically hurt at his question. I wanted him to not be involved so badly that I willed it and would be willing to make a deal with the devil. But it did no good. He was a part of the scandal and it was my decision to balance that knowledge with the man who'd helped keep me sane most of my life. "That would be awesome. I wasn't planning on going back to the house, so this would be a mini escape."

"Perfect. I hoped you'd agree. We always have fun and we can talk about your plans after graduation, eh? Get your resume polished and ready to go. I can help you with your search, hm?"

It was like swallowing a fistful of cotton when I tried to get my throat to work. My *doubts* had doubts about his intentions and my voice was gruff when I responded, "Yeah, sounds good."

"Ah, well, I need to go. Have a business meeting, but I'll see you soon, okay? I think I'll be in the area within a week, Ambar. Stay out of trouble."

"You too!" I almost shouted at him. He hung up, but my pulse pounded in my ears for a couple of minutes when I calmed down from the call. *Is it always going to be this way? Me faking it?*

The poor lining in my stomach wasn't going to survive this whole ordeal. I grabbed a packet of crackers and a soda from downstairs to settle the almost acid-like feeling in there, and Laney cornered me with a suspicious look. "Yes?"

"I have a huge favor to ask of you."

"I'm listening," I responded, hesitant to agree without hearing her out completely. She was clever as hell and had once got me to take out the trash for an entire week and that was not happening again. "But none of your fancy words."

She rolled her eyes and leaned onto the doorway with an almost shy look. "This guy I'm into invited me over to a pre-game tonight and said to bring some friends. I have no idea if this is a huge party or intimate, but would you come with me? Marissa's internship is too stressful and she gave up going out for two months."

"That's why you looked all nervous? Yes, of course I'll go with you." I laughed at all the other things she could've asked me and tilted my head as her words hit me. "Who is this guy, by the way? I've heard nothing about him."

"Well," she began, and I succumbed to sitting down at the table and letting her rave about him for a good fifteen minutes.

* * * *

Dressed in skinny jeans and a casual sweater that was tighter than I liked, I chose to wear my red lacy bralette that made me feel good underneath it. It was easier to accept how I was built when I'd avoided my mom's calls for almost two weeks, but I wasn't sure how much longer I could hold off on talking to her. So I was going to enjoy the little confidence while I could. Laney looped her arm through mine as we walked toward the house located about five blocks away from ours and the wind blasted our faces. The goddamn cold was getting out of control and I made plans to not leave the house for the rest of the weekend. *Unless Jeff wants to meet up.*

Just the thought of him had me warm and I checked my phone to see if he'd responded to my text from earlier. He hadn't and the absence of his reply could mean a lot of things. Like, he was busy, at a team meeting of sorts, talking to his coach…or *with another girl.*

God damn it. No. Not that thought.

Ambar: My uncle called and I'm probably visiting him during spring break. I'm so nervous talking to him now, it's sad. What if he knows, I know…? Anyway, you have plans tonight?

That was all I'd said. Nothing too demanding or clingy or anything, really. But it was okay. He'd text when he could and that was good enough for me.

"Liam better be worth this trek," Laney said, her teeth chattering and I agreed with her. We were shivering by the time we knocked on the old wooden door of a three-story house. It was similar to the houses on our block, but this one almost looked like a former fraternity with the large windows and shutters on the sides.

"Ladies." A kid with a huge toothy smile answered the door and ushered us inside. "Welcome! Everyone's downstairs. Just head through that door."

"Great, thank you!" Laney almost skipped inside and ran to the open archway that led below. Music blared and shook the walls as we descended and I didn't have the heart to tell Laney that this was not an intimate pre-game. It was a house party, plain and simple, and it didn't shock me when we were greeted by a large, already intoxicated crowd.

Laney didn't let her discomfort show though. Not my confident best friend. She waved at a handsome guy and dragged us toward the couch where she introduced me to Liam. I had never seen her blush like that before and I had to fight a grin. "I'll be right back. I'm going to find a water."

"Head to the back room down there. We have a fridge with water," Liam said, not looking away from Laney. *Someone is smitten.*

I saluted them and found my way down the hall and had to choose between three doors. The first was a bathroom and the second was locked. The third one opened when I pushed it and I gasped when Jeff and a tall brunette stood really close together. The image of the way her hand rested on his arm and the way his face was tilted toward hers with interest burned into my mind.

Have we defined the relationship?

Is this why he didn't text back?

Can I even be mad?

Oh my god, *say something*. It's been ten seconds. "Uh, I'm sorry? Water. I was looking for water." I pretended to look around the room and ran into the doorframe on my escape. "Shit."

Get out. Go to Laney. I'd barely got five steps away from the door when Jeff's voice sounded right behind me and he wrapped his fingers around my wrist. "Ambar, hey, hold on."

He spun me around to face him with ease, but I focused on his beautiful broad shoulders instead of his face. My adrenaline spiked, making my words come out fast and jammed together. "Hey, what's up? What's going on?"

"Jessica is a junior on the volleyball team." He widened his eyes and gestured to her as she left the room. He smiled at her. "Thanks for talking to me. We won't use any names."

"That's all I ask." She huffed and gave me a tight smile. "I need a beer."

She didn't say more before walking back to the main area of the basement and I turned to follow her when Jeff tightened his grip on my arm. "Henderson, get in that room."

I felt all sorts of stupid for a variety of reasons and my entire body burned when I walked into the bedroom and faced him. Instead of trying to talk through the wedge in my throat, I smiled goofily at him. He laughed and put both of his hands on my shoulders, an amused expression on his face.

"I didn't take you for jealous. It was kinda cute."

"Ugh," I groaned and placed my head on his chest. "I wasn't… I'm not… Maybe. Just, you're free to do whatever you want. We aren't anything, really. We've slept together a couple of times." I still refused to look him in the eye and the silence made me keep babbling. "We haven't DTRed and, according to Laney, that's a thing people do, but I don't know that because I don't do this sort of thing. You probably do, so maybe you know."

"You're fucking cute."

"Me?" I looked up and it felt like the ground shifted beneath me at the tenderness on his face…all directed at me.

"Yes." He moved his hands up from my shoulders to my face, cupping my cheeks. "Tell me, did you like seeing me with Jessica?"

"Um, no?" I scrunched my nose and hated admitting it. "But you're allowed…you can do anything…you don't owe me anything."

"I sure as hell don't want to see you with another guy." His jaw tightened and he ran his thumb over my bottom lip, his gaze heating when he stared at it. "We never talked about it, really, but while we continue our investigation, I'd like to be exclusive, if you'd agree."

"We only hook up with each other?"

"Yes, Henderson. Just you and me." He moved his thumb again and moved closer. "I'm having way too much fun exploring you to share."

I gulped and heated at his words. "Okay."

"You're taking up way too many thoughts in my mind for me to get with anyone else. I found Jessica through a mutual friend and got great information from her that will help our case."

"Yeah?" I lost my train of thought when he dropped his lips to the spot beneath my ear. "Not…here? People are out there."

"I know," he hummed, pressing his mouth against mine for a quick, passionate kiss that didn't last nearly long enough. "Just wanted to remind you that your mouth drives me crazy."

"Oh." *God, that's a good line.* "Yours too. For me."

"I know. I love getting you flustered."

"It's embarrassing," I admitted. I fidgeted with my sweater and tried smoothing it down to busy my hands with something, but he stopped me.

"No, it's not. It's real and endearing. I'm a fan of it." He let his gaze drop from my face to eye my outfit and his grin grew. "You look good. I was hoping to convince you to let me stop by tonight, but this is perfect. Are you staying here long?"

"I came with Laney, so I'll see what she wants to do first." *Ask about the text. Just do it.* "Uh, did you get my text earlier? About my uncle?"

"What?" Alarm crossed his face and he searched his pockets, front and back, as the line between his eyebrows grew and his frown deepened. "My phone isn't on me. What the hell?"

"Did you drop it?" I moved to search where he'd stood earlier but his rigid posture made me nervous. "What is it?"

"I had it at practice…talking to my coach." His face paled and he slowly shook his head. "We were in his office. What did your text say, Ambar?"

"Shit. Shit!" I paced the room. I showed him my phone and he hissed out some cuss words. "What do we do?"

"We hope he doesn't read it and we head there in the morning."

Chapter Twenty-One

Jeff

I had to be on fire—my body was sweating like crazy and I wondered if Aaron had broken the furnace or something to spew fire into our house. I sat up and paused when hair spilled across my chest and legs tangled in mine. *Ambar.* I stayed over with Ambar.

When was the last time I'd crashed at a chick's place? Years? I snorted at the realization and didn't think twice about the lack of worry I had over it. Lying back down, I pushed her hair out of her face and studied her. She slept on her side and had one hand under her cheek with her lips slightly parted and I couldn't stop my smile. She was naturally beautiful and so different from my usual type. I shouldn't be thinking about kissing her awake. But that was what I wanted to do. I started at her neck—the spot that drove her crazy—and pressed feather-light kisses along her collarbone, moving down low to tease her dusky-pink nipple that peaked out from the covers and it was then she stirred next to me.

God she's so fucking sexy with her sounds. I sucked the tip into my mouth and pulled on it with my teeth, copying the move on her other breast and admiring how wet and perky they were when I was done. Small tits were now on my list of favorite things, specifically hers. I kissed down her soft stomach and stopped when she lifted her head. "What feels so good?"

"My mouth on you." I kissed just above her where her legs parted and flicked my tongue against the one spot that would send her over the edge. "You taste great in the morning."

"You spent the night." She pushed herself up to her elbows and stared down at me with a combination of confusion and heat in her eyes. I held the contact when I dragged my tongue deeper into her and sucked her clit hard. She moaned, threw her head back and clutched the sheets in her hand. "Jeff, oh."

"That's right, Ambar. Come in my mouth." I slid two fingers inside her and matched the pace of in and out with my tongue. She squirmed beneath me and I continued licking and teasing her until her body tensed. My dick throbbed each time she mumbled my name or whimpered with pleasure. I almost exploded when she convulsed around me. She moved her legs to wrap around my head, almost trapping me against her, and I fucking loved it. I deepened my taste as she rode out the orgasm and felt an immense sense of pride that I'd put that satisfied look on her face. With one final kiss on her pussy, I smiled up at her. "Good morning."

"I'll say," she replied and fell back onto her pillow. "My legs are still trembling."

"Good." I slid up her body and ground my hardness against her. "How long do you need to wait before having another?"

Her eyes lit up and she ran her tongue over her bottom lip. "Oh, I'm ready."

"Greedy girl," I laughed and reached over her to grab a condom from the nightstand. I let her put it on me and grabbed her hips to flip her so she was straddling me. "Ride me. I want to see your tits bounce when I thrust into you."

"W-what?" she stuttered and red splotches appeared on her chest. "Let me turn the lights off."

"No." I ran a hand down her chest, over her soft curves and back up to her face. "I want to see all of you. Your body is sexy. Feel how hard I am for you." I arched my hips and she glanced down at my dick with a hungry look. "You're in control now."

It took her a couple of minutes to position herself to slide down my shaft, sucking me into her, and I groaned at how fucking good she felt. She clawed her nails into my chest when she tentatively moved her hips back and forth. It was slow, almost like torture, but I let her set the pace. Her eyes were squeezed shut and that wasn't good enough for me. "I want to see your eyes, Ambar."

She opened them, unease and worry etched into them, and something tightened in my chest. *She's unsure, but why?*

I reached up to play with her tits, telling her how perfect they were, and moved down her body to circle her clit with my thumb. She moaned and quickened her pace, the hesitation leaving her face and a new expression taking over. *Passion.* "That's my girl. Ride me hard."

She did and sweat pooled where our bodies met and it was the hottest fucking thing. She grunted and fell onto my chest so I grabbed her hips and thrust, giving her the needed change and she fell apart. "Jeff…god…yes!"

Hearing her say my name in such a whimper sent me over the edge and I spilled into her, pleasure spreading through my veins to the point my ears rang. I slammed my mouth on hers, demanding she kiss me with everything she had, and she did as I rode out the most intense orgasm. When my hips stopped thrusting, she ended our kiss and carefully lifted her weight off me. The absence of her heat upset me, but I shook off the weird feeling. "Let me clean up," I said, earning an unreadable look from her.

I disposed of the condom in her bathroom and returned to the bed. She sat there, uncovered and naked, and had a dazed look on her face. "What's going on in your head, Henderson?"

She frowned and met my eyes. "I've never woken up with someone before."

"Is it safe to say you enjoyed it?" I teased, scooting next to her and dropping a kiss on her bare shoulder. "I sure as hell did."

"It was…amazing." She grinned sheepishly at me and moved so she could put her fingers on my pecs. "I didn't know it could be like this between two people."

My stomach swooped at the meaning of her words and I nodded. "I know what you mean. It's been pretty fucking excellent with you."

"Yeah," she replied, pushing herself up from the bed and throwing on a baggie t-shirt from the bottom drawer of her dresser. "I don't know the protocol for this. My go-to was kicking dudes out after we were done or I'd leave as soon as I got what I wanted."

I laughed because my own mantra was similar. "We can figure it out together, because I sure as shit don't know what any protocol is. I just liked waking up to you naked and wouldn't mind it again."

I mean it, too, and it doesn't freak me out.

She arched one eyebrow. "You…you haven't done the morning-after thing either?"

"Nope. This is a first for me, too."

"Hm." She crossed her arms and returned to the bed. "I figured you'd… I don't know, have all these experiences."

"I won't lie about my past. I do have a lot of experience, but like you, I didn't like putting myself in a vulnerable position by staying the night. Especially after all that shit that happened with Aaron. Trusting people is difficult."

She blew out a breath and fixed her hair into something looking like a hive on top of her head. "I understand. It's kinda nice to know I'm not the only one experiencing new things with you."

"Henderson," I replied warmly, "there's a whole slew of new shit I'm experiencing with you."

My words pleased her and she gave me one of her real smiles that reached her eyes. She glanced at the clock on the wall and the warmth was replaced with worry. The temperature in the room changed and I knew why. My coach had my phone. She ran a hand over her arm and asked, "What's the plan for today?"

"We head to the stadium and get my phone." I shrugged, but every cell in my body was on high alert at what the result of my dumbass mistake could be. "I think you should go with me and keep an eye out for anything that I could've missed. Do you feel comfortable doing that?"

"Yes. Do you have practice today? Will other players be there?"

"We have offense this afternoon and I'm sure guys will be there early. Why?"

"To use them as a cover if I need to. It might seem strange to your coach if me, the niece of Martin, shows up at the stadium for the first time ever after you left your phone with a message from me on it."

She had a great point, like she always did, and I made the move to start getting dressed. "I'm glad I have you on my team."

Her face warmed and we got dressed within a minute. "Let's grab some food and head there."

"You read my mind."

* * * *

My teammates' cars were scattered around the stadium parking lot and my coach's blue Chevy stood in the same spot it always did, right in the front. "I didn't even think about making sure you get home. It's too cold to walk back."

"I'm bundled up and the walk will be good for me." She zipped her coat up to her chin and shut the car door before matching my stride. "I'm curious. What's a normal practice for you?"

Normal? Hm. "Running defense drills, working with pitchers and hitting. We watch film of our previous at-bats to analyze our swing and work with the necessary coaches depending on what needs work."

"Sounds intense. What kind of coaches focus on what?" She pursed her lips in thought. "I'm trying to get a picture of how much interaction all the players have with each coach. Like your head coach—he works with every player, yes?"

"He runs the ship, yeah." We marched through the double doors and sounds of the batting cages being used echoed down the hall. The familiar smell of rubber and leather greeted me like a hug, as it did every time I walked into the stadium, but the nostalgia had more of a bitterness to it now. *My experience is tainted by this scandal.*

I hoped I'd get over how betrayed I felt in time, but it wasn't the moment to dwell. We needed my phone. Ambar eyed each wall, hugging her notebook close to her chest, and cleared her throat.

"Well? How many coaches?"

"Right. Uh, we have a pitching coach, catching coach, hitting, infield and outfield coaches, some specialized in base running, a bullpen coach and our head, who is also the manager of the team."

She nodded and made a note. "That's a lot of coaches. Say, could a player not interact with one of those coaches, ever? Go four years and not have to work with a specific one?"

I thought about it and frowned. "I guess so. If you're an outfielder, I guess you'd only work with base running, outfield and hitting." I scratched my neck and nodded at two of the younger guys on the team who walked by us. They had the fresh-faced awe that I used to wear and it made me sad to know my days at this campus were numbered. Ambar remained quiet as we walked farther into the stadium and passed one of the weight rooms. We approached the end of the hallway where my coach's office was and I stopped her. "I'm going to see if he's in there."

"Should I wait for you?" She bit down on her lip and glanced down the hallway. "I am the only non-athlete here and my goal is to remain unnoticed."

"Yes, wait here." I hated the worry lines that appeared around her eyes and I didn't think twice before reaching out and placing my hand on her arm. "It'll be fine, I promise."

She gave me a weak smile and leaned against the wall and I took a deep breath before knocking on his door. "Come in," carried through and I entered. He glanced up and widened his eyes. *He isn't expecting me.*

"Hey, Coach." I stood at the entrance, not quite moving closer to his desk but not standing in the doorway. My nerves buzzed as I tried to read him for any clues. "I think I left my phone here yesterday."

He sighed, sounding older than he had in the years I'd known him, and ran a hand over his face. "I'm surprised you lasted this long without it. Aren't you all addicted to those damn things?"

I forced a laugh. "I survived."

He stood and moved toward his line of file cabinets and opened the top shelf. "Here. I didn't want to mess with it and wasn't sure whose it was. Couldn't figure out how to turn the damn thing off, either."

He passed it to me and the screen lit up with texts and notifications from social media. Relief coursed through my blood. *He didn't read her text.* There was no way, not with the hundreds of notifications and his blatant lack of technology skills I had witnessed my four year on the team. "Thank you."

"Be careful with your phone, son, you don't want the wrong people getting hold of it."

I tensed. Did he tone change, or was it just me? His weathered expression remained blank as he stared at me and sweat dripped down my forehead, despite the freezing temperatures. "No kidding. I'll be more careful."

"Good. Now, did you think about what we talked about yesterday?"

The draft, my future, telling my teammates. "Honestly, no."

"The sooner you get it out in the open, the better you'll feel. You're walking around tense with the weight of the world on your shoulders and I can't have one of my captains distracted with our first game weeks away."

The fact he'd chosen me captain made everything worse. The lead in my stomach weighed me down and I almost felt sick. "I'll do it soon."

"What's the worst that can happen?"

"They don't understand my choice."

My coach scoffed and leveled his gaze with me. "That's not what's bothering you. What's the real reason you don't want to tell them?"

I glanced at the door, making sure no one was there, and lowered my voice. The truth flowed out of me because I was desperate and relieved to talk about *this* rather than the investigation. "That I won't be one of them anymore. We've all had the same goal all these years and learning mine's different…it could change things."

He relaxed into his chair and gave me a look that reminded me of my dad so much that I had to force myself to focus on the face he was involved in this bullshit somehow. "Jeff, everyone changes and grows up. You're a hell of a leader and you're going to lead this team whether or not you continue after our season. If this was my last year coaching, would you take me any less seriously?"

"No."

"Exactly. It's the same thing. Go hit the gym or do something that'll get relax you soon because I'm stressed just looking at you." He hit the top of his desk and smiled. "Make sure you check in with Mac before practice. He wants to talk to you about something."

"Will do." I moved to leave his office and turned to give him what I hoped was a reassuring smile. "Thank you."

"Anytime, Jeff. You know I got your back." His eyes sparked when he said it, but I attributed it to excitement for the season. I wanted to see how much Ambar heard and get her take on everything. Maybe she'd have good advice for me, but when I walked into the hallway, she was nowhere to be found.

Chapter Twenty-Two

Ambar

'That I won't be one of them anymore.'

Jeff's words caused a pang in my chest and hearing him sound so vulnerable opened up feelings I'd shoved down deep. *Like maybe I'm growing real feelings for him beyond lust.* He wasn't just the confident, good-looking guy who eased through life. He had his own insecurities and worries that plagued him just as I had mine. Maybe we weren't so different after all.

Laughter traveled down the hallway and shoes clicked on the cement floor as two shadows danced on the wall nearing the office. One of the men said something, causing the other to respond and that voice sent a chill down my spine. I knew who that voice belonged to and the tiniest of hopes that I had to clear his name disappeared. My face tingled with fear. *Uncle Martin.*

He can't see me here.

What do I do?

I darted down the hallway that we'd come in and tried every door I found, but they were all locked. Even with a hard jiggle, the handles wouldn't budge and the chances of him not seeing me got lower and lower each second I wasted. *Shit!* Panic clawed at my throat and my heart beat so fast it physically hurt as each attempt at hiding failed. The voices got louder and I sprinted down the narrow pathway to the entrance and almost ran face-first into Brandon's hard chest. He caught me, but I released a loud *oomph* at the contact.

"Ambar?" he asked, a confused smile on his face as he eyed down the direction I can from. "Are you okay?"

"I need to-to go," I panted, looking over my shoulder and trying to get out of his grip. I had a minute tops before they came into view. "The doors. Come on."

"Seriously, what's going on? You're freaking out right now." He moved a hand behind my back and gently pushed me in the direction I needed to be going. "Your face is flushed."

"Yeah, I remembered something." I started running when I saw the wide doors leading outside, but Brandon followed. "I'm good, I swear."

"Hold the hell on." He reached out to put his hand on my arm, holding me just outside the exit, and he spoke with an authority that surprised me. "I'm not the kind of guy who is going to let a girl run out of there looking like she saw a fucking ghost. Please, tell me what happened. I want to make sure you're okay."

I used my free hand to push my hair out of my face and sighed in semi-relief. We were outside, my uncle was not, and I was probably in the clear. I hopped down four more steps—to make a getaway easier if needed—and Brandon's face was hard with concern. It warmed me to see him care, but the timing couldn't have been worse. "I didn't want someone to see me."

"Why? Did they hurt you?" He looked back toward the building with a frown and I drew his attention back to me.

"No. No one hurt me. I promise."

He released his hold on me and ran a hand through his hair. "Something's not right. Why were you here? It's Saturday and most of the guys aren't here yet."

I didn't get time to answer. The doors swung open and my Uncle Martin walked out with his arm around the shoulders of a middle-aged man I hadn't seen before. Every part in my body froze in place, unable to move or make a sound when his jovial face froze mid-laugh as his gaze landed on mine. Time stopped for ten seconds when we each stared at each other. *What do I do? What is normal? Does he know?*

No answer came to me. My mouth hung open and it wasn't until Brandon cleared his throat that I snapped out of it. "Uncle Martin? What are you doing here?"

"I could ask you the same thing, Ambar!" He transformed his face into a smile and closed the distance to give me a huge hug—like he always did. My spine tingled at his fake grin. It looked demonic. "It's too damn cold for us to be talking out here."

"Agreed. I was just finishing an interview with Brandon for one of my assignments. I'd love a cup of coffee to warm up if you have time?" I avoided Brandon's curious stare as best I could, but with one quick glance, I saw him put some pieces together.

"Actually, I'm not sure I like my answer to the last question. Can we go over it again, if you don't mind, sir? It's my first year on the team and I really want to look good in her article," Brandon said, moving closer to me and addressing my uncle.

"Of course. We have plans soon anyway." He patted my cheeks and gave Brandon a nod before turning back to the man he walked out with. "Until next time, Tony."

Tony, whoever he was, didn't respond. He didn't spare us a glance before marching back through the doors, leaving the two of us alone with the wind whipping around us. Brandon waited until the doors closed before eyeing me. "You didn't want your uncle to see you. Why?"

"Notice how he didn't say why he was here?"

"I did catch that." He frowned and jutted his chin toward the doors. "I'm freezing my ass off. Let's go in."

I didn't wait a second before running back to the warmth and sighed at the heat. Between the wind-chill and the adrenaline, my teeth chattered. Brandon joined me a second later, just as Jeff came into view down the hall. His shoulders were stiff and he walked with a purpose. His gaze found mine, worried and concerned, before landing on Brandon. His expression hardened and his jaw tensed. "There you are, Ambar."

"I'm sorry, a lot happened." I gave him a warning look, but he ignored it and stared at Brandon. "Brandon helped me out from a potentially awkward situation."

"Yeah, what's that?" He crossed his arms over his chest and displeasure oozed off him. He did not like me standing next to Brandon. *Interesting.*

"Let's talk later, okay?" I spoke softer than normal, hoping he'd get the hint.

"You're interviewing Jeff for the article too, right?" Brandon asked, moving closer to me so ours arms touched.

"Um, yes?"

"I can see you're uncomfortable about everything that happened, but I'd like to know why I covered for you. Can I meet up with you after practice?" he asked in a kind, unpresuming way, and I felt terrible when Jeff answered for me.

"I'll explain it for you if you tell me what happened."

"You?" he asked, his gaze flicking to Jeff with confusion etched on his forehead. "You weren't even here. How would—"

"We're together, man. Ambar and I. Figured you should know," Jeff said, not using a kind or patient tone. His words shocked me because they weren't exactly untrue, but they were crass and meant to send a message.

Brandon's face fell, but he resigned himself with a long sigh and smile sadly at me. "Knew it was a long shot asking you out, but now I know."

"I wasn't playing games with you."

"I know," he said, giving my arm one more squeeze. "Still doesn't explain what the hell just happened out there."

I gave Jeff a look and shrugged. "It's your call, Jeff. Tell him what you want. I'm heading home."

"Can we talk first?" His perceptive eyes swept over my face and his frown deepened. "Please?"

Brandon cleared his throat and said, "I'm heading to the cages. I'm glad you're okay, Ambar. Really."

"Thanks again."

He nodded and left Jeff and I in the hallway, the tension somewhat uncomfortable as he moved toward me. He placed his hands on my face and said, "What the fuck happened? Why are you so pale?"

"My uncle was here," I whispered. "I heard him outside your coach's office and I ran to avoid him, about running smack into Brandon. He helped cover for me when my uncle saw me."

"He asked you out."

"How did you…yes. Brandon did. Weeks ago. How is this relevant?"

His eyes darkened and he moved his hands from my cheeks to my shoulders. "You have a soft spot for him."

"He's a nice guy." I laughed at the disgruntled expression on his face. "Jeff…are you…jealous?"

"Yes. He stood very close to you and touched you."

No one has ever been jealous over me before. Ever. Warmth and annoyance combined into an adrenaline rush and I took a couple of seconds to think of a response. "So that's why you told him we were together—to keep him away from me."

"I felt it was time to tell him. I'll tell the team, too."

"We aren't together though, are we? I mean, I guess we sorta are but—"

"We are together, Henderson." He dropped his head so his lips teased mine. "We are together."

"Okayyy," I muttered, blushing from head to toe and hating how my body betrayed me with those simple words. "Still don't think now is the time to talk about it."

"We can talk about it later, if you want. Preferably in bed with way less clothes." He smirked and looked real pleased with himself and I found myself grinning back at him. We were bantering. Jeff and I.

And it feels natural and amazing.

"You're insatiable, really." I pushed my hair out of my face and willed my skin to not redden at his attention. "This morning wasn't enough?"

His face softened. "Not with you."

I cleared my throat and glanced at the floor for a second to catch my breath. This was a lot to handle. My uncle, Brandon, then Jeff saying we were together. *I need a drink.* "Well, I'm going to head out, but maybe if you want to stop over after practice, we can talk?"

"Already planned on it." He looked outside and winced. "Are you sure you don't want to get an Uber or something?"

"No. The cold will do me good with all the heated looks you're giving me," I teased, earning an appreciative grin. "By the way, is there a coach named Tony?"

"Tony? Not that I know of. Why?"

"He's the guy I saw walking with my uncle. He called him Tony."

* * * *

The internet had hundreds of photos of the baseball team, the players, even the coaches, but there were no pictures of the middle-aged man I'd seen walking with my Uncle Martin. I even searched for an hour through the hockey team photos and volleyball to see if the guy's face would pop up in anything. While it was frustrating, it didn't surprise me.

My uncle's reaction to seeing me there with him had sparked something in my gut. Tony mattered in all of this and I had no idea how. I twirled my pen around in my hand for a minute before sketching out my initial thoughts.

Someone is going to these high schools and or meeting with parents to discuss some sort of deal.

Someone is involved in baseball, volleyball and hockey organizations at some point within the past four years. Potentially other sports.

One hockey coach quit two years ago and nothing shady reported since.

The stories of the fake-athletes all match.

We have a phone number of one of them.

Uncle Martin is involved.

Some sort of dean is involved.

We had enough to write an initial report…but where to start? Did I focus on the fake-athletes, their parents, the money or the coaches? Hell, did I go after the deans in an article, calling for them to explain it? I needed to understand how spots were determined for each sport and how they were recruited. That meant I needed to talk to the Dean of Athletics.

I rubbed my temples and eyed my list of actual homework that I hadn't started. My final project remained a blank document and I couldn't recall why I couldn't use this article as my final. The requirements all pertained to the research I'd been doing with Jeff and it would save me hours of time. I was about to jot down how I could tweak my notes and interview transcripts when the doorbell rang.

Laney was at yoga still and my pulse picked up. *Jeff. It's too early for practice to be out though.*

I skipped downstairs with a huge smile on my face as I opened the door. "Hey, stranger."

It wasn't Jeff.

It was my Uncle Martin and he looked pissed.

Chapter Twenty-Three

Jeff

With our first game in two weeks, practice was more relaxed that I'd anticipated for a Saturday. Everyone was in good spirits, laughing and busting ass to prepare for our opener against our rivals. Zade was throwing fire on the mound, Tanner playing with a fierceness I hadn't seen before in the outfield and Hilly, he took his role of leader on the field seriously. He'd always covered a lot of ground at shortstop, but he seemed bigger this year, diving and back-handing grounders better than I had seen before. I had never been prouder of my best friends and teammates and a wave of complete regret startled me as we were picking up equipment for the day. My final season with them, with the sport itself, and the last time we would all be on the field together was coming to a close.

Can I really walk away from this?

"Maddow, come here for a second." Coach Tee gestured with his large hand and I nodded before walking toward him. He'd played minor league baseball for a couple of years and had incredible insight when it came to calling pitches. "You seemed tense today. What's going on?"

Am I just walking around with a fucking stick up my ass?

"I'm good, man. Thought we had a great practice." I shrugged and saw our head coach looking over at us, eyebrows furrowed together. "I think the younger guys are picking up on blocking the plate significantly better than last year."

"Yeah," he said, his gaze not really focused on anything for a second. Then he crossed his arms and leaned against the wall. "Hey, you having girl problems or any shit like that? Some of these guys are so caught up in their chicks I'm afraid a stupid fight will throw off their game."

Tee liked to talk shit from time to time, but it always veered toward our opposing team or the Dodgers—his least favorite team in the National League—so for him to talk about our teammates caught my attention. "They've never let their outside life affect their game. They're professionals, Tee. You know this."

He slid me a glance and barked out a laugh that showcased his years of smoking cigars. "You're not seeing that Henderson girl? Heard she's doing some interviews on the guys and one of the freshmen went on about her."

Brandon. I fought an eye roll and nodded. It wasn't unusual for coaches to know a lot about our personal lives, but everything had me on edge, especially after Ambar's uncle had been at the stadium. It felt wrong to want to lie to him about it, to protect her, but I did it anyway. "Nah, we're just friends. I don't have time for any of that with my final season coming up."

"Don't blame you, son. Enjoy being young and single. When you're married and my age, life is not nearly as fun." He clapped my back and sighed. "Sorry to keep you. Head on home and I'll see you Monday."

"Sounds good."

I took off to set the buckets of balls in the dugout closet and found my roommates fucking around in the hall instead of leaving. "What are you clowns doing?"

"Waiting for you," Zade replied, a shit-eating grin on his face. "Word on the street is you and Ambar are finally a thing."

"Christ." I pinched the bridge of my nose. "How the hell does everyone know this shit? I didn't even know it until this morning."

"Finally got himself snatched up," Tanner replied, throwing his arm around my shoulders and pulling me in for a hug. "The lone wolf is no more."

"Thought monogamy wasn't for you, hm?" Hilly asked, the amusement in his eyes counterbalancing how much they were annoying me. This was karma, really, for all the bullshit I gave them about their ladies.

"Okay, okay, everyone settle down. Yes, I deserve all the grief you're throwing my way, but Ambar and I are just… together. We aren't dating or boyfriend-girlfriend shit. Not like all your pathetic asses." I shoved Tanner off me and flipped them off. "Don't make a big deal out of it."

"*Ohhh,* he's sensitive about it. A classic sign. This is serious," Zade chimed in and shoved my shoulder. Tanner and Aaron slewed insults and jabs back to back, and soon enough, I had Zade in a headlock and we were all laughing.

"I wondered what the hell the racket was out here. It's just you four." Our coach joined us with a shadow of a smile on his face and it was a major déjà vu moment for me. It was like a flashback from freshman year, the four of us messing around before practice and him walking into us mid-fighting. The same nostalgic feeling I'd been carrying around hit me and it was one of the moments I wish I could stop time and Pause, just for a second longer.

"Sorry, Coach, we'll head out soon." Zade straightened and masked his face of the insult that was surely on the tip of his tongue. "Our professional bachelor here got himself a lady friend and we're busting his balls."

"That is newsworthy." His stare bore into me, his words from earlier repeating in my head at his expression. *Tell them, your conscious will be cleared.* "Well, head out. Enjoy your free time while you have it."

"Will do, Coach." Aaron nodded and we followed suit, picking up our stuff and heading out of the doors into the freezing air. The sun still shone on our campus, but the bitter cold hung around. "I'm off to the bar to see Greta. Catch you fuckers later."

That left me with Tanner and Zade and the words were almost there, the truth about everything, but I stopped myself. I needed to check in with Ambar and see what we could do about speeding up the process. If her uncle was here, with a dude named Tony, it didn't look good. "If you need a ride back to the house, I'm heading there to drop shit off before going to Ambar's."

"Loverboy is busy. How precious."

"Fuck off, Zade." I laughed and ignored the side comments before jumping into my car. They didn't take my offer and they could walk in the cold. Fine by me. I barely got the car started before they jumped into the passenger and back seat and started talking about the younger players on the team and who they thought was going to step it up this year.

It was easy to chime in and comment every minute or so on the short drive and when I pulled onto our street, a shiny black SUV sat in Ambar's driveway. I never remembered seeing that car there before and I drove a little faster. If they noticed, they didn't say anything and I parked in a hurry. "Catch ya later."

"Remember when you were that desperate for ass, too?" Tanner asked Zade.

Zade muttered something offensive, but I ignored them. My skin tingled, not in the good way, and I jogged to her door. It could be her parents, someone visiting her roommates, but in my gut, I knew it wasn't good. Voices carried from the house, but I couldn't decipher if it was Ambar or Laney. My nerves picked up and I fidgeted in the cold, waiting for her to open the door. Thirty seconds went by and I knocked again.

I was about to pound it even harder when Ambar opened the door with wide eyes, red cheeks and a worried smile. She made a face and gestured behind her, but I didn't care. I barged in and wanted to make sure she was okay.

"Jeff. Hi. I'm kinda busy right now."

"Are you okay?" I asked, needing to touch her and make sure. She had her arms wrapped around her middle and the right side of her bottom lip was red—a sure sign she was gnawing on it.

"Y-yeah, of course." She cleared her throat and pushed my hand away when I reached up to touch her. "I have some family here. I'll call you later, okay?"

I looked around the small foyer and didn't see anyone. I did not fucking like how she wanted me to leave with *family* being here. It had to be him. Martin Rhett. It was the only explanation why she was pushing me out. I mouthed, *your uncle,* and she nodded with a fearful look in her eyes.

"Ambar? Do you have company?"

Her eyes darkened and she released a quick rush of breath. "Shit." She lowered her voice and whispered, "Go with what I say."

I nodded and didn't want to tell her I was goddamn thankful she didn't kick me out. Martin Rhett intrigued me and I wanted to meet the man responsible for so much of the shit going on. *And to learn why Ambar is so afraid.*

She took a deep breath and gave me a long look that I couldn't decipher. She moved past me into the view of whoever was in the living room and I followed. She'd changed into jeans that hugged her curves in some sort of way and lifted her hand to motion to the clean-cut man standing next to the sofa. "Uncle Martin, this is one of my friends. Jeff, this is my uncle."

"Jeff Maddow, from the baseball team?" he asked, a large smile on his face. His teeth were super-white and his skin very tan. "It's great to meet you."

"Nice to meet you, as well." I shook his hand that he held out and I took a minute to study his outfit. Fitted jacket, expensive-looking slacks and shoes, and a Rolex that reflected the sun shining through the window. "You a fan of the baseball team here?"

"I follow all the Big Ten sports. Baseball and football are my teams though. Played in high school and college. Sure miss it." He jutted his chin to Ambar. "How do you know my girl here?"

"We're friends, Uncle. I told you." She spoke in an annoyed tone and a million questions went through my mind. Like, what happened before I got there and what the hell do I say to his questions?

"Are you a part of the article she's completing for one of her classes? Media bias when it comes to athletes, yes?" Martin asked, moving to sit down on the coach without any indication he was leaving. Ambar's jaw started tensing and I followed his action, sitting on the couch hoping she would relax and join me. She did.

"Yeah." I casually crossed one leg over the other knee and looked at Ambar. "How much have you talked about the project yet? I don't want to bore him with details."

She blinked twice before catching on to my question. "Oh, just the differences between starters and non-starters."

"Weren't you going to add a section about the senior life versus freshman year? That punk Brandon was going on about his questions with you. Seems the kid thinks he's going to be a celebrity now."

"Ambar does have an incredible talent at writing," her uncle praised, and no alarm bells went off in my head. As tense as the air was in the room, he seemed right at home and not worried. "The freshman experience in comparison to the senior. That's an interesting take. Just the clout on the team has to be vastly different."

"You would think these young'uns would know the drill when they come onto the team, but they're all big fish coming from tiny ponds. The egos don't last long."

"Yes, that is very true, I imagine." He sighed and looked at Amber with a fondness that contradicted the worry in her eyes. "You'll have to send me the article when you're done, Ambar. I'm sure your family would be proud of you."

Her eyes flashed and she let out a hard laugh. "Right. Because they love when I'm successful at anything."

Her sarcasm wasn't lost on me and I appreciated the way her uncle dismissed her. "Her mother favors her two older brothers, and her father is too busy working to realize it. That's where I come in. She has me on her team."

"Uncle Martin," she warned, but I slid her a look and reached out to squeeze her arm. She pulled back like my touch was fire, but I didn't care. If what he said was true, it made sense. She lacked confidence about who she was and it would come through in small moments—something I never had an issue with.

"You have support here too. You know this," I said, using a tone I rarely used. She blinked a couple of times and gave me a weak smile. "Your family should be damn proud of you, but what's most important is that you're proud of yourself."

"That's what I've been telling her," her uncle said, moving from the couch to stand up. "I'm glad you have a friend here supporting you, Ambar. I'll leave you two. An older guy can still read the room." He winked and held out a hand to me again. "It was nice meeting you, Jeff. Hopefully, our paths will cross again soon."

"You as well." I shook his hand and watched when he hugged Ambar tight. Her face almost crumpled when he walked out of the door and I barely held my arms open before she flung herself at me. She squeezed me tight around my middle and I rested my chin on the top of her head. It felt perfect. The way her body fitted against mine, the way her hair smelled and how I could offer her even a little bit of comfort felt right. "Do you want to talk about it?"

"Just… Let me enjoy this a little longer."

So we stood there, hugging without an inch between us, for a good long while. I didn't care about anything else but holding her and the thought didn't freak me out. If anything, it caused me to squeeze her tighter.

"I can't breathe, Jeff." She laughed against my chest and looked up at me with the most vulnerable expression on her face. "Let's go talk. I think it's time this goes public."

Chapter Twenty-Four

Ambar

Jeff wore sweats and a large sweatshirt that had seen better days and the laid-back clothes had never looked so good on him. He was the embodiment of a cuddle and when he leaned against my headboard and motioned for me to scoot right up next to him, I didn't hesitate. I had my notebook in my lap and his arm wrapped around my shoulder—if I could've stayed in that position for a week without moving I would have been content. But life had to move on and that meant talking about the demise of my Uncle Martin.

"My uncle explained that Tony, the middle-aged man I saw him talking with at the stadium, is an old friend of his from his college days. I searched online for a good two hours for any pictures of him from the baseball coaching staff, hockey, even football and came up empty."

"Do you buy it?"

"I don't know." I sighed and Jeff ran his hand up and down my arm in comfort. "You've seen how charming and manipulative he is. He would've had you in the palm of his hand if you didn't know about all the shady stuff, hm?"

"I could see it. He's a very likeable guy and, I gotta say, I liked the way he supports you."

"God damn, I know. It makes this so much harder. I have a feeling that was his intention coming to see me today."

"To remind you he supports you?"

"Yes." I leaned my head to rest on Jeff's shoulder. "He came here with gifts, saying he was going to surprise me after meeting up with an old friend. Sending me gifts isn't anything new, but a part of me wonders if this was a manipulative trick to get me to love him. He went on about how talented I am and asked to see my article on the baseball team."

"Shit."

"Yeah, I explained that it's still in outlining and I tend to binge-write on the weekends, but I did bullshit enough until you showed up. He knows something's going on and did a damn good job diverting the conversation to how he'll always support me."

"Did you press him on this Tony guy?"

"I tried. I asked if he worked with the baseball team and he ignored it. He asked a lot about my relationship with Brandon and Aaron. That's why I was so worried when you got there because he didn't know we were connected."

He sighed for a second but then tensed. "One of my coaches was asking about me and you today. Said Brandon was going on about you at practice, but that doesn't sound legit, does it? I talked with him after you left and filled him in on some shit and asked him to be quiet until you figured it out."

I sat up and turn to start at Jeff. "A coach asked specifically about me?"

'"You with that Henderson girl?' That's what he asked." Jeff spoke faster. "Fuck. Could he be in on it, too?"

"At this point, anyone could be. What's this guy's name?"

"We just call him Coach Tee. Let me think... Humphries. Tee Humphries."

I wrote the name on my list and circled it. "Any chance his real name is Tony? Tee could be short for that?"

"You're not wrong." He moved to grab his phone and started typing furiously. "Let me try and find a picture of him to see if this is the guy you saw."

I nodded and reveled in the thrill of the chase. We were close. My blood tingled with the hunt and I shoved any regrets about my uncle down deep. It wasn't the time to second-guess my entire relationship with him. It was time to nail these assholes and get the ball moving—whatever that meant. "I'm going to start writing it. The only other piece I really need is to talk to the Dean of Athletics, Dean Sanders."

"Woah, if he's involved, it could tip him off about everything." Jeff's face tightened and he shook his head quickly. "I don't like you putting yourself in that position."

"Jeff," I said, reveling in his worry over me, "I should be okay if I spin it the right way. My plan is to get my professor's recommendation to interview him and set it up through that class so it's less suspicious. Get a couple of email chains going so it's documented and time stamped."

"Brilliant." He pulled me in for a hug and kissed the top of my head. "Anything I can do to help? Our first game is in two weeks and once the season starts, I'll barely have any free time."

"Hm." I sucked my lip into my mouth and thought about what we really needed to guarantee people would take this article seriously. "Pictures. Evidence. Proof. I know we talked about it before, but any pictures putting these guys places could help. I want to find this Tony guy and how he relates to this."

"Pictures…what kind?"

"The most incriminating part of this entire thing is these guys—however many are involved—talking to high school kids and/or their parents, securing money somehow, and staging the release from the team. After the fake injury, their part is essentially done."

His face became grim and he handed me his phone. "I got another text with a warning."

I yanked it into my hands and frantically read the message.

UNKNOWN: You have too much to lose. Let this go.

"Shit." I glanced at Jeff and hated the pit of fear in my gut. "When was this sent?"

"This morning…about an hour after you left the stadium."

I closed my eyes and refused to let fear motivate me. "We're close. That's what this means."

"I know." He let out a resigned sigh and I felt the weight of his stress in my bones. I didn't want to ask the question, terrified of what his answer might be, so I took a couple seconds to garner enough courage.

"Is there any chance you could lose your scholarship from this? These guys are high-ups and if you want to wait until your season is over, I don't mind." I reached out and ran my fingers through his thick hair. He hummed at my touch and gave me a beautiful half-smile.

"It's something that has been weighing on my mind and I can't, with good conscious, not let you write this article because of what maybe could happen to me. This is unfair and illegal. If I lose my scholarship, I'll financially be okay."

"But the team?"

"I have less to lose than the other guys. They have the draft to plan for and I don't. I'm just glad it's me who figured this out. I can handle some bastards coming after me."

"Jeff," I replied softly. He was being the silent leader, suffering so his teammates could thrive. I placed my hand on his chest, right over his heart, and said, "You're incredible taking one for the team, figuratively and literally, but it's still your senior season and you deserve to play."

He covered my hand with his and looked a little broken. "It's a chance I'm willing to take."

"I think you need to tell your teammates. Maybe not all of them, but your roommates for sure," I said, tensing as I waited for his reaction. If he realized I'd overheard him and his coach talking, he didn't let me know, but it was bold for me to give him my opinion without him asking. "I'm not just talking about the investigation. I'm talking everything."

"I know. They deserve a heads-up if everything changes."

"They deserve to hear it from one of their best friends. You're suffering through this whether you want to admit it or not and they'll support you. I know it." I smiled and he cupped my face, leaning in for a soft kiss. It was pleasant at first, his soft lips connecting with mine, but then it turned heated when he slipped his tongue inside my mouth. "Mm, Jeff…"

He rolled me over so his body was on top of mine, his elbows holding him up just above my face. He deepened the kiss as a low growl came from his chest. This kiss was different from all the others somehow. The urgency and passion was there, but the way he took his time exploring my mouth, the way he touched me was softer and the tenderness in his eyes was new. My body burned at his attention when he slid his hands up my shirt to cup my breasts. It was too much emotion and I needed a little distance.

"Wh-what are you doing?" I asked, breathlessly. "Shouldn't we keep…keep talking about everything?"

My voice hitched when he pinched both my nipples and grinned down at me. "We can keep talking."

He slid my shirt off in one quick pull and brought his mouth down, sucking and biting like he had that morning. He trailed kisses over my collarbone, down the center of my chest, and bit down on the skin over my belly button. "What's on your mind, Ambar?"

"Uh…" I mumbled, unable to form words now that he removed my pants and slid two fingers inside me. In and out, fast and slow. I panted, an orgasm so close, but he stopped when my body tensed. "Hm?"

"Okay, let's talk." He stopped touching me and moved to lean against the wall, a coy smile on his lips. "What should we do next?"

My brain lost focus. His bulge pressed his jeans and my nerves were on fire—desperate for the release I craved. Licking my lips, I crawled over him and undid the waistband of his jeans. He stopped me. "You wanted to talk, Ambar."

"Why are you... You're teasing me." I pouted and kept removing his pants. This time, he let me and his beautifully hard cock sprung out. He wanted to play a game and I was fine with it. But two could play. I leaned forward and took him in my mouth. I sucked four times, taking him as deep as my mouth would let me, and he bucked when I carefully bit down on the head.

"Fuck..." he moaned and gripped my hair in his hand. "God, your mouth is fucking heaven."

I cupped his balls with my hand and continued sucking him and when his legs tensed, I dropped, licking all the way up his shaft and stopped. "Mm, that was a nice taste."

His eyes looked feral when I got up and licked my lips, all while holding an intense eye contact. Never had I ever stood completely naked in front of a guy in broad daylight and goddamn, it felt good to see him so hungry for me. "Ambar," he warned.

"Yes?" I teased, moving away from the bed and going to the closet. We were both on edge and I knew just the trick to make it even crazier. "You ready to talk still?"

"I'm seconds away from attacking you. Do you feel how hard I am for you?" He stood and followed me into my closet, his hands comings around my hips and moving my ass directly over his erection. "What I would give to just slip inside right now and watch you pant."

"How about you take your impatient ass and get back to the bed, hm?" I said, bolder and more confident than I had ever been in my life. I pushed his naked chest and wiggled my eyebrows. "Bed."

He smirked and marched his fine ass back to my room and I scrambled to find a pair of old pantyhose. I had some black ones that I rarely wore because they had a run in them and I slid the material up my legs. Scissors were still sitting on the dresser since I'd had to cut off tags the week before and I used them to cut a hole right in the crotch. Wearing just the pantyhose, I walked back to my bed. "I think we had a bet to settle, am I right?"

"Fuck me," he groaned and bit down on his knuckle. "You're the hottest fucking thing. Get your ass over here."

I giggled—because I did that now—and crawled onto the bed real slow, loving how he twitched when I ran my hand down the length of him. "You're ready for me?"

"Christ, I'm barely hanging on." He moved fast, grabbing a condom from the night stand and sliding it on himself within thirty seconds. "I won't last long with you looking how you do."

"Better make it worth it then," I challenged.

He met the challenge head on. He sat on the edge of the bed with his feet on the ground and he picked me up to sit on his lap facing away from him. He held my weight completely to prevent me from falling forward and I gasped when he slid himself inside me. "Fuck, Ambar." He paused his movement and rested his forehead against my upper back. He used his fingers to tease my nipples and bit my neck as he thrust upward. I bucked when he did it again and again, stretching out my walls and combining the sensation of his cock and his hands.

"Jeff, this is…" I moaned and let my head fall back onto his shoulder. He wrapped his arms around my middle and held me close.

"I know."

We moved together like that, back to chest, his dick sliding in and out a torturously slow pace that had us both panting. "I'm so close," I whispered, every cell in my body on edge for the release only he could give me. He brought his fingers down to my clit and swirled against it fast. It didn't take long and I fell apart on him. The sensation spread through my body, from my core to my limbs, and I cried out his name. He growled in my ear and picked up his pace, moving his hands to my hips to force me up and down harder on him.

"Ambar, I'm going to come," he warned before grunting one last time. "Christ, baby." His thrusting slowed, then he did a final two times before he stopped and held me tight against him. His heartbeat pounded against my back—the furious pace matching mine—and we remained pressed together until we caught our breath. He pressed one kiss on my spine before picking me up and removing himself from me. "Amazing."

"Agreed," I replied, feeling dazed and high from him. "And…I'm getting some real stockings."

"The fuck you better." He laughed and disposed of the condom in the bathroom before returning to my room. It was normal now to see him naked in my bedroom and I tried not to think about how much I liked having him there. He threw on his boxers and crawled back into the bed. I got up to remove the pantyhose and put on something more comfortable—loose shorts and an oversize sweatshirt—and I joined him.

"There are still a couple of things we need to talk about," I said, not quite meeting his eyes. Now that our bodies were sated, it didn't exactly make it easier to bring up the other topic on my mind. "Brandon."

"Him." Jeff made a face like he'd eaten sour fruit and it made him look kinda cute. "What about him?"

"You told him we're together."

"Still on that?" He laughed and pulled me against his chest. "After what we just did, you're telling me we *aren't* together?"

"No?" I had no idea how to answer his question nor what it meant for the future.

"We're both serial non-daters, right? I'm way too busy with my final season and you're swamped with your final project and writing a major fucking article that could change a lot about our college. It works between us and I'd like to keep it that way as long as we can."

"So…we're dating?"

"If you want to say that. I don't like labels or that shit but if you prefer it, then yeah." He ran a hand down my arm again and yawned. "Can I nap here with you? You're comfy and today wiped me out."

Something like heat radiated through my chest at his words and I snuggled deeper to him. "A nap sounds great."

Chapter Twenty-Five

Jeff

One week left until our season started and the energy in the house was erratic. It was almost tangible. Zade hummed constantly as he paced and rearranged books on our shelf while Aaron and Tanner threw insult after insult while they played video games. It was normal for us to get amped up before a season, but this felt heavier. I was spending more time with Ambar because she was the perfect distraction from the mess in my head, but it still didn't help me sleep. My dreams were filled with nightmares of me disappointing the team, losing the game or ruining the season for everyone. Guilt took its form in a variety of ways and mine rooted itself in my stomach, tearing at the lining until I broke. "Guys, can I talk to you about something?"

"Do you even need to ask?" Zade responded, eyeing two different books to make sure they were equal distance apart. "Are you about to explain the weird mood you've been in? Because I thought with a chick you'd mellow out a bit. We've heard you and Ambar. You're not quiet."

"Okay, *Zade*. You're one to talk." Tanner rolled his eyes and paused the game. He was in a tricky spot since he was dating Aaron's little sister so we couldn't joke around with him if Hilly was around. It was like poking a bear who hadn't eaten in a year. "What's going on, Jeff?"

I rolled my shoulders, hoping it was help with the tension, but it didn't. Ambar had encouraged me to share everything with them, whatever I felt comfortable with, but it still felt wrong to talk about it without her here. She'd holed herself in the library to start writing without disruptions—which included me—so I found myself sitting with my roommates reading to spill my fucking guts. They looked at me without judgment, just curiosity, and I plopped onto the couch. "I don't want to play baseball after this season."

They all reacted differently, but not overtly. Zade furrowed his eyebrows, Aaron shifted his position on the couch and Tanner ran a hand over his jaw. No one asked why, or said I was an idiot, so I continued. "Playing overseas last year really fucked with me. It wasn't what I envisioned and I know it's different playing in the minors, but my heart isn't in it anymore."

"Dude, that's why you're so uptight?" Hilly asked, scoffing and shaking his head at me. "You were afraid of telling us that?"

"Well, yeah." My face burned with embarrassment for a minute before I started to relax. "It's been the goal all these years. All four of us. Playing our asses off, enjoying college and making it to the big leagues. It's what brought us together freshman year and me losing the same collective goal freaked me out."

"I understand the worry, but it's unnecessary. It wasn't the draft that brought us together, man—it was the friendship. The brotherhood." Zade got up and put a hand on my shoulder. "I hate you couldn't tell us that, but I get it. We all deal with shit differently."

"I didn't realize it fully until the past couple of months. I've been looking up law schools and want to start studying for the LSAT after the final season. It makes me sound privileged, but money isn't an issue for me." I stopped and winced. "I can take the time to figure out a different future for myself."

"You gotta do what's best for you." Tanner gave me a reassuring smile and added, "You'd make a hell of a lawyer."

My heart swelled with pride as my teammates asked more questions, like what schools I was looking at or what type of law I was interested in, and there wasn't one judgmental question about my lack of Dedication. It didn't matter than no one said it, I still felt the need to clarify myself. "This doesn't change how hard I'm going to play this season. This team is still my family and I'm gonna play like hell."

"No shit," Hilly said with a laugh. "We'd kick your tall ass if you didn't."

"This changes nothing, by the way. Not how we treat you, not how we're gonna play on the field, nor what we tell anybody. This is your choice and your business and it'll stay that way," Zade said, stepping up to be the leader he had always been. "Thanks for telling us."

Do I tell them? Will it make it worse or better? Ambar's words about owing them a warning repeated in my head.

If the situation was reversed, I'd want to know. "There's something else."

"What is it?" Zade asked.

"The reason Ambar and I even got together is because something fishy is going on in sports." They all sat up straighter and gave me their undivided attention. "Involving baseball...and more."

"Wait—what the hell do you mean by that?" Zade asked, sharing a concerned look with Hilly.

"It's something illegal."

"Go on," Hilly urged when I paused.

"We have reason to believe players, not legit ones, are buying their way onto team rosters and into the school." I ran my hand over the back of my neck and waited for their reaction. Would they believe me? Laugh at me? Mock me?

"Jeff, that's... That sounds—" Zade stopped and cast a look at Hilly. Then they both said together, "Tell us how we can help."

* * * *

My mood reached an all-time high after sharing everything with my teammates. Relief loosened the muscles in my neck and I thought about Ambar on my walk to the library. I couldn't wait to tell her about their reactions, and willingness to help, and I wondered how much work she'd gotten done. My effort to find pictures had resulted in discovering just one that could've been her uncle at a high school three years ago—so not really helpful. She'd said she had an idea and I trusted her to find something useful.

I smiled, not caring I probably looked like a weirdo smiling to myself, at how incredible her work had been.

I would be a fool to think the investigation was fifty-fifty. She had done a lot of the work and I owed her big-time. She texted me her location on the lowest floor and I found her super focused, hair piled on top of her head and a large frown on her face. *God she's cute.* She wore a loose sweater that hung off one of her shoulders and she chewed on her bottom lip, clearly interested in whatever she was reading on her computer. A part of me wanted to watch her, but people were staring at me and I didn't want to be weird. "Hey, Henderson."

She looked up and her face changed. It softened completely for me and I'd be damned if it didn't make me feel something inside my chest. "Sit down."

"Yes, ma'am." I obeyed and moved to the chair next to her. "You should boss me around in the bedroom more often."

She ignored my comment and I laughed. It had been two days since we'd spent the night together—her choice, not mine—and just being near her had me thinking dirty thoughts. "Look at this."

She pointed at her computer screen and scrolled through five pictures. Each one of them had her uncle in the background. It wasn't clear where the pictures were taken, but it was definitely him. "Where are these from?"

She lowered her voice to a whisper and it forced me to lean closer to her. I wasn't mad about it and fought the urge to kiss her. "I spent hours creeping on some of the guys involved and their signing, because most kids who get any legit partial-scholarship have a signing day at school, right? But since these are under the radar, I had to go deep. Three of these pictures are of the guys we talked to in the beginning and my Uncle Martin is there. But get this, I can't find any proof these guys made a big deal out of getting a spot on an athletic team. So why was he there? And I'm pretty sure this Tony guy is this dude." She pointed at a blurred figure of a man, but he didn't look familiar to me. But Martin Rhett was definitely in the shots with the fake-athletes.

"Holy shit, Ambar. This is incredible work." I put my hand on her knee and squeezed it. "This is part of that evidence we need."

"I know." She pushed some crazy escaped hairs behind her ear and leaned back. "I have an appointment to meet with the Dean of Athletics tomorrow and after that, I think I can have the first draft done by your first game."

"You're amazing." *Fuck it.* I dipped low enough to kiss her and she hummed in response. "Please tell me you aren't busy tonight."

"Why? What did you have in mind?" She wiggled her brows at me.

"We grab dinner, take a break from all this shit. You deserve a nice dinner and I want to take you out."

"Yeah?" She blushed and scrunched her nose. "We're going on a date. You and me."

I thought about it for a second and shrugged. "Yes. I'm taking you on a date."

"Should I wear stockings?"

"Fuck me, Ambar." I groaned into my fist and ran my hand up her leg. She wore jeans, but she got the message. "You're killing me."

"Better get used to it if we're going to continue this once your games start. You'll have many-a-night with your good ole hand." She laughed at her own joke and paled when she saw my face. "Oh shit. Did I ruin it by suggesting we continue?"

If I'm this obsessed with her now, what will it be like during the season? Can I even fit her in? Do I want to try?

"Ignore me, Jeff. I know how crazy your season will be and I'm pretty sure we agreed to only let this continue until the story is done." She blinked quite a bit and red splotches appeared on her neck. "Seriously, forget I said anything."

"I want to continue this." I scooted my chair closer so her side pressed into mine and I felt awful at her momentary embarrassment. "It'll be tough and new for me, but I'd like to try."

"You sure?"

"Yes, I'm sure," I said, enjoying the way she molded into my side. She let out the littlest sigh when I put my arm around her shoulder and it felt right. "We just need to be honest with each other."

"I can do honesty." She looked up at me with so much warmth and love that my breath caught in my throat. I coughed at the unfamiliar sensation and she frowned. "I have some water. Here, take a sip."

She pulled out a water bottle and handed it to me. She took care of people she cared about and I wanted to be the one to take care of her. "Thank you. Listen, are you sure you want to write this knowing it'll cause a lot of issues for your family? I know what your uncle means to you."

"I can't be complicit in his actions. He made his choices and I can deal with the fall-out. I've always been the black sheep of my family, loved less than my brothers and ignored by most of my extended family because of my dumb choices as a teen. Nothing would change except my relationship with him and I've been questioning that lately anyway. Was he fooling me this entire time?"

"No." I shook my head. "I heard the way he talked about your talents that day. He cares about you and regardless of his actions, that shouldn't affect his support of you."

"I guess we'll see." She brought her fingers to her lips and pulled on the side. "It's crazy how much we've uncovered and yet there is still so much we don't know."

"My goal was always to expose them and let the higher-ups deal with the details. Even if we can put something on their radar and get traction… Hey, I told the guys everything this morning."

"Really?" Her grin stretched from ear to ear and she patted my hand. "I'm so glad you told them. How do you feel?"

She didn't ask what they said or their reaction. She asked about me and it felt nice to have someone care. "Guilt free and like the weight on my shoulders lifted. I practically skipped here to tell you."

"I'm sure they were accepting of your choice and willing to help. Am I right?"

"Yes," I said, pulling her in for another hug. "They offered to help anyway they can. I brought up some of the younger guys and they remembered the same shady shit that went down. It validated everything I had been feeling."

"Good. We might need help spreading the article and bringing awareness to it with their social media followings."

My phone went off and glanced to see a text from Zade. I almost ignored it, but I saw Ambar's name.

Zade: Been thinking about what you told us. Never thought anything of it but Coach Tee was asking me this week if I was involved in the article by the Henderson girl. Could mean something, or not, but it felt weird to have him ask me.

Jeff: Thanks man. If you think of anything else, let me know.

"Look at this. He was asking me about you, too."

She read it and clicked her tongue a couple of times. "It's safe to say Tee is involved in this too, not just your head coach."

"My head coach has been alone with me a handful of times the past month or two and hasn't once asked me about your article. You think it's an act?"

"He could be drawing suspicions away from himself and using his assistant coaches to try and gauge how much you know." She sighed and continued, "Or, he wants you to still trust him. You said he didn't read my text on your phone. Do you believe him?"

"The man still has a flip phone, so yes. But he has issued a couple of grave warnings that had me on edge. He knows I know something." The tingling sensation of being watched caused me to look around the library. "The sooner we get this out in the open, the better. Maybe I can relax then."

"You and me both."

"Want me to leave you alone for a bit and pick you up in a couple hours for our date?"

"Yeah. I'd like that."

"Wear stockings." I stood, kissing her more passionately than I should've for being in public, and grinned at the heat in her eyes.

Chapter Twenty-Six

Ambar

Jeff wearing a collared shirt and jacket did things to me I didn't expect. His broad shoulders filled the material perfectly and I wanted to run my fingers up and down his body for hours without stopping. He'd even shaved and looked so good I had a hard time focusing on the delicious Italian food. He glanced up at me, humor in his eyes, and smirked. "You're staring at me."

"You look gorgeous. You should wear stuff like that more often." I gulped and took a long swig of water. The temperatures were still cold outside, but in the small corner of the restaurant, I was overheating. "It's dangerous."

"We wanna talk about dangerous." He stopped and darted his gaze to the low dip of my dress. "You in stockings and that dress. I meant it when I said we could order take-in and just get naked immediately."

"It's good for you to wait." I grinned and ran my tongue over my lip. He followed the movement and his entire jaw tensed. A thrill went through me. *This is easy, the flirting and teasing.*

"I disagree but whatever," he quipped, adding on a wink at the end. He took another bite of his pasta and gave me a long look. "What's next for you? The article is coming together and you'll be able to use it for your senior project. What's after?"

"Hm, great question." I'd thought about what was next, in the back of my mind, but never verbalized it to myself or any other person. But Jeff's face was so intent on my answer, a light smile playing on his lips, I found myself blabbing. "Investigative journalism woke me up."

"Yeah? What do you mean?"

"The past four weeks…I haven't felt a thrill like this before in any of my classwork. The research and questioning were intense and even going undercover at times." My voice rose with excitement. "It gave me a purpose that I was lacking. Graduation doesn't seem as scary now. It sounds cheesy, I know."

"No," he said, covering my hand with his. "This article could help you make a name for yourself beyond this campus. If it gets into the hands of the right people, it could go viral."

I hadn't thought of that and I dazed off in thought. *Viral? My family will see it and everyone would know I turned on family?* I shook the thought away. This was bigger than my uncle and me. "It would help me get into grad school if I go that route. Hell, maybe even help me get a job."

"You want to go to grad school?" His eyes lit up and he leaned closer to me. He did that often, positioned himself closer to me when I spoke. It was endearing.

"I'm toying with the idea. Majoring in communication is fine, but I never chose a focus. Again, I coasted by hoping something would work out."

"And it did." He smiled and held up his wine glass. "You busted your ass and impressed me a million different ways during this. Cheers to you, Ambar."

He held eye contact when I hit my water glass with his and felt his stare all the way to my heart. *Tender. Care. Love.* All those emotions swirled in his eyes and a nervous sweat formed on my forehead. *Are we moving too fast? Is this real?* He cleared his throat and replaced the warm look with a flirty one. "Along the theme of celebrating you, I'd like to say it has been amazing to watch your confidence grow in the bedroom."

"Jeff," I warned, but he ignored it.

"You're a real badass, Ambar, and I'm glad I decided to come yell at you that day."

"Oh, are you?" I said sarcastically. We both laughed and he leaned over to press a kiss to my cheek. I almost melted off the booth at his gesture and blinked up at him. "What was that for?"

"You've kinda snuck your way into my life. I didn't want you there at first but now, I want to keep you in it."

I blushed so hard at his words, I had to look down at the table. "You're being awful swoony tonight. Makes a girl feel a lot of things."

"Is wet one of them?"

"Find out yourself, handsome," I fired back. His face froze and I chuckled. The sentimental words made me unsure of how to respond but his comment about my sexuality was true. I had grown more confident and I brought my foot up to his crotch and teased him. "I like making you suffer sometimes."

"I know," he grunted and reached under the table to feel my pantyhose. He'd asked numerous times if they were the same ones from before—with the hole—but I refused to answer. The tablecloth hid his hand from anyone else and he trailed his finger up my thigh and paused. I didn't stop him and he scooted closer. "Ambar," he said with a groan.

"You've been asking all night. Find out yourself." I forced myself to remain still and to not show anything on my face as he brought his finger closer and closer to the center of my legs. Not only was I wearing real stockings—they were all I wore underneath the dress.

He hissed when he found out and let loose a long cuss word when he realized I was commando. "Oh, *Christ.*"

I smirked but the smile fell from my lips when he slid one finger inside me, clearly not giving a damn we were sitting in a public restaurant. "Jeff," I warned, but he didn't stop. "Wh-what…"

"You're playing with fire, babe. God, you are wet. Is it from what I said?"

"Y-yes." I bit down on my lip hard to prevent myself from moaning as he moved his finger in and out. His face gave nothing away. The only indication he felt anything was his quickened breathing and flared nostrils. "I like teasing you."

"I've noticed." He slid a second finger inside and found a steady rhythm. "So did you enjoy the food?"

"Uh-huh." I held on to the table top, trying to calm my breathing. He moved closer and used his other hand to grab his wine glass. His throat bobbed when he swallowed and I had never been so turned on in my entire life. "How can… How can you act so normal?"

"Am I acting normal?" he said in a husky, dangerous tone. "I'm on edge, Ambar. If I got up, everyone in this place would see my dick straining against my pants."

I whimpered and he gave me a wicked grin. He stared intently at me when he added his thumb against my clit, swirling and flicking it just the way I liked. My body tensed with anticipation of the orgasm he would surely give me in public, but he stopped. "Hm?"

"You're so beautiful, Ambar." He kissed my forehead and raised his other hand to grab our waitress' attention. "I don't want you getting off in a restaurant where anyone can see you. I want hours with you tonight."

I couldn't respond. My body shook with a taut desperation, almost to the point of pain when he denied my orgasm. The waitress appeared with the check and Jeff threw a couple twenties on the table in a hurry. His hand remained under the table and he carefully removed it from beneath my clothes. "Are we leaving?"

"You bet your fine ass we are." He took my hand and dragged me from the booth. "You were done eating, right?"

I laughed at his frantic pace and he almost picked me up to run to the car with me. "Jeff, you're acting insane."

"Am I?" He stopped and pressed my back against the restaurant wall. It was just us, on a cold February night, and something about it was magical. He looked back and forth between my eyes, as if unsure of what he wanted to say, before he whispered in the softest tone, "I can't get enough of you, Henderson. It's driving me insane."

Then he kissed me. He claimed my mouth and turned any resolve I had into mush. I clung to his jacket when he slid his tongue inside my mouth, tasting and exploring it. He moaned into my mouth and I had never felt so drunk on being wanted. "Jeff, let's go home."

He grinned and bit my lip playfully before grabbing my hand and running to his parked car. He almost tossed me into the passenger seat and I had to yell at him to be careful. "Just want to get home and pleasure my woman."

I'm his woman?

Does that make him my man?

He kept a hand on my leg the entire drive back and he didn't ask if we were going to his place or mine. He parked in his driveway and waited for me before picking me up. "Jeff! Don't hurt yourself."

"Please, Henderson. Don't insult my muscles." He opened the front door and stopped us on the bottom of the stairs for a soul-searing kiss. "Are you still tight and ready for me?"

"You got me on the brink of an orgasm at the restaurant before stopping. It was a bit cruel," I joked, but a line formed between his eyebrows. "You need to make up for it."

"How do you want your orgasms, then?" he asked in a deadly serious tone.

"Mm, I like options," I said, already backing up the stairs to his bedroom. He followed and I started removing an item of clothing on each stair. First it was my heels, then my jacket. "Watch me undress right there."

He gulped and nodded. His grip on the banister was almost white and I took my time undoing the halter of my dress. I let it slide down my body and pool at my feet so I stood there in nothing but the stockings and a flimsy see-through bra. I sat down on the top stair and spread my legs—his eyes almost bulged out of his head and he begged for me. "Please, let me touch you."

If I could get that on a recording and listen to it every day for the rest of my life, I'd be happy. I nodded and Jeff pounced. His hands and mouth were everywhere, pleasuring me and giving me what he'd promised at the restaurant. It took no time for him to bring me to orgasm with just his fingers and I arched my back, crying out his name when he brought his tongue into action.

"Will two orgasms satisfy you enough?"

"Mm, let's find out."

He ate me out with a furious passion and my thighs shook hard around his head when he flicked my clit with his tongue for the final push. My body was goo after the second orgasm but he didn't stop there. He lifted me up and carried me to his room, carefully setting me on the bed. "I love your body, Ambar. Your perfectly small tits." He bent down and kissed each nipple, slowly sucking it into his mouth. "Your curves."

He licked down the center and ended between my legs. "Your pussy—sweet god, it's perfect. These legs." He kissed each thigh and came back up to my mouth. "I love making you feel good."

I blinked back tears at the tenderness in his voice and when he put on a condom and slid into me, it felt different. This was slow, the way he kissed me between each thrust, and told me how beautiful I was. It was almost like…we were making love.

Everything slipped from my mind as our bodies sweated against each other and I wrapped myself around him tight when he convulsed, groaning out my name. It was sweeter, gentler and unlike anything I had experienced. I leaned up to kiss him on the cheek, as a thank you, and I was met with a goofy smile. "That was…"

"I know," he said, kissing me on the mouth again. "Let me get you a shirt to sleep in. I'm not done with you tonight."

* * * *

It was difficult leaving a sleeping Jeff. His eyelashes fanned over his cheek and my heart lurched at the strength of my feelings for him. I brushed his hair out of his face and he stirred, opening his sleepy eyes and smiling. "Morning."

"Morning to you," he said, before yawning. "Where you sneaking off to?"

"My meeting with the dean."

"Right." He groaned and tried to sit up, but I stopped him.

"It's early. Sleep. I'll let you know how it goes."

"Call me after." He moved and cupped my chin with his hand. "Be careful."

"I will." I leaned into his hand and bent my head to kiss him. He hummed against my mouth and it took all my effort to not turn into a silly girl gushing over how much she liked a guy. "We can meet up later, yeah?"

"As soon as I get out of practice, I'll be over."

I smiled at him, wishing I could stay in the warmth of his bed but knowing I couldn't. I ran home to freshen up and change into my business outfit—black slacks and a red button-down. It made me feel professional and I even listened to my pump-up tunes on my walk to the building. My professor had helped set up the meeting last week so there was nothing worrying about this meet-up—if this guy was involved in the entire scandal. I wanted to know how recruitment worked, who handled the money and if athletes were monitored. *Like were these fake-athletes still paying for a spot in school, without having anything to do with sports?*

The thought angered me but I masked my emotions when I entered the pristine building located on the northern part of our campus. A very perky woman glanced up at me from behind the welcome desk and smiled. "Hello there."

"Hi, I'm here to meet with Dean Sanders."

"Sign in, please." She indicated the clipboard and I hesitated before writing my name. It was stupid to feel under watch, but the hairs on the back of my neck tingled. *Is my uncle here?* I looked discreetly around the foyer, hoping like hell I didn't see the familiar dark hair, and released a pent-up breath when it was just us. I printed my name and gave her a tight smile. "Thank you, Ms. Henderson. Go on through the doors and his assistant will direct you."

I followed her directions, pushed open the door and the air left my lungs when Tony, my uncle's *friend,* stood against another welcome desk in a charcoal suit. I ducked my head down, pretending to look at something on the ground, and tried to think of what to do. *He either works here or is visiting.* Both were equally troubling and my heart was in my throat. *Maybe he won't recognize me.* Thirty seconds went by and I was still crouched on the floor, pretending to tie a shoelace that didn't exist, and I stood tall. It wasn't as though he could do anything about it here, in front of people, but just as I stood, someone reached out and gripped my arm. "Come with me."

The head baseball coach had a look that would make the bravest player cower. The intensity of his face had me nodding and I followed him out through the doors I'd entered a minute ago. We walked past the welcome desk and through another set—where Dean Sanders sat with a forlorn look. "Ms. Henderson, just the person we were looking for."

"What's going on?" I yanked my arm out of the coach's grip and tried to analyze the situation. My gut churned at the possibilities. *They're in it together and going to blackmail me. Or blackmail Jeff. Or the team. Or threaten me.* I prepared for all the possibilities. "Regardless of what either of you say, the article is getting published. There is not a threat or offer that will sway me."

Dean Sanders smiled and chuckled. "You weren't kidding. She is headstrong."

The coach relaxed into a chair but leveled his gaze with me. "You're going to want to sit down."

"I'll stand, thank you." I gripped the edge of the leather seat. "Well?"

"We need you to wait a couple more weeks before you post the article."

"And why would I do that? To give you time to cover your asses?"

"Ha, no." Dean Sanders shared a look with the coach. "You and Jeff Maddow aren't the only ones aware of what's going on. What we're about to tell you… It must stay here."

"Why would I agree to that?"

"This affects Jeff. You want to help him, don't you?"

"Why don't you tell me what you know first, hm?" I fired back, hoping they couldn't see how hard my fingers shook. If something happened to Jeff…I couldn't handle it.

Chapter Twenty-Seven

Jeff

After telling the guys everything, I expected there to be a slight difference in how they treated me once we got to practice the next day. I kept waiting for it to come, a subtle hint like my time in the cages wasn't as important as theirs or a comment about how much pressure they were under. That never happened and I smothered the guilty feeling that I'd underestimated my friends.

It's because Ambar is meeting with the dean and I'm on edge. That was what I told myself.

"I think Coach has shown up late to practice once in the four years I've been here." Aaron scanned the field and blew onto his fists to get warm. "Wonder where he is."

"Ten bucks says it's wife trouble," Tanner said.

"Nah, I'd say fighting with our trainer over something. Him and Nicole get into it once a week."

Zade nodded to himself. "Plus, we start practice ourselves anyway."

"Yeah, but he's always around, watching how we react with other players and if we give it our all every stretch. You know his motto, players are given opportunities to advance on fifty percent skill, fifty percent character. He's probably watching from somewhere," Aaron said before going into a sprint.

They were all probably right in their assumptions, but my gut told me it was something more. He hadn't shown up to check in with the captains or to give us any updates that tended to be about the focus of the day. It wasn't entirely uncommon for him to stroll in five minutes late with a stern look and a clipboard, but his timing wasn't great for my nerves.

Is it Ambar? Is she okay? I snuck to my catching bag and glanced at my phone resting on the side pocket. We weren't allowed phones unless it was an emergency and while no one would agree with me, this felt like one. My screen showed no messages, just the time.

She should be out by now.

"Jeff, let's go throw a little," Zade yelled, and I forced myself to not be annoyed. We were at practice and my job was to be a leader. Pitchers and catchers were supposed to work together every other day and Zade had to throw a certain number of pitches before we could move onto the next drill.

I dressed in my full gear—something our coach wanted me to get used to before the season started—and got lost in the routine of it all. The sound the ball made when it hit my glove, the whirl of Zade's pitches and the smell of the catching gear I had worn all these years. It comforted me to not think about Ambar or my coach and to just catch, throw and repeat. It went on for an hour and

Zade went to see Nicole, giving me a spare minute to scan the field for our coach.

Still nothing.

"Where the fuck is he?"

"Who?" Brandon asked, matching my aggressive stride as I head into the dugout. Of all the people to hear me talk to myself, I didn't want it to be him.

"Our coach."

"Something's going on, I think." He stopped walking when I put my arm in front of his chest, preventing him from going farther. "Dude."

"What do you mean, something is going on?" I asked in a lower voice, noting how two of our other coaches stared at us.

"I heard shouting coming from his office and Tee and Mac have been real dicks so far today. They're usually chill but I think it has something to—" His eyes widened and he whispered, "Do you…do you think it has something to do with *you know what*?"

"I don't fucking know, but Ambar is in the middle of it. I can feel it."

"Because her uncle—"

"Yes, but don't talk about it here." I cut him off and ran my hand over my face, suddenly exhausted at balancing it all. We still had some time running through plays on the field, which could last two hours if we really got into it, and my body sagged. I wanted to find out what happened with Ambar and to not be in a constant state of worry.

"Maddow!" A stern voice had me looking up and I didn't expect to see Nicole glaring at me. "Get over here."

I shared a worried glance with Brandon and adjusted the strap on my shoulder. "Yes, ma'am."

She crossed her arms over her chest and jutted her chin toward her office. I caught up to her but whatever had her pissed off radiated in the air and I remained quiet. Normally, she'd be busting my balls about what I was eating or drinking before the season, but this time, the quiet unnerved me.

Does she know what's going on, too?

"Get in." She almost forced me into her office before shutting the door. She stomped to her desk and slammed her hands on the top of it. "Are you shitting me? Seriously? Senior year, Jeff? You? Yeah, you were kinda a dipshit for a bit, but you got your head on straight." She put her head in her hands and gave me the saddest, most disappointed look I had ever seen in my life. "You failed the drug test."

No.

No way.

I laughed. "Uh, come again?"

"You failed your drug test, Jeff." She showed me a piece of paper just as the door slammed open and my coach walked in with a lethal look on his face. "Coach."

"I told you to wait, *Nicole*." His gaze never left my face and his tone sent a tremor of terror through my body. "Get your stuff and meet me in my office."

My throat closed up and my body froze in place. He added, "*Now*."

My legs could barely move, like my shoes filled with cement with each step I took. Some of the guys on the team stared at us, but I could only look at the ground. *Failed? How? How could I fail the drug test?*

"Tee—end practice early and have everyone report back here first thing in the morning."

"Yes, sir."

I glanced up to Coach Tee and my entire body tensed at the almost happy expression on his face. His eyes bore into mine and I swore he winked. *He's framing me.* "Coach, listen—"

"No, you listen." He slammed his office door when I got inside and pinched the bridge of his nose. "We will retest you at the end of the week but until then, go to the house and stay low."

"There has to be a misunderstanding. I think—" I paused, unsure if I should continue. He could be in on it, too, but I never imagined he'd let Coach Tee frame me for a failed drug test. I swallowed, the action feeling like nails in my throat, and hated how my voice trembled. "I don't do drugs, dir."

"You'll come back Friday to test again. Don't say anything to your roommates until they get home. You understand?"

"No. No, I don't fucking understand." I stood up, on the edge of hysteria at the bullshit going on. "Someone framed me."

"And why would anyone *frame* you, Jeff?" he asked, a glint appearing in his hard eyes. "Who would have motivation or the time?"

My voice stopped working. I wanted to tell him it had to be Coach Tee unless it was him. But I had no proof. The anger pouring off him scared me to the point where I thought I might throw up and my phone felt like ten pounds in my pocket.

The texts.

If I could find out who'd sent the warning texts than I'd have a leg to stand on. In a scratchy voice that sounded like I had been living in the desert for a week, I said, "I don't know, sir."

"Then own your results. You're lucky I'm letting you test a second time." His jaw tensed and he appeared much older than I was used to seeing. "Now leave."

Without another word, I left his office and kept my head down on the walk to the car. My mind swirled with anxieties and my throat burned. I knew it was a possibility that I'd piss someone off, but fucking with my scholarship and playing time?

Who are these people?

"Fuck!" I screamed and slammed my fist against the steering wheel. *Lost.* I felt lost and I fumbled with my phone and called Ambar. It rang for a full minute before it went to voicemail—so I tried again. This time, she answered and relief flooded my senses, causing me to relax for the first time since she left me that morning. "Ambar, Christ, I need… Where are you? Are you okay?"

"I'm walking home. What's wrong?"

"They framed me." My voice cracked at the end and I rested my forehead on the top of the wheel. "Can I come over, please?"

"S-sure. Give me ten minutes."

I gave her eight and waited on her front door step. The cold didn't bother me. A terrifying numbness took over and when she walked up to me and put a hand on my face, I almost fell apart. I yanked her against my chest and held her tight. She hugged me back and I focused on the familiar comforting scent of her hair. It calmed my breathing.

"Come on, let's make something warm for you." She took my hand and led me inside, taking charge of removing my coat. "You're freezing."

"I waited outside for you."

"You're still in your practice gear." She frowned and busied herself with making something from the kettle. It rattled around when she held it and I hated to see her shaking with worry over me.

"I've never fucked around with steroids my entire life. There's no way I failed the drug test. It has to be them, Ambar." I hung my head and she returned to the couch and cradled me against her chest, rubbing her hands up and down my back.

"It'll be okay, Jeff." She kissed the top of my head. "There has to be a mistake."

"My coach told me to go home and not come back until Friday to retest. I don't… What if he's in on it? A second time doesn't mean shit if they were willing to forge this one. I just…" I squeezed my eyes tight and focused on her. "Are you okay? Please tell me they aren't fucking with you, too. I can't handle it if they are."

"I'm okay," she said softly. A weird expression formed on her face, one I didn't recognize. She pressed her lips against mine and I wished I could rewind my life by a couple of hours. "Tell me more about what exactly happened."

I sighed and told her everything. Instead of being raging pissed on my behalf, she nodded. "That's interesting."

"I tell you all that shit and you think it's just *interesting*?" My voice rose and my temper flared.

"The timing of it all. Your first game is in a week. They could've done this at any point, but now? It's interesting." She patted my face and gave me almost a pitying smile before getting up. "I think I'm going to wait to post the article until this plays out."

"No! Go after these fuckers now. I'm already screwed."

"Trust me, Jeff. Waiting will be a good thing."

Her eyes had a glint in them that was unfamiliar, and the way she said *trust me* reminded me of something someone else had said. I couldn't figure out what my mind was trying to tell me and I sank farther into her couch. The words were easy to say, but difficult to mean and I ignored the warning bell in my gut. "Okay. I'll trust you."

Chapter Twenty-Eight

Ambar

Three days later, the guilt of lying to Jeff almost had me throwing up. I washed my face and used mouthwash, delaying the time until I went back into my bedroom where Jeff remained. He had refused to go to classes the first day, but I'd gone with him earlier this morning and his mood hadn't changed.

Angry. Rightfully slighted. Confused and lost. My heart broke for him and I couldn't do anything about it until his coach reached out to me. That was the deal to ensure the bastards were caught and Jeff's future with baseball was secured. It just sucked seeing him suffer when I knew it would be over soon. *And if he finds out I knew this whole time, he'll never forgive me.*

My phone buzzed with an unknown number and my pulse spiked. *It has to be the coach.* I ran downstairs as quietly as I could and went into the basement. "Hello?"

"Ambar, it's Coach. How's he doing?"

"He's a mess."

Coach sighed and I knew we both cared about Jeff and what this was doing to him. "You getting the article ready? You got the photoshopped pictures I forwarded you?"

"Yes, I think focusing on the three players for baseball will be the best angle. The fake photos of Max, Cooper and Dillon playing on fake teams will have the most impact. I never got the emails you mentioned, though. The ones between the parents and Tony?"

"I'll forward those over to you today once I can." He cleared his throat and spoke in a lower voice. "Your proof of Martin and Tony being at those high schools was phenomenal. Joining alumni associations to search through hundreds, if not thousands of photos and articles… It's admirable and thorough. Sanders said he's close to finding the money trail. Days away, so just make sure our guy is doing well, all right?"

"I'm trying, Coach."

"Write the article even with the missing pieces. You can add those later. As soon as you can publish it, do it. Don't wait for me—go ahead."

"I know," I replied, thankful he called but frustrated there was no new information.

I fought a wave of nausea and tiptoed back into my room. Jeff had fallen asleep—which suited me well because I could get back to what I wanted. That was writing the damn article and avoiding lying to him about how much I knew. His coach had filled in the missing pieces and I had myself a full-blown piece that would showcase the illegal and shady transactions the athletics department had been doing for at least four years…I just couldn't tell Jeff yet.

I didn't have proof of the money but that was where Dean Sanders came in. He could trace the dollar amounts and provide me more details for my article. It would be easy to bask in the accomplishment that Jeff and I had uncovered more details regarding the activities than he had, but again, his focus was on the misuse of finances. I fired up my laptop near my desk and eyed the rough outline of how I'd framed the story. It wasn't salacious or for show. If anything, it was one of the driest pieces I'd ever written and it didn't worry me.

It was enlightening to find excitement and motivation in a piece that was so out of my wheelhouse and the high of finally getting to write it almost outweighed the worry I had over Jeff.

He sighed in his sleep and my heart tightened in my chest. He looked awful with large bags under his eyes and a vacant expression. His teammates had tried cheering him up, assuring him the second drug test on Friday would show he was clean because they, too, assumed the results had been faked by the guys behind the scandal.

When he went on about his coaches framing him, it hurt to pretend I knew nothing, but it was what had to be done. I thought about curling up next to him and enjoying my time with him.

He rolled over and slowly opened his sleepy eyes. His voice was all husky and gruff when he asked, "You watching me sleep?"

Busted. "Maybe?"

"Join me." He moved to the back of the bed and painted a perfect image with his messy hair, clear gray eyes and playful smirk. The smile was new and I shut the laptop to move into his inviting arms. His body heat comforted me when he wrapped his large arms around me, snuggling his nose into my neck. "Mm, you smell good."

"Thank you," I said, hating how the longer the lie went on, the more it physically affected my insides. "I didn't wake you, did I? You were sleeping so peacefully."

"You didn't, but I wouldn't have minded you waking me up." He began kissing along my neck and bit down on my earlobe. Goosebumps broke out all over my arms and he giggled, all low and deep. "I love your body's reaction to me."

"She betrays any resolve I have." I squirmed when he moved his hands up my shirt and caressed my bare skin. It felt so damn good. "Are-are you sure you shouldn't be sleeping?"

"Ambar," he said in a very serious tone. "You're about the only thing in my life right now that is good. I want to enjoy you and forget about the shitstorm we started."

Pain began in the back of my throat at the tender way he looked at me. He meant those words and I forced myself to close my eyes to prevent tears leaking out. *I'm protecting him. That's why I'm not telling him.* His lips parted and he looked like he was about to say something and I couldn't handle hearing anything else. I gripped the back of his neck and brought his face down to mine, capturing his lips in the most passionate kiss I could. It was hard to try and apologize and show him I would do anything to protect him without words, but I gave it my all.

"Christ, Ambar," he moaned into my mouth and the soft touches turned harder, more possessive and animalistic. I ripped his shirt off and dragged my hands over his muscles, enjoying the way they felt in my hands. His frenzied pace matched mine when he pinched my pebbled nipples, bringing me to the desperate place where I lost all rational thoughts.

We scrambled to get each other naked, each using the other as an escape. I moaned when he used his tongue to cover every inch of my skin and let the feelings I bottled up explode when he slowed and held my gaze. "You're amazing. I hope you know that."

"You are, too," I replied, hoping he didn't hear the crack in my voice. It was too much—the way he took his time pleasuring me, the soft touches mixed with teasing that brought me over the edge and the controlled patience when he slid inside me. "*Jeff*."

"I feel it, too," he mumbled into my hair. There was nothing between our bodies. Our chests pressed tight against each other and every movement he made had my entire body trembling. This wasn't an escape of lust. It was making love and it was unlike any other experience I had ever had in my life. Each look was precious, as though it could be the last, and each touch was like flames on my skin. Jeff was in no hurry and he thrust in and out, making sure I felt every inch of him as he brought his lips to mine. We found a rhythm we hadn't had before and it was unparalleled. My eyes stung when he switched positions so he could move his fingers to my clit. The combined pressure of his cock and leisurely swirling thumb sparked the orgasm to start at my core, slowing spreading through my body and ending at my limbs. I trembled from the force of it, but Jeff held me tighter and squeezed his hold on my hips. "*Ambar*."

His chest heaved when he too was brought to orgasm, but the difference this time was the way he watched me the entire time. It felt more intimate, more serious than anything before and I bit down on the side of my cheek to stop myself from saying something stupid. "Thank you," he said before pressing a kiss on my forehead.

"Thank you?" I repeated, unsure why he'd said those words.

"Yes." He laughed and pushed himself up on the bed. "Thank you for it all. The past couple of weeks have been a combination of awful, new, exciting, and it all brought me you. So thank you."

My throat swelled and I couldn't hide the tears in my eyes. His face softened and he cupped one side of my face. My bottom lip trembled the longer he gave me that sweet face. "Jeff… everything will work out for you. I know it."

"It's out of my control at this point." He shrugged and it was then I noticed the lack of tension around his eyes. *Maybe I can distract him with sex until everything unfolds.* "I was thinking today…I'm glad it's me and not my teammates. If I get benched half the season, it won't affect my future like it would theirs."

"You're a good leader." I pulled the sheet up and snuggled deeper into my bed, hating everything about the secret I kept. "Not very many people would say they were glad it's them."

"It's the truth." He cleaned up and put on his boxers before joining me in the bed. "This whole thing started when my buddy back home, Jaime Smith, didn't get offered a spot on the team or financial help because these scammers took his spot. Look at it now. It blew up and if I can find the silver lining in all of this, it's knowing my teammates aren't affected."

I leaned my head on his shoulder and wrapped an arm around him, squeezing. "You're one of the best."

He chuckled but stopped when my phone went off. I wasn't late, about nine at night, but very few people actually called me. I stilled. *If it's his coach, I have no way of explaining.* "I'll uh, let it go to voicemail."

Jeff frowned but let it go. I released a sigh of relief, but my phone rang again. This time, he reached over to the side table and handed it to me. "You should get it."

"Why?" *Shit. Shit. Shit!*

"It's your uncle."

Oh god. Uncle Martin. *Be chill. He doesn't know what I know.* "Shit. Okay, yeah. I should answer, huh?"

Jeff nodded and his gaze clouded.

"Hello?"

"Ambar, my favorite family member. How are you doing?" His voice sounded the same, nothing off about it, but he spoke faster than normal. I sat up straighter in my bed and held eye contact with Jeff.

"Having a boring night, actually, but otherwise good. What about you? This is a random time to call." I swallowed, hard, and felt confident I sounded normal to him. Jeff gave me a slight nod and I clutched the phone tighter against my ear.

"I wanted to ask you about…this article."

Damn.

He knew I knew.

My pulse quickened and Jeff must've sensed the change. He moved closer to me and furrowed his dark brows. "What about it?"

"It's for your senior class, you said?"

His voice changed now. It wasn't friendly or upbeat like I was used to. He ended each syllable with a hardness I hadn't heard before and for the first time since we'd started this thing, I was scared of my uncle. "It's one of the reasons."

"And the others?"

"Why don't you ask me what's really on your mind, Uncle?" I fired back.

"How did you find out?"

"Be more specific."

"Me, Ambar. How did you find out about me?"

I glanced at Jeff. The truth was all him. There was no way this would've ever caught my attention or gotten on my radar if it weren't for Jeff, but he'd already suffered enough. It physically felt like my heart broke in half, one for betraying my own family and the other for lying to Jeff. "Why does it matter *how* I found out?"

"Because I can think of exactly one person who lives in the sports world. It isn't you." His words became sloppy and someone else was in the background. It was distinctively male, but I had no idea who the muffled voice belonged to.

"Uncle Martin…" I let my vulnerable side show. He was used to this Ambar, a sad and low-confidence girl. He would underestimate this version and I wanted him to downplay how much I knew. "People were always going to find out."

"How much do you know?"

"That doesn't matter."

"What proof do you have?"

"Again, that doesn't matter." I shifted uncomfortably and knew I had to speed up the process. The article had to be posted as soon as possible. "I sought the truth and discovered things on the way. This isn't personal."

"You're going to publish an article that will hurt your family? The one person who supported you your entire life? The man who helped get you into this college when you had very little to offer?" he seethed, and I could almost imagine the spit flying from his mouth. "We need to talk. In person."

My voice shook for real this time. "I don't know if we do."

"Yes, Ambar. You wouldn't want anything to happen to *you* or your *friend*, would you?"

"Did...did you threaten me?"

"I'll be in town tomorrow." He hung up and I sat there, mouth agape, disgusted, hurt and wanting to cry. Jeff ran his hand up and down my back and pulled me into his arms.

Everything felt wrong. My uncle threatening me, Jeff comforting me without knowing the entire truth and the weight of carrying the story that hurt so many people. I had enough regrets in my life to have second thoughts about posting the article, but a part of me hated the damaged relationships. *My uncle and I, Jeff and Coach Tee, Dean Sanders and Assistant Dean Tony, and Jeff and I.*

"I'll be here with you tomorrow, so you won't be alone. I won't allow it," Jeff said as I clung to him. "He's trying to rile you up, Ambar. Don't listen to him, okay?"

I couldn't be strong anymore. Tears fell and Jeff let me wet the entire part of his shirt. I was the worst and I couldn't do a damn thing about it. "I just want to sleep and forget about all of this."

"Then let's do that. Come here, Henderson." He moved us to lie side by side in my bed, his comforting arms holding me against his chest, and I had never felt safer. He ran his fingers through my hair for a good five minutes, helping me relax. "We'll get through this together."

I just hoped it was true.

Chapter Twenty-Nine

Jeff

I imagined heartbreak felt similar to the funk I'd woken up in four days in a row. Each morning was the same. I'd wake up, realize what had happened, get angry, furious, sad and lie in bed without motivation for much. Ambar helped with the essential grieving process of potentially losing my senior year of baseball, but the loss of something so crucial to my life physically hurt.

But today was different.

Ambar woke up in a hurry and rushed off to class, leaving me in her bed. I appreciated being able to relax here, away from the baseball house, because none of us knew what to say to one another. I had no doubt they believed me in my innocence, but the fact they went to practice every day made me pissed off. Ambar's was safer for my sanity and theirs. They had the draft to worry about. I didn't.

Today was about finding a loophole or a way to prove that I didn't fail my drug test, which meant researching ways drug tests could be falsified. It was worth a shot but after ten minutes of reading on my small phone screen, I texted Ambar.

Jeff: Can I use your laptop to research something real quick? I'm still in your bed.

Ambar: Sure, I should be back soon anyway.

Ambar: Stay in my bed.

Jeff: Only if you boss me around later.

I smiled at her demand and thought about how we got to where we were at. There was a part of me that wondered how different my life would be if I hadn't seen that document on my coach's desk and found out Martin Rhett was her uncle. I wanted to think I would've found my way to Ambar somehow but I knew it wasn't true. I'd judged her without knowing who she really was and I would never regret the investigation, because it had gotten me her.

Now, I needed to fix the drug test bullshit and move on with my life.

I fired up her laptop and started looking up articles about procedures and alternative ways to get tested for steroids. My family wasn't incredibly wealthy, but we could afford a lawyer if it came down to it. I preferred to not involve anyone else in this. They didn't need any stress and, until the final test Friday, no news was better. Ten minutes in, a *ping* went off showcasing a text message. Ambar must've had her Mac connected to her iPhone and I tried to ignore it because I trusted her and wasn't that guy, but I recognized the number.

It was a number I had only called three times in my four years there, but it was one we were told to memorize in case we ever got into trouble.

Coach.

Why the fuck was he texting Ambar? My palms started sweating as my brain traveled through every scenario that made sense, but none did. Clicking on the notification box, I read through the messages and a flash of anger and curiosity stormed through my body.

Coach: I saw you called.

Ambar: I'm stopping by your office. It's crucial.

Coach: I told you a couple more days.

Ambar: Can't wait that long.

Coach: Does Jeff know?

Ambar: No. He's doing what you asked.

Coach: I'll be there in fifteen minutes.

My blood ran cold and I had the overwhelming urge to punch a wall. Dialing Ambar's number, I forced myself to take deep breaths until she explained what the hell that meant. Her phone rang and rang before going to voicemail.

I tried again. Same response.

Jeff: What is going on?

Ambar: Got caught up talking with a professor, call you in a bit.

A professor?

Fuck that.

If they were going to be meeting in my coach's office in fifteen minutes, then I was going to be there too.

Twenty minutes later, I thought I was going to get sick. A part of me hoped there was a miscommunication or something explanatory about what was going on, but the more I thought about the texts, the angrier I got.

Does Jeff know?

No.

Do I know what? That was what bothered me. My coach could be involved in this entire thing and while I understood her uncle's threat the night before might've spooked her, meeting up with my coach was out of left field.

How did she even have his number? Did she steal it from my phone when I was sleeping? The amount of questions I had clouded my patience and the second I saw Ambar walking into the stadium, I bolted from my car. She had a notebook held tight against her chest like she always did and looked over her shoulder every couple of seconds. *She's worried.*

A part of me was glad she was. She was lying to me and I wanted to fucking know why. I hid behind a car until she went through the double doors and almost ran straight into Brandon in the process.

"Dude! You're cleared?"

"No. Don't tell anyone you saw me." I must've looked terrifying because he flinched and cowered away from me. He nodded and I continued my path to my coach's office. The walk seemed ten times longer than normal as each step was like a punch in the gut. Ambar was here, with my coach, discussing something about me they felt I shouldn't know.

The door was shut, but it didn't block angry voices from carrying through it. I took my fist and pounded on the door four times, debating the first thing I would say. Would I shout? Yell? Accuse them of…something. The voices quieted in the seconds between my knock and waiting, and soon enough, Coach opened the door and his expression went from concern to confusion.

"Jeff, why are you here?" He made no moves to open the door wider. "I told you to be at home."

"Why is Ambar here?" I pushed past him and forced my way in. Ambar sat, wide- eyed and paler than I had ever seen her, on a chair in the corner next to a middle-aged man dressed in a suit. "Is this your *professor* you mentioned?"

She blinked and looked at my coach instead of me, as though she was going off his lead, and it pissed me off. "Ambar. Why did you lie? Why are you *here*?"

My coach shut the door, locked it and moved to sit behind his desk. Tension filled the room as the silence went on and I had to grip the back of a chair to give my adrenaline a way to escape. "Someone tell me what the hell is going on, I swear to god."

"Jeff, this is Dean Sanders, head of the university's athletics department. He's here to discuss the investigation that you and Ms. Henderson started regarding bribery and scams happening with our athletic teams."

I glanced at Ambar and found her staring at me with pleading eyes. She seemed to have forgotten to tell me she was on speaking terms with the fucking dean and my coach. "Okay. Why am I not a part of this?" I asked her.

"Because the Tony I saw my uncle with is one of the associate deans." She stood and walked a few steps closer to me. Not enough to touch me but enough for me to see her reddened cheeks and shaking fingers. "None of this was to keep things from you or lie. This was all about protecting you."

"You meeting with *my coach* and the dean was to protect me? Even when I was terrified he was involved in the entire thing?" I yelled, not giving any more fucks about who was in the room. "Please explain your reasoning to me."

"Jeff, sit down." My coach's command didn't register and I remained standing with my hands on a chair. "I'll explain."

"Start explaining."

Dean Sanders spoke first. "It seems about the same time you brought the story to Ambar's attention, your coach found a document with various student athlete names and dollar amounts that were not permitted for his recruitment allocation. He came to me to start looking discreetly at the paper trail and up until this morning, we couldn't find anything." He spoke in an even manner, as though this was old news, but I did note the tired look on his face.

He continued, "When Ambar went through her professor to set up a meeting with me Monday, I called your coach in to be there so we could pull her aside to find out what she knew. We're not imbeciles and caught on that you two knew something. I don't want to speak for your coach when he is here, so why don't you touch upon things you picked up?"

"You've been tense around me for two months, Jeff, but what really led me to believe you were involved was overhearing one of our coaches mention Dillon Cage a couple of weeks after I saw it on a sheet of paper. Turns out, the punk got scared you asked him questions and reported back to Coach Tee."

"I knew Coach Tee was fucking involved. He looked way too happy about the drug test. He framed me or falsified it or something, I swear it," I said, praying he would finally believe me now that everything was out in the open.

"I know it was fake. It was actually our idea to do that."

"What?" I asked, unsure if I heard him correctly. "Your idea?"

"When we talked Monday, Ambar told us about the threatening texts you'd gotten and how a coach paid too much attention to you. We came up with a plan to pull you from practice so Tee wouldn't be able to do anything to hurt you."

"So you all put me through misery for four fucking days and didn't tell me," I said, each syllable difficult to get out because of the ball in the back of my throat. "You knew, Ambar?"

"Yes." She recoiled and gave me an odd look, like I was an idiot.

"You watched me be miserable all week and you couldn't give me a fucking clue it was planned? After everything?"

"I was told not to until they could find a paper trail of money. Then I could post the article and tell you everything." She continued to glance at me and instead of the fiery passion I was used to seeing in her eyes, it was a bleakness. "After my uncle called and threatened me last night, I demanded the three of us meet to plan to move forward. Martin will be here tonight and I want the article set up to go live tomorrow regardless of what he says."

I finally sat in the chair and rested my face in my hands. I was a smart enough guy to put all their confessions together and it made sense. But it was all too much. Ambar getting threatened, her keeping crucial information from me, my coach knowing this entire time and not telling me? I didn't look at any of them when I asked, "Since I'm out of the loop, what happens now?"

"Jeff," my coach said, using a tone I hadn't heard before. "Look at me."

I did but not without showing my frustration and hurt on my face. His mouth turned down on the sides and he looked older than I had ever seen him, but I was comfortable staying in my own pity party to realize how all this affected him. "Yes, Coach?"

"Starting tomorrow, Coach Tee will be put on leave while the athletic department undergoes their own investigation. Until he is pulled, you are still 'off' because of the drug test. Now you know it is bullshit and I will make sure to tell the team everything."

"Fine." The adrenaline channeled my anger by causing my legs to bounce up and down against the floor and I didn't care I sounded like an ass. "Still don't understand why you couldn't have given me a goddamn clue."

"That was my idea, not your coach's."

I sneered at Ambar, hurt and betrayed by the one person keeping me sane. She wouldn't look up at me and focused on the ground, wringing her small hands together. An hour ago, I would've felt bad for her. It was clear she was uncomfortable but right now? I was fucking disgusted. She gave me a heartbreakingly sad look and said, "I don't regret it, Jeff. I know you're pissed—rightfully so—but it was terrifying seeing that

Tony guy in a position of power. He could've done something worse to you and I-I couldn't handle it."

Her shaking voice and hurt eyes wouldn't work on me. I ignored her and looked at the dean and my coach. "So the article will go live tomorrow, Coach Tee will be suspended and dealt with at a higher level, but what happens to Ambar's uncle and the parents of the fake-athletes?"

"That will all be handled at the dean's level. The school will hire an attorney and press charges." My coach paused and jutted his chin toward the dean.

"There is a chance you and Ambar will be called in as witnesses. If that is the case, our attorney will work with you to prep for it." Dean Sanders eyed his watch and walked over to put a hand on my shoulder. "You and Ms. Henderson have done incredible work when none of this was your responsibility. I'd like to think your coach or I would've found all this out eventually, but you two sped up the process. Be proud."

I didn't have anything to say to him so I nodded. He made arrangements to meet with Ambar the following week and he left, leaving me in the office with two people who'd lied to me. It was confusing to feel relief my coach wasn't involved in the scandal, but also a different type of betrayed that he'd known what we were doing this entire time and didn't mention it. I gripped the sides of the chair to the point where it hurt my fingers, and let out a long sigh.

"Jeff, be mad, but you'll understand why the choices we all made were in your best interest." He, too, moved and placed a hand on my shoulder. "I need to get to the field before the guys show up. It'll be hard pretending to be normal to Coach Tee, but I need you to head out without being seen. Ambar, you too. Wait ten minutes and leave through the back door."

"We will," she said.

My coach left us alone in the room and as soon as it was the two of us, I turned and glared at her. "We promised no lies, do you remember that?"

"Yes." She stood to her fullest height and looked perfectly pretty in her fitted black dress. My chest felt tight, like it was hard to breathe. "Jeff…"

"No." I backed away from her touch and shook my head at her. "You lied. You knew my coach wasn't involved, you knew Coach Tee was and it was your fucking idea to fake the drug test. I can barely fucking look at you right now."

Her bottom lip trembled and she didn't hide her tears. "I understand."

"No begging or pleading with me? That's a little disappointing," I fired at her. I wanted her to feel hurt like I was. To feel betrayed and played by people she trusted. "I guess this was all a way to further your career since you didn't have one?"

"You know that's not true." She wiped her eyes and spoke in a louder voice. "You're upset right now and I get it. But please, don't say anything that will ruin what we have. I'm sick thinking about—"

"Ruin what we have? I don't need to do that. You did that all by yourself, Ambar. You hid information and didn't trust me. Great job." *Fuck it.* I needed to get the hell out of there and run the feelings out of my system. *The gym. I need the fucking gym.* "Good luck with everything."

"That's it, then?"

I opened the door and gave her a fake smile. "That's it." Her face crumpled and that was the final image of Ambar in my brain. While it felt good to know she was hurt, it did nothing to ease the pain in my chest and stomach.

Chapter Thirty

Ambar

I'm fine. I'm totally fine.

My stomach hurt something fierce, a constant churning that threatened to come up. I wrapped my arms around my middle and did my best to settle my breathing. I'd done the right thing to protect Jeff. There wasn't room for regrets because these men were dangerous.

But what if I would've told him everything Monday night? Would he have played along just as well? Rolling onto my front side, I buried my face in the pillow on our couch and that was how Laney found me.

"Uh, you okay girl?" She sat on one end and put her hand on my back. "You're not hungover, are you?"

"No." I didn't move and spoke into the pillow. "Jeff and I are done."

"Are you sure? He's been almost living here and wearing a stupid smile on his face every time you're around. Wasn't he here this morning?"

"Yes, but there's a bunch of stuff I haven't shared with you." I wiggled myself to flip over and she made an amused face. "It's been a fucking couple of weeks."

"What have you kept from me?" she asked, not in an accusatory way.

"The article I've been working on has been a cover. I wasn't really writing about the baseball experience or Jeff. It was about a scandal Jeff uncovered. My Uncle Martin, along with a dean and a coach on the baseball team, was providing fake spots on sports teams to students who weren't athletes to help them get into school. We don't know the dollar amounts involved but they were taking bribes. It's going live today, what I wrote, and Dean Sanders is going to be taking care of the rest."

"Holy shit." She leaned back into the couch and had a dazed look on her face. "So you and Jeff weren't hooking up then?"

"I tell you all that and you ask about Jeff." I rolled my eyes and caught her smiling. "We were. We got together because of all the time we were hanging out and well, at some point, it got pretty heavy. I think I was falling in love with him."

"Oh, Ambar." She squeezed my hand and asked, "What happened then? It sounds like you uncovered a lot together."

"I had to lie to him for almost a week to protect him." The familiar sting in my eyes returned and the knot in my chest intensified. It was almost as if the thought of losing Jeff made it hard to breathe. "He was getting threatening texts from an unknown number and when my uncle—holy shit!" I jumped from the couch and moved to look out of the window. "My uncle is in on it and threatened me last night. He said he's coming over today to talk."

"He threatened you?" Her voice rose in my defense and my heart swelled at her loyalty. "Like how?"

"Like he was in a position of power to do something to my career or place at school here." My adrenaline spiked and I started picking up anything out of place. The stack of books, the remote, the extra coasters. They all went back into the coffee table while Laney looked nervous watching me. "Are you able to be here tonight? Not downstairs but in the house, just in case..."

"Yes." She nodded with too much aggression and an overwhelming urge to hug her took over. I went to her, arms open, and she met my rare form of affection. "Wow, this has you messed up, huh?"

"Just accept my hug. I appreciate you," I said into her hair and sighed at the contact. It hadn't even been a full day and the thought of not hugging or touching Jeff again hurt me.

"I'd do anything for you, just as you would for me. That's why we're best friends." She pulled back and smiled, patting my cheek with her hand. "I'll make sure I'm here all day and I'll have a bat ready if I need to hit your uncle, even if he is hot..."

I shoved her away and laughed at her audacity, but the smile left my face when someone knocked on the door. "Shit."

Fear and uncertainty had always been a part of my life, but never with my uncle, and my body's reaction to it was insane. I had numb fingers, panting breath, sweaty palms and an uncomfortable pit in my gut that wouldn't go away. "That must be him."

Laney reached out and squeezed my hand before she went upstairs. I took a deep breath, pushed my hair behind my ears and told myself he wouldn't actually hurt me. I opened the door with my heart in my throat and stared at my favorite family member. "Uncle."

He didn't say anything when I gestured for him to come in. I snuck a glance toward Jeff's baseball house and found him staring right at me from his driveway. It only lasted about three seconds, our stare-down, but the urge to cry hit me hard and it took a monumental effort to not break down there. *Deal with Martin first. Then talk to Jeff.*

"Ambar, I don't know where to start." He collapsed onto the couch and put his head in his hands. He spoke with a desperate sadness and when he looked up at me, his eyes were red and…remorseful? *How dare he try to act sad after what he said to me.* My fear turned to anger and I channeled that to get through this conversation.

"How about the fact you threatened me last night?" I fired back, surprising myself with the confidence in my tone.

"I didn't have a choice. I would never… Tony was with me and forced me. He knew we were at the end of our con and he is truly in a position to hurt you and told me to threaten you. To scare you or he would. I would *never* do anything to hurt you." His voice came out strong when he said that and a part of me wanted so badly to believe him.

"Well, you were successful."

A loud banging on the front door interrupted us and I got up, already knowing who it was. My voice was breathless, holding on to a little hope when his gaze met mine. "Jeff."

"Five minutes." He stormed into the house, past me and into the living room where he leveled his gaze at my uncle and spoke in a tone I had rarely heard. "You get five fucking minutes of her time then I'm throwing your ass out of here."

My uncle blinked twice before nodding. "Understood."

"I'm waiting in the kitchen, Ambar. The timer starts now." He barely looked at me before stomping into the other room and that left my uncle and me alone.

He groaned and rubbed his palms against his eyes. "I deserve him kicking my ass. All of it is true. Taking money from parents with or sometimes without their kids knowing about it to guarantee them a spot at school. Working with Tony…knowing it was wrong."

I ignored the thrill of seeing Jeff defend me and focused on what Martin said. "I know it's true. The article goes live today where everyone will know. Plus, Dean Sanders already started a legal investigation."

"You want to know what's funny?" He barked out a fake laugh. "I've accepted I'm going to jail. My entire life has been built on lies and cons. It's why your mother hates me so much." He gave me a sad smile and leaned back farther onto the couch. "But one thing that is true, is that you are still my favorite family member, Ambar. You can ask me anything you want and I'll be honest. Knowing I scared you…" He shuddered. "I'll never forgive myself."

He looked pathetic with his tired eyes and wrinkled clothes. I had a million questions for him, all important to the article, but the draft was done and more would be uncovered as the investigation came out. The question I had in the back of my mind was selfish. I cleared my throat and said to hell with it. "Did your scheme get me into this school?"

"What?" He tilted his head and frowned. "No. We focused on wanna-be athletes and parents who enable them."

"You said on the phone you helped me get into this school when I didn't have a lot to offer."

"Ambar." His voice broke and he shook his head. "I never paid a dime for your acceptance. Yes, I bought you gifts because your mother is selfish and superficial and I wanted you to feel loved, but no, I never touched your education."

"Then why would you say that?"

"Because I know your weakness and used it to scare you." He hung his head again and wiped his palms on his pants. "Will you ever forgive me?"

"I can't really say yet." It was the truth. There were so many emotions and thoughts about him, what he did, what he said he didn't do, and right now, I needed to focus on getting through the week. "It's not a yes or no. It's a maybe."

"I understand." He stood and looked at me with warmth. "I won't keep you. If Tony is watching, he'll think I followed through. Be careful, Ambar. There are a lot of moving pieces to this system and once your name is on the article…"

"It's a risk I'm willing to take."

"You brave girl. If I separate myself from it all, I'm filled with so much pride in what you did. Learning so much when we thought we were covering our tracks. You've always had an edge to you and I wasn't sure where you would land, but this… You did good."

"Thank you," I said, tears finally spilling down my cheeks. "I'm not sorry for uncovering everything but I am sorry you were involved."

"I know. It was my choice and I'll deal with it." He moved toward me and pulled me into a hug. It would probably be the last hug for a long while and we both held a little tighter than normal. "I'm glad that young man is on your side. Whatever happens now, please know I'm still rooting for you."

"Thanks, Uncle Martin," I mumbled to his chest. We ended the hug and he left, leaving me in an even more confused state. Heartbroken over Jeff, heartbroken over losing the one family member who loved and supported me, and worried about who else was involved beyond the handful of men we'd found. I rubbed my chest with my hand, taking deep breaths and trying to settle my heartbeat down, when Jeff came back from the kitchen.

"Is your uncle gone?"

"Yeah, he just left." My initial happiness of him being here started trickling away when I took in how hard his expression was, and how he seemed to move closer to the front door and away from me. "Thank you for coming here to defend me."

He sighed and asked without changing his expression. "Did he threaten you again?"

"No." I leaned against the doorway and longed to touch him, to comfort him and to have him give me some of his strength. My eyes stung at how much I wished I could be with Jeff and with the combination of my uncle's admittance… my emotions took over.

"Why are you crying?" He furrowed his brows but made no movement to comfort me. It was pathetic how much I missed his touch.

"Because…he apologized for hurting me, threatening me, just being involved in the entire thing and shattering our relationship. The associate dean forced him to threaten me last night on the phone—"

"You believe him?" he asked, his voice rising. "He's a fucking con artist."

"I know, Jeff, but I think I do believe him. He looked broken."

Jeff made a sarcastic face and shifted his weight from the left to the right. "You're fine, then?"

"Not really." I sniffed and laid it all out on the table, something I never did, and it was more terrifying that posting the article live. "Jeff, can we please talk upstairs? It's been killing me thinking about us not hanging out anymore. You have to know I did everything with the sole intention of protecting you." My voice broke, but his face remained unmoved. "Through all this time, I've grown to care about you more than I imagined and… I don't want this to end. You and me. I think we're good together."

"I can't get over the fact you comforted me, used your body to distract me, when you fucking knew the truth." He shook his head and looked at me with so much disappointment, I knew, this was it. He was a strong-willed person and he'd made up his mind. "I just… I'm glad you're safe. I wanted to make sure when I saw your uncle here, but nothing more." He removed his hands from his pockets and backed up toward the sidewalk.

This is it. He's gone. The brief restraint I had on my emotions broke at the expression on his face and I stopped holding it in. A sob escaped me and I covered my mouth with my hand. Two people who'd snuck into my life, helped me grow my confidence and showed in different ways how they loved, had left me. Jeff met my eyes one last time, the tortured expression in his almost giving me a sliver of hope, but Laney came outside and pulled me into her arms. "Sweetie…you can't fall for a guy who doesn't understand you'd do *anything* for the people you love."

She shut the door, closing off whatever response Jeff might've had, and I wanted nothing more than to sleep and cry for a week. *This. This is why I don't date. The heartbreak isn't worth it.*

Chapter Thirty-One

Jeff

My goddamn left arm hurt and I made a couple of arm circles, stretching it for a full minute and trying not to wince. My game had never been better, but my muscles and mindset could use some work. *Stop thinking about her.*

"Maddow, my man, you are the definition of beastmode," Brandon said, clapping his hand on my back and speaking way too loudly. "Throwing out two runners and almost hitting a cycle…dude."

"Thanks," I mumbled, wishing I was back home in my bed away from everyone. We'd won our first game and I'd played great—yet celebrating with the team was the last thing I wanted to do. They would want to talk about *it*, the article, and ask questions. It had been a full week and the buzz remained. Losing a dean and an assistant coach was a huge deal, and other coaches from other teams getting suspended while a real investigation took place was huge fucking news. Our school name had appeared in the news no less than a million times in the past seven days and because of her article, that meant people were talking about Ambar—something I was not ready to do.

"You heading out with the rest of the guys tonight?" Brandon asked, and I had to force myself not to snap at him. He was too young to go to bars, but I wasn't a total asshole to crush his bubble.

"Nah, I'll head home." I shouldered my bag, walking by him and whatever question he was about to ask. All the goddamn questions were driving me crazy. *How did you figure it out? What undercover work did you do? How did Ambar do it? What was it like? Were you scared? Was she?*

It was enough to drive anyone crazy. With the intention to drink alone and zone out, I'd started the walk to my car when my coach barked my name. Things had been tense between us since that showdown in his office. On the field, I showed every ounce of respect and would follow him to the end of time, but once the game ended, a switch went off inside me and resentment bubbled up to the point I couldn't talk to him.

"Yes?" I asked, not facing him but at least stopping my pace.

"Let's chat."

I sighed and prepared myself for some check-in. *How are you doing? Are you okay?* The guys at the house had asked me at least twice a day since it all happened and while I appreciated their concern for me, it was just another thing that irritated me. Zade nodded at me with an encouraging smile when I passed him on the way to Coach's office and I tried to return it, but it was forced. Everything had been forced the past week and I couldn't get the feeling to go away. No matter what happened, I was in a shit mood and everything I tried made it worse or remained the same.

"What's this about?" I asked when he indicated the chair for me to sit down. He shut the door and took his time moving behind his desk. When he joined me, he crossed his arms over his chest and narrowed his eyes at me with almost a scowl on his face. "What?"

"You about done?" he barked out a laugh and shook his head in disappointment. "You've been pouting around here all week. Say whatever you need to get off your chest, right now. Don't hold anything back."

I gritted my teeth. "I haven't been pouting."

"Good comeback." He pulled up the article on his computer and moved the screen to face me. "Have you even read it yet? Seen how much this blew up and how good of a job Ambar did?"

I shook my head and adjusted my jaw so my neck didn't start hurting. "I don't need to read it. I helped get that information."

"You pissed your name isn't in the byline?"

"What? No." I scoffed at his question and eyed the clock. If I could get out of here within an hour, I could have a beer by eight.

"Jeff," he snapped and used a tone I'd only heard used on players messing around. "What is it that you are so goddamn mad about? You pissed at me for not telling you I knew you were poking around? You mad that Ambar came up with the idea that I supported to fake the drug test? You've been an unpleasant shit since last week and I'm tired of it."

"You and Ambar lied to me."

"That's it, then?" He nodded to himself a couple of times and whistled. "Why don't you ask me what happened that day we cornered her?"

"Why?"

"Ask me."

My skin started to itch with irritation and I obliged, just to get the fuck out of there. "What happened then?"

"We ambushed her, Jeff. I pulled her into a room and she held her ground. Not once did she back down from what she was doing and she refused to give us any information. We went back and forth for a good while and she stood strong against us, protecting you from being involved. Sanders and I had no idea how detailed the entire thing went until we cracked her." He stopped and motioned with his hand. "Ask me how we cracked her."

"How?" I tried to act indifferent, but a little spark lit up. I desperately wanted to know how they'd gotten her to talk.

"We threatened you. She didn't know if we were involved or not but as soon as we said your name, she changed from being an aggressive journalist to one more amenable to working with us." He let me digest the words before he asked, "Now why do you think she'd do that?"

Laney's words repeated in my head from the last time I'd seen Ambar. *'You can't fall for a guy who doesn't understand you'd do* anything *for the people you love.'* The vision of her crying had almost broken me, but I'd compartmentalized it and stopped myself from thinking about it too long. But now…it came rushing back with an overwhelming force and my heartbeat sped at the insinuation of my coach's words. "For me."

"Yeah, dumbass." He chuckled at his own insult and the first sign of a smile broke out on my face. "After that, the truth came out and she helped come up with the plan to fake a failed drug test until we could find the paper trail. I was naïve and only thought this was happening with baseball until her and Sanders confirmed it was more. Now, with the threat of something happening to you, Ambar made the decision to not tell you and I think that was the right move. As your coach, I hated lying to you but I'm at the liberty to do anything to protect my team and my family. You are a part of that, Jeff, and I understand you're pissed, but I'd do it again in a heartbeat."

"That's what Ambar said."

"I imagine she did." He leaned back into his chair. "Well? You done pouting?"

Am I? Does Ambar really…love me? Could she still…? Do I love her? I sighed and almost felt the possibility of things going back to normal spark a little hope. My muscles started to relax and a different kind of worry took over. "Do you think I blew it with her?"

"I think you behaved like an idiot who could apologize a hell of a lot. But no, the way she defended you, kid, I don't think you blew it."

I stood up and held out my hand, emotion clogging my voice. "Thank you, Coach. There are not enough words to tell you the kind of mentor you are to all of us. I'm sorry for *pouting* for a week and I'm grateful you knocked my ass out of it."

"Baseball is family." He took my hand and gave it a hard shake. "I'm almost ready to forgive you for the fact you actually thought I had something to do with this entire thing."

Color left my face and I stumbled for words. But he laughed and said, "I'm messing with you. Get out of here, go talk to Ambar and try and enjoy your senior season."

"Yes, sir."

My breathing came out heavier, as if I'd sprinted around the bases, as I walked to my car. *Is this why I'm acting like an idiot? Ambar? Is this a fucking heartbreak?*

Yes.

I knew the answer but had avoided thinking about it all week because it hurt. She was the first person I thought about when I woke up, and anytime something happened, whether it was funny or stupid, I wanted to tell her. I missed her smile and sleeping next to her… *Fuck.*

I had to talk to her. Before starting the car, I typed out ten different messages to send her first but stopped. She might not respond or want to respond and I didn't want to chance it. Instead, I sped toward her place, parked and made my way to her house. It was dark out for a spring evening, but the weather had finally warmed up enough to not freeze to death. It didn't matter now though—sweat dripped down my back as my nerves grew.

I didn't know what to say and didn't think about it until I knocked on the door. Ambar answered and looked so goddamn beautiful in a simple off-the-shoulder black sweater and jeans. Emotions rushed through my body—the need to hold her, protect her, promise her I'd never be an idiot again—but none of that came out in words.

"I miss you," I said, trying to gauge her reaction to seeing me. She looked sad, but not the same way I felt inside. It was like a little of the light had left her eyes and I hated knowing I had a part in that. "I'm fucking sorry and I hope you can forgive me and I want to hold you, sleep next to you again, tell you all the dumb shit that happens all the time, talk about the future with you, and—"

"Jeff," she interrupted and I swore a small smile played on her lips. "Do you want to come inside?"

"Yes. Yes please. I do."

Like I had done many times before, I walked past her and was struck by how much I loved how she smelled. It was a mixture of comfort and enticement and I put my hands in my pockets to prevent myself from hugging the shit out of her. "Uh, should I stay in the living room or—?"

"We can talk upstairs." Her tone sounded happy and I took that as a good sign. We went up the stairs and into her room, where she sat on the edge of her bed and left me to stand in front of her, pacing and trying to find the right words.

"Ambar…look." My throat got tight and I knelt on the floor so I could place my hands on each of her knees. She didn't push them away and I was so fucking glad. She looked up at me with her dark eyes and long lashes, and my chest physically hurt at the amount of emotion I felt for her. Suddenly, I knew what to say. "I've never had a relationship before, not like one we had…have. Not like one we have. This all-consuming feeling where I think about you constantly…it's insane. It's new to me and when the thing with my coach came out…I refused to see anything but the fact you lied."

"You have to know why I did, though." Her voice sounded so sad. I moved my hands up to her face and ran my thumbs over her soft cheeks.

"I do. I really do, but I'm an idiot and it took a bit of time. I didn't realize the hurt and anger I've been carrying around was actually my own fault." I swallowed, hard, and went for it. This was the girl who thought on her feet, who supported me when I told her my real dreams, made me laugh, who turned me on like no other and shared the excitement about the unknowns of the future. "I'm pretty sure I'm in love with you. The crazy, can't sleep, want to be near you all the time love and it's terrifying."

"It is, isn't it?" she replied, a smile growing on her face when she reached out and mirrored my position with her hands on my face. "That's why I agreed to keep something from you. Because I *do* love you and couldn't stand the thought of something happening to you during your senior year."

"What do I have to do to get you back?" My voice cracked.

"I never left, but some groveling would work," she teased. She ran her fingers through my hair and I moaned at her touch. "Relationships are new to me, too, and I'm probably going to mess up at some point."

"I'll forgive you." I brought my lips to her mouth, the sensation of finally kissing her setting off an explosion inside me. She tasted so damn sweet and warm and she opened her mouth and slid her tongue inside mine, bringing my tender kiss to fiery real quick. She bit down on my bottom lip, dragged her teeth over it and the urge to be naked with her was almost animalistic. "I take it I'm forgiven?"

"Um," she said, reaching to the edge of my shirt and pulling it over my head. "It depends."

"Name it and I'll do it." I fumbled with the edge of her sweater, wanting to see her skin and touch every inch of her. She was braless, typical of her, and I leaned her back onto the bed so I could lick each breast just how she liked. "Fuck, I missed your body."

"Show me."

Oh, I can do that. I grinned and sucked one nipple hard into my mouth, circling it to the point she squirmed beneath me. Then I did the other and licked from her neck to her belly button, not giving her a chance to catch her breath. "I love how soft your skin is, and how good it always tastes."

She moaned and I undid her jeans and slid them down along with her panties to expose her sex. Here she was, my girl, legs spread wide for me to show her how much I missed her. I inserted two fingers and pumped her for a couple minutes before adding my mouth to the mix. She pulled at my hair and whined my name when I flicked my tongue against her clit at the pace that brought her to climax. She rode out the orgasm, her legs bucking around my head as I held her down. When she stilled, I kissed the inside of each thigh. "So fucking perfect."

She sighed and looked at me with sated eyes. Pride filling me because I damn well knew I did that to her. "You're halfway to being forgiven."

"Well then, I'll put in more work." I bent down again, but she stilled.

"No, I want you inside me. I missed your body, too. The way it felt against mine." The way she said it was like a sucker punch to the heart. It was so sweet and innocent, as if she had never said those words to anyone else in the world, and I wanted to pound my chest like a caveman.

The pace changed when I slid out of my practice shorts and rushed to put on a condom. This wasn't rushed. This was showing her how much I cared for her. I took my time, kissing her and teasing her neck before gliding into her. But I didn't go fast. I went real slow and waited until her gaze landed on me. "I love you, Ambar. I want more of this with you as long as you'll have me."

She blinked back some moisture before she nodded with a huge smile on her face. "I love you, too. Just promise me you won't disappear again. Even if you're mad. I can't have that again. You've become one of my best friends."

The words tortured me as much as they comforted me and I promised her. I promised to always be honest, just as I started thrusting into her. I promised to never go that long without talking again, just before I nipped her ear. And I promised to do everything I could to never hurt her.

She held on tight when I picked up the pace, coaxing her with my body and my words, and she dug her nails into my back when she got close. I reached down with my hand and gave her the added pressure she needed, and she arched her hips when she orgasmed for the second time. Her cries started deep in her throat, coming out sexier than hell, and I just watched and admired her. She didn't hold back in the bedroom with me anymore and each time with her felt better and different, like we were exploring new ground together, and it thrilled me.

"Fuck," I groaned when the base of my spine tingled. Just seeing her pleasure was enough to set me off and I pumped a final three times before spilling into her. "Ambar…" I kissed her collarbone, her face, her forehead and pushed myself up. "Can I sleep over with you tonight?"

"Yes," she replied with a sweet giggle. "I'm not sure how much sleeping we'll do. You got me addicted to you."

"You say the perfect things sometimes." I tickled her side and disposed of the condom. "Thank you for giving me another chance. I'm not sure what I would've done."

"Well, what can I say, you're just such a catch with all your baseball muscles and perfect hair," she teased. She patted her bed and moved over so I could join her. "I need to fill you in on some stuff, but we can talk tomorrow since you don't have practice or a game. Let's just enjoy each other tonight, okay?"

"God, my girlfriend is the best."

"Yeah, I guess I am," she mumbled against my chest when I pulled her into my side. It was the first time in…forever I'd felt good. There wasn't a single worry and I wasn't afraid for the other shoe to drop. She nuzzled closer to me. "Mm, this is perfect."

I smiled even though she couldn't see me. It was perfect.

Epilogue

Ambar
Four months later

"Henderson." Jeff's voice caught my attention and I looked up from my nook in the library to find him walking toward me with a huge smile. It never got old, seeing him look at me that way, or the fact we were together. *Us.* A real couple who said I love you's and held hands. "I brought you something."

"A cookie?" I asked, trying to see what he held. He smirked and bent down to give me a quick kiss. Each time was a thrill and he sat on the chair next to me, scooting it closer to me so our legs touched. *Look at us showing PDA and not caring!*

"Not a cookie." He straightened and a serious look crossed his face. "Just, take a look at this and let me know what you think." He handed me a brochure and looked more nervous that I had seen him in months.

"What is this, Jeff? Why are you worried?"

He didn't respond and jutted his chin to the brochure when he reached under the table to put his hand on my knee. I was a little concerned with his silence and opened the brochure. It was for an apartment complex just north of campus, a small one bedroom with a den.

"Are you moving?" My voice dropped a bit because the fact our lease was up on the house at the end of June—only five weeks away—meant making big decisions and I loved living two houses down from him. This would be miles away. "Have you toured it?"

"You're taking a year off before applying to grad school. I'm taking a year to study for the LSAT and apply next year." He spoke like he was checking off a list.

"Yes, we've talked about this, Jeff." I gulped and butterflies exploded in my stomach. My initial thoughts were insecurities about the investigation, or if he was second guessing our relationship…but that didn't make sense. Things had been so good between us. "It'll be risky for us, but I think getting some part-time jobs and with the explosion of the blog, I can freelance my writing. I'm sure we can do it, or at least take out loans."

"Have you thought about where you're living after your lease is up?"

I made a face and shook my head. "I've been avoiding it, actually. Laney is moving to Chicago and Marissa is moving back home until she can save some money and, well…" I paused and held his gaze. "Truthfully, I wanted to see what you were going to do first."

"God, I love you." He grabbed my face and kissed me hard. "We're on the same page and now I feel silly for not just asking."

"Asking what?"

"Ambar Henderson, will you move into this apartment with me? I know it's kinda fast, but at this point, I know what future I want and you're in it. If you're game…I say we do it."

I eyed his hesitant smile and the warmth in his eyes and breathed a sigh of relief. I didn't realize this was what I had been waiting for when I'd put off making any decisions and I threw my arms around him. Now it made sense. "Let's do it."

"So yes?"

"Yes, Jeff." I laughed against his neck and felt weightless. "We can eat macaroni every day and fight over who hogs the blankets more."

"Can't fucking wait to celebrate this with you." He pulled back and kissed me long and hard, right in the library. Onlookers watched us, but I didn't really care. It was a new normal for me to have people recognize me after the article went out, but my close friend circle had never changed. Jeff glanced at the binder on the table and tilted his head. "Shit, sorry. I interrupted whatever it was you were doing."

"A little late for that, punk." I leaned into him and closed my notebook. "This is a better distraction that looking for scholarships and part-time jobs."

He nodded, because he, too, would be in the same boat, and lowered his voice like he always did before he asked, "Have you heard from your uncle since the trial started?"

"Just one letter." It sat in my nightstand drawer and would remain there. "Nothing new, but he did have enough information to get a better deal than the others."

"Will you visit him?" He ran his hand over my collarbone and gave me a little squeeze. It was those little touches that meant so much to me, as though he knew when I needed a little extra strength so he gave me some of his. "I can go with you."

This is why I love him. "In time, yes. It's too soon and for the first time, my mom and I are on decent speaking terms. I'll write to him, but the wound needs to heal."

"I understand. It's admirable you're able to still find a way to have a relationship with him. You impress me."

"Are you trying to sweet-talk me to do inappropriate things in the conference room, Jeff Maddow?" I teased.

"Is it working?" He grinned his goofiest smile, making his eyes bug out, and I snorted.

"Nope."

"Well, when you're ready to head out, we're having a get together at the house tonight with all the guys. The draft is next week and I'm not sure where we're all going to be. It'll be our final pre-draft party."

"No regrets?" I asked, like I did every time he brought up the draft. He was playing the best he had all four years, but it didn't sway him.

"None." He kissed me again and stood. "I'm excited about the future being unknown to me. For the first time, I want to enjoy the surprises and ups and downs and I want to explore them with you."

"Don't get sappy on me," I replied, feeling more emotional than I expected. "You know, you've been really good at this boyfriend thing."

"I'll be even better as a roommate." He winked and gave me an expectant look. "Are you staying for a while or ready to wrap up?"

"I'll leave with you." We packed my things in my backpack and set off, but just as we left the library, someone pointed at us and whispered to the person next to them.

"Hey, that's that girl who wrote the article I was telling you about!"

"Really? No way!

"Yeah, it made national news. She's a legend now."

I smiled so damn big my cheeks hurt. It was me, not Jeff, who they were talking about and I had never felt cooler. Jeff heard it too and slung his arm around me. "Guess I'll have to get used to people knowing you everywhere we go. Especially the more you write and uncover. I have no doubt you're gonna be famous one day."

"You think you can handle me getting all that attention, Mr. Hotshot Baseball Boy?"

"Oh yeah. I can see us now. Lawyer and investigative journalist."

The pure joy and anticipation of the future in his voice eased any self-doubt I had. It would be hard, I knew, but my entire life had led to this point and I was going to enjoy every damn second of it. "We'll make a good team."

"Yes, we will, Henderson."

Want to see more from this author? Here's a taster for you to enjoy!

Out of the Park: Evening the Score

Jaqueline Snowe

Excerpt

"Shut the fuck up. *The* baseball-playing star of my fantasies Gideon Titan?" Spit left my mouth and my pulse raced at the thought of that perfect specimen of a man. His poster hung in my room. He had starred in my dreams more than a handful of times. His eyes, abs and smile…I shivered. Wishes did come true. The receptionist at the Los Soles stadium gawked at me and I held up a hand. "Forgive my language. But please clarify. Who will I be coaching with again?"

Her gaze darted to the door as a blush crept up her neck. "Uh, Gideon Titan. He's volunteering for the season for the fourteen and under baseball team. You're paired together."

"Cool." *Ohmigod.* "Thank you." I tried my best to remain calm and smiled while she printed off the schedule. She chewed on her bottom lip so damn much I wanted to smack her. I couldn't be the first person to lose their shit at the chance to meet Gideon Titan.

He defined the term *masculine*. He put all men to shame. For a baseball-lovin' southwest chick, he was it. When he was in full form, he was the epitome of perfection. Even with his injury and slight limp, I would take any invitation he offered. I left her desk with the practice schedule, reading about the forty games within four months, four games a week after two weeks of full practice.

Fucking Jade. Amazing, beautiful Jade. I called my pseudo-boss from the non-profit I had volunteered at for the last four years. She was my best friend, mentor and the version of a sister I'd thought my real sisters would be. She answered on the first ring her voice cheery. "Lo?"

"Gideon Titan."

Jade's breathy laugh traveled through the phone. "Surprise?"

"Hell, yeah. Best surprise ever. When I asked to get involved with youth sports, I was thinking more like pee-wee soccer. Not baseball. How did you do this?" The fresh air hit my face as I barged through the exit and I couldn't contain my grin. November in Phoenix had perfect weather—I intended to enjoy every drop of it.

"Well, I know a guy who knows a guy…plus, you've put a lot of work into our programs that focus on high school kids. You're great with them and this will be a good fit. You can talk about the dangers of texting and driving *and* get to coach one-on-one with Gideon Titan. I see this as a win-win."

The stab of pain came and went—I was used to the wave of grief whenever Justin crossed my mind. It got easier to not react to it. I cleared my throat and wiped my suddenly sweaty palms on my jeans. "Thanks for thinking of me for this. I'm grateful. And hello? Gideon. Freaking. Titan."

"Yeah. I heard he can be a real asshole, but I want every detail."

My brain wasn't in the right place to fully comprehend her words. I laughed it off. With a face like Gideon's, he could ramble on and on about stupid, irrelevant information and I'd still be happy. "You misheard it. I'm sure they meant to say he's a hot piece of ass."

Jade sighed, ignoring me. *Typical Jade.* "Anyway, crazy. We need to talk about that job offer that is still unanswered."

My throat closed and I let out an awkward grunt. "Mm, yeah. Sure."

"I'll let you go enjoy your moment to think about Gideon, but I need an answer, Fi. See you at the office soon?"

"Yup." I hung up, took a deep breath and started the drive to the shitty two-bedroom apartment I'd moved into a month ago with a former co-worker. I'd made enough the two years before, waitressing at an IHOP, and had saved every last penny to be able to live on my own my senior year. I adored my mom and my childhood home but shit—I needed to cut the cord and live my life. Her meddling personality got in the way, despite her good intentions. I wasn't a bitch, but I wanted to be independent even if it killed me. Yeah—I had a stubborn thing going and I was damn proud of it.

Jade's words weighed heavy on me the entire drive. Volunteering at Texting Too Late had started out small to help me cope with Justin's death. But it had grown into more. Once a month had become twice, and twice a week had become almost daily. The foundation was amazing and it gave me a fulfillment I needed to deal with the guilt, but could I accept a full-time position knowing damn well every day would remind me of him, and my secret?

I gripped the wheel tighter and scoffed at all the couples holding hands. *What the fuck? It's like noon on a Tuesday – why are they just strolling down our shitty street?* I parked in the covered carport, spying Michelle's Toyota, and checked my phone before heading into our modest place.

Jade: You would get to see me every day.

Jade: Diane knows you kick ass with all the money stuff I avoid.

Fiona: Keep the compliments coming. It's good for my ego.

Jade: You could pick the music station?

Fiona: I would choose 2000s R&B and it's still a maybe.

I pocketed my phone and pulled my hair up into a ponytail before walking inside. I was quite proud of the way I handled donations to TTL and that our rating had gone up in the past three months. I allocated about fifteen percent of all donations for maintenance, freelance work and advertising, but Jade had proposed moving it to twenty and keeping me on full-time with pay. Diane—the president and founder—agreed.

It had insurance, great benefits and a good salary for a non-profit. I would work with Jade, who was pretty fucking awesome, and have a job on the table before graduating.

But…*Justin.*

Nah. Not today, grief. I straightened my shoulders, pushing down the negative spiral I was sure to have. I avoided feelings. Tied up, sewed shut. I hadn't had a relationship that amounted to more than awesome, gravity-defying sex since I was eighteen, but that didn't really count, and I was okay with it. Sex was easy. Attention was easy. Feelings were not. Feelings did not lead to happiness. I came across as wild, reckless or cold to most, but it didn't bother me. It was safer, smarter and survival. Light rock music carried from our place and I plowed through our front door. I had news and Michelle Benning needed to hear it.

"Michelle. Get your ass out here right now."

"What is it?" She waltzed out of her room, just to the right of the kitchen. She wore the ugly blue apron and had her hair done up. We both had our secrets, our pasts that defined the core pieces of us. But I hadn't asked her what hers were, nor had she asked me. We enjoyed each other's company and I didn't require much more than that from my first roommate besides my mom.

"Guess who the fuck I got paired with to coach this team. Guess." I plopped onto our long-standing burgundy couch. It had been a family piece and my mom had given it to us. It smelled like an old basement, of stale popcorn with a mix of lemon furniture polish. I loved it. Michelle ran her manicured red nails over her chin, humming in thought.

"My mind is blank. Tell me."

"Gideon Titan." I smirked, pulling up a picture of him on my phone. "*The* Gideon Titan."

"Fuck me sideways." She snatched the phone out of my hands. "I want to sit on his face."

"Girl, join the club. I want him to sit on *my* face." I fanned myself with my free hand. "I have to send him an email, or reach out to him somehow. Practices are four times a week! Then, forty games."

"I hate you." Her dark brown eyes widened, her hand going to her heart. "I'm not one of those jealous bitches. But I could cut you right now."

I snickered. "I don't blame you. Here, will you help me type out an email to him? Or should I call? What do you think?"

She took the schedule from my hands and skimmed the bottom line—*contact me for details*. She pursed her lips. "He left a number and email. What would you rather do?"

"It makes more sense to text, right?" Nerves took over. I would be texting someone whose face was plastered all over our city. *Wow. But what if he's driving?*

"I think so. If this wasn't Gideon Titan but some random person, you would text, right?"

"I'd rather call. I'd want to talk about logistics and division of coaching duties. It'd be easier to talk than type." I wiped my palms on my jeans. "Shit."

"Girl, this is insane. Call now. I want to hear his voice." She grasped my hand, with her face a little too happy, a little too eager. I couldn't blame her, though. My excitement and nerves took center stage and the reality of the situation had me stiff. "Call."

"Okay, okay!" I skimmed the informational sheet the woman had given me and his number sat at the bottom. Gideon Titan's number. I dialed it, hesitating for a second before pressing call. Then it rang. "Shit. Ah!"

It rang three times, each tone causing more sweat to form on my brow. The fourth ring, he answered.

"It's Gideon."

His voice was rough and strangled, but my body reacted to it anyway. My legs clenched together, the deep tone affecting me way too much. Michelle said something to get my attention and I cleared my throat. "Hi, Gideon Titan. My name is Fiona—"

"Who fucking gave you my number?"

His sudden verbal attack made me jump. My tremulous voice gave me away, I was sure. "Los Soles, sir."

"Why?" Something shuffled in the background, the accusation clear as day. "What do you want?"

"We-we got paired to coach the fourteen-blue team." *Goddamn my nerves.*

"Christ." He released a long, aggravated sigh. "I don't need another coach. Tell them you can't do it and never call this number again."

Then he hung up.

The first spark of anger began in my stomach. It worked its way up to my chest, then to my neck. I wanted to *murder* this guy. He was an asshole of epic proportions. Michelle's eyes were the size of small saucers.

"Did he for real just do that?" Her brittle voice matched mine.

"Yeah. The fucker hung up on me." I fisted the paper into a crumpled ball. "Fuck him."

I hit redial, his rough voice answering the same. "Listen, asshole. I'm coaching with you. I want this opportunity. So fuck off. I'll see you at the first practice."

Then I hung up.

"Oh my god. What did I do?" I threw my phone onto the small coffee table. Michelle's face remained unmoving, as though my actions had frozen time. *Whoever cusses at Gideon Titan?*

"When is the first practice?" she asked.

I unfolded the paper, glancing at the date and times. "In five days. That should be enough time for everyone to cool down, yeah?"

"Sure, hon." Michelle got up, shaking her head at me a little bit. "I knew I liked you for a reason. Your balls are bigger than most men I know."

I laughed. "Then you aren't around decent guys. Ball size is everything."

She cackled, shouldering her purse and reapplying lipstick. "Balls are a deal breaker for me."

"Dude, I know." I leaned farther back into the couch, wishing it would swallow me up. Regret and embarrassment would hit me later, with Michelle at work and no one to distract me. "I've said it all the time, *but* balls are weird. Guys have to have them, but where do they go when they ride a bike?"

"Right! Or when they sit? Do they squish them to the side or flatten them?"

"How can they cross their legs?" I added. "And why must they touch them all the damn time? And do the reach-down-then-smell-their-fingers thing?"

"Why do they ball tap each other? I don't mind a titty twister now and again, but I don't greet my friends with a boob grab every time."

I laughed—Michelle had a great point. "I mean, the thought they walk around with a stick hanging out boggles my mind. But add two squishy sacks of skin next to it? Why?" I closed my eyes, thoughts of balls and penises overtaking my mind.

Michelle snickered and headed toward the door. She had to work and the thought of doing homework alone depressed me. "I'll be home later than normal. I might be staying until breakfast."

"Damn, well, be safe. I'll be here thinking about balls."

"God." She shook her head. "I'm glad we're roomies. See you."

She shut the door and I smiled. I liked Michelle as much as I could like someone outside my family. Hope blossomed in my chest that maybe, just *maybe,* I could let her in.

About the Author

Jaqueline Snowe lives in Arizona where the 'dry heat' really isn't that bad. She enjoys making lists with colorful Post-it notes and sipping coffee all day. She has been a custodian, a waitress, a landscaper, a coach and a teacher. Her life revolves around binge-watching Netflix, her two dogs who don't realize they aren't humans and her wonderful baseball-loving husband.

Jaqueline loves to hear from readers. You can find her contact information, website details and author profile page at https://www.totallybound.com